Melvin L. Severy

The Darrow Enigma

Leseklassiker

Melvin L. Severy

The Darrow Enigma

ISBN/EAN: 9783955630225

Auflage: 1

Erscheinungsjahr: 2013

Erscheinungsort: Bremen, Deutschland

Leseklassiker

CONTENTS

THE EPISODE OF THE DARKENED ROOM

CHAPTER I

What shall we say when Dream-Pictures leave their frames of night and push us from the waking world?

As the part I played in the events I am about to narrate was rather that of a passive observer than of an active participant, I need say little of myself. I am a graduate of a Western university and, by profession, a physician. My practice is now extensive, owing to my blundering into fame in a somewhat singular manner, but a year ago I had, I assure you, little enough to do. Inasmuch as my practice is now secure, I feel perfectly free to confess that the cure I effected in the now celebrated case of Mrs. P – was altogether the result of chance, and not, as I was then only too glad to have people believe, due to an almost supernatural power of diagnosis.

Mrs. P – was not more surprised at the happy result than was I; the only difference being that she showed her astonishment, while I endeavoured to conceal mine, and affected to look upon the whole thing as a matter of course.

My fame spread; the case got into the medical journals, where my skill was much lauded, and my practice became enormous. There is but one thing further I need mention regarding myself: that is, that I am possessed of a memory which my friends are pleased to consider phenomenal. I can repeat a lecture, sermon, or conversation almost word for word after once hearing it, provided always, that the subject commands my interest. My humble abilities in this direction have never ceased to be a source of wonderment to my acquaintance, though I confess, for my own part, when I compare them with those of Blind Tom, or of the man who, after a single reading, could correctly repeat the London Times, advertisements and all, they seem modest indeed.

It was about the time when, owing to the blessed Mrs. P – , my creditors were beginning to receive some attention, that I first met George Maitland. He had need, he said, of my professional services; he felt much under the weather; could I give him something which would brace him up a bit; he had some important chemical work on hand which he could not afford to put by; in fact, he didn't mind saying that he was at work upon a table of atomical pitches to match Dalton's atomic weights; if he succeeded in what he had undertaken he would have solved the secret of the love and hatred of atoms, and unions hitherto unknown could easily be effected.

I do not know how long he would have continued had not my interest in the subject caused me to interrupt him. I was something of an experimenter myself, and here was a man who could help me.

It was a dream of mine that the great majority of ailments could be cured by analysing a patient's blood, and then injecting into his veins such chemicals as were found wanting, or were necessary to counteract the influence of any deleterious matter present. There were, of course, difficulties in the way, but had they not already at Cornell University done much the same for vegetable life? And did not those plants which had been set in sea sand out of which every particle of nutriment had been roasted, and which were then artificially fed with a solution of the chemicals of which they were known to be composed, grow twice as rank as those which had been set in the soil ordinarily supposed to be best adapted to them? What was the difference between a human cell and a plant cell? Yes, since my patient was a chemist, I would cultivate his acquaintance.

He proceeded to tell me how he felt, but I could make nothing of it, so I forthwith did the regulation thing; what should we doctors do without it! I looked at his tongue, pulled down his eyelid, and pronounced him bilious. Yes, there were the little brown spots under his skin – freckles, perhaps – and probably he had an occasional ringing in his ears. He was willing to admit that he was dizzy on suddenly rising from a stooping posture, and that eggs, milk, and coffee were poison to him; and he afterward told me he should have said the same of any other three articles I might have mentioned, for he looked so hale and vigorous, and felt so disgracefully well, that he was ashamed of himself. We have had many a laugh over it since. The fact of the matter is the only affliction from which he was suffering was an inordinate desire to make my acquaintance. Not for my own sake – oh, dear, no! – but because I was John Darrow's family physician, and would be reasonably sure to know Gwen Darrow, that gentleman's daughter. He had first met her, he told me after we had become intimate, at an exhibition of paintings by

William T. Richards, – but, as you will soon be wondering if it were, on his part, a case of love at first sight, I had best relate the incident to you in his own words as he told it to me. This will relieve me of passing any judgment upon the matter, for you will then know as much about it as I, and, doubtless, be quite as capable of answering the question, for candour compels me to own that my knowledge of the human heart is entirely professional. Think of searching for Cupid's darts with a stethoscope!

"I was standing," Maitland said, "before a masterpiece of sea and rock, such as only Richards can paint. It was a view of Land's End, Cornwall, and in the artist's very best vein. My admiration made me totally unmindful of my surroundings, so much so, indeed, that, although the gallery was crowded, I caught myself expressing my delight in a perfectly audible undertone. My enthusiasm, since it was addressed to no one, soon began to attract attention, and people stopped looking at the pictures to look at me. I was conscious of this in a vague, far-off way, much as one is conscious of a conversation which seems to have followed him across the borderland of sleep, and I even thought that I ought to be embarrassed. How long I remained thus transported I do not know. The first thing I remember is hearing someone close beside me take a quick, deep breath, one of those full inhalations natural to all sensitive natures when they come suddenly upon something sublime. I turned and looked. I have said I was transported by that canvas of sea and rocks, and have, therefore, no word left to describe the emotion with which I gazed upon the exquisite, living, palpitating picture beside me. A composite photograph of all the Madonnas ever painted, from the Sistine to Bodenhausen's, could not have been more lovely, more ineffably womanly than that young girl, radiant with the divine glow of artistic delight – at least, that is my opinion, which, by the bye, I should, perhaps, have stated a little more gingerly, inasmuch as you are yourself acquainted with the young lady. Now, don't look incredulous [noticing my surprise]. Black hair – not brown, black; clear pink and white complexion; large, deep violet eyes with a remarkable poise to them." – Here I continued the description for him: "Slight of figure; a full, honest waist, without a suggestion of that execrable death-trap, Dame Fashion's hideous cuirass; a little above middle height; deliberate, and therefore graceful, in all her movements; carries herself in a way to impress one with the idea that she is innocent, without that time-honoured concomitant, ignorance; half girl, half woman; shy, yet strong; and in a word, very beautiful – that's Gwen Darrow." I paused here, and Maitland went on somewhat dubiously: "Yes, it's not hard to locate such a woman. She makes her presence as clearly felt among a million of her sex as does a grain of fuchsine in a hogshead of water. If, with a few ounces of this, Tyndall could colour Lake Geneva, so with Gwen Darrow one might, such is the power of the ideal, change the ethical status of a continent."

He then told me how he had made a study of Miss Darrow's movements, and had met her many times since; in fact, so often that he fancied, from something in her manner, that she had begun to

wonder if his frequent appearance were not something more than a coincidence. The fear that she
might think him dogging her footsteps worried him,
and he began as sedulously to avoid the places he
knew she frequented, as he previously had sought
them. This, he confessed, made him utterly miserable. He had, to be sure, never spoken to her, but it
was everything to be able to see her. When he could
endure it no longer he had come to me under pre-
tence of feeling ill, that he might, when he had made
my acquaintance, get me to introduce him to the
Darrows.

You will understand, of course, that I did not
learn all this at our first interview. Maitland did not
take me into his confidence until we had had a con-
ference at his laboratory devoted entirely to scientific
speculations. On this occasion he surprised me not a
little by turning to me suddenly and saying: "Some
of the grandest sacrifices the world has ever known,
if one may judge by the fortitude they require, and
the pain they cause, have occurred in the laboratory." I looked at him inquiringly, and he continued:
"When a man, simply for the great love of truth that
is in him, has given his life to the solution of some
problem, and has at last arrived, after years of closest
application, at some magnificent generalisation –
when he has, perhaps, published his conclusions,
and received the grateful homage of all lovers of
truth, his life has, indeed, borne fruit. Of him may it
then be justly said that his

"'. . . life hath blossomed downward like
The purple bell-flower.'

But suddenly, in the privacy of his laboratory, a single fact arises from the test-tube in his trembling hand and confronts him! His brain reels; the glass torment falls upon the floor, and shatters into countless pieces, but he is not conscious of it, for he feels it thrust through his heart. When he recovers from the first shock, he can only ejaculate: 'Is it possible?' After a little he is able to reason. 'I was fatigued,' he says; 'perhaps my senses erred. I can repeat the experiment again, and be sure. But if it overthrow those conclusions for which I have given my life?' he gasps. 'My generalisation is firmly established in the minds of all – all but myself – no one will ever chance upon this particular experiment, and it may not disprove my theory after all; better, much better, that the floor there keep the secret of it all both from me and from others!' But even as he says this to himself he has taken a new tube from the rack and crawled – ten years older for that last ten minutes – to his chemical case. The life-long habit of truth is so strong in him that self-interest cannot submerge it. He repeats the experiment, and confirms his fears. The battle between his life and a few drops of liquid in a test-tube has been mercilessly fought, and he has lost! The elasticity of the man is gone forever, and the only indication the world ever receives of this terrible conflict between a human soul and its destiny is some half a dozen lines in Nature, giving the experiment and stating that it utterly refutes its author's previous conclusions. Half a dozen lines – the epitaph of a dead, though unburied, life!"

My companion paused there, but I found myself unable to reply. He had spoken with such intensity, such dramatic fervour, that I was completely swept away by his eloquence; so much so, indeed, that it did not even occur to me to ask myself why he should have burst out in this peculiar strain. I have given you the incident in order that you may see the strange moods into which Maitland occasionally relapsed – at least, at that time. After a quick glance at me he continued, in a quieter vein: "All of us men of science have felt something, however little, of this, and I believe, as a class, scientists transcend all other men in their respect for absolute truth." He cast another one of his searching glances at me, and said quickly: "This is precisely why I am going to confide in you and rely upon your assistance in a matter, the successful termination of which would please me as much as the discovery of an absolute standard of measurement."

He then made the confession which I have already given you, and ended by asking me to secure him an introduction to Miss Darrow. I cheerfully promised to bring this about at the first opportunity. He asked me if I thought, on account of his having met her so frequently, she would be likely to think it was all a "put up job."

"I do not know," I replied. "Miss Darrow is a singularly close observer. On the whole I think you had better reach her through her father. Do you play croquet?" He replied that he was considered something of an expert in that line. That, then, was surely the best way. John Darrow was known in the neighbourhood as a "crank" on the subject of croquet. He had spent many hundreds of dollars on his grounds. His wickets were fastened to hard pine planks, and these were then carefully buried two feet deep. The surface of the ground, he was wont to descant, must be of a particular sort of gravel, sifted just so, and rolled to a nicety. The balls must be of hard rubber, and have just one-eighth inch clearance in passing through the wickets, with the exception of the two wires forming the "cage," where it was imperative that this clearance should be reduced to one-sixteenth of an inch – but I need not state more to show how he came to be considered a "crank" upon the subject.

It was easy enough to bring Maitland and Darrow together. "My friend is himself much interested in the game; he heard of your superb ground; may he be permitted to examine it closely?" Darrow was all attention. He would be delighted to show it. Suppose they make a practical test of it by playing a game. This they did and Maitland played superbly, but he was hardly a match for the old gentleman, who sought to palliate his defeat by saying: "You play an excellent game, sir; but I am a trifle too much for you on my own ground. Now, if you can spare the time, I should like to witness a game between you and my daughter; I think you will be pretty evenly matched."

If he could spare the time! I laughed outright at the idea. Why, with the prospect of meeting Gwen Darrow before him, an absolute unit of measure, with a snail's pace, would have made good its escape from him. As it is a trick of poor humanity to refuse when offered the very thing one has been madly scheming to obtain, I hastened to accept Darrow's invitation for my friend, and to assure him on my own responsibility, that time was just then hanging heavily on Maitland's hands. Well, the game was played, but Maitland was so unnerved by the girl's presence that he played execrably, so poorly, indeed, that the always polite Darrow remarked: "You must charge your easy victory, Gwen, to your opponent's gallantry, not to his lack of skill, for I assure you he gave me a much harder rub." The young lady cast a quick glance at Maitland, which said so plainly that she preferred a fair field and no favour that he hastened to say: "Your father puts too high an estimate upon my play. I did my best to win, but – but I was a little nervous; I see, however, that you would have defeated me though I had been in my best form." Gwen gave him one of those short, searching looks, so peculiarly her own, which seem to read, with mathematical certainty, one's innermost thoughts, – and the poor fellow blushed to the tips of his ears. – But he was no boy, this Maitland, and betrayed no other sign of the tempest that was raging within him. His utterance remained as usual, deliberate and incisive, and I thought this perplexed the young lady. Before leaving, both Maitland and I were invited to become parties to a six-handed game to be played the following week, after the grounds had been redressed with gravel.

Maitland looked forward to this second meeting with Miss Darrow with an eagerness which made every hour seem interminably long, and he was in such a flutter of expectancy that I was sure if

"We live . . . in thoughts, not breaths;
In feelings, not in figures on a dial
We should count time by heart-throbs,"

he must have passed through a period as long as that separating the Siege of Troy from the "late unpleasantness." The afternoon came at last, however. The party consisted, besides Darrow and his daughter, Maitland and myself, of two young gentlemen with whom personally I had but a slight acquaintance, although I knew them somewhat by reputation. The younger one, Clinton Browne, is a young artist whose landscapes were beginning to attract wide attention in Boston, and the elder, Charles Herne, a Western gentleman of some literary attainments, but comparatively unknown here in the East. There is nothing about Mr. Herne that would challenge more than passing attention. If you had said of him, "He is well-fleshed, well-groomed, and intellectually well-thatched," you would have voiced the opinion of most of his acquaintances.

This somewhat elaborately upholstered old world has a deal of mere filling of one kind and another, and Mr. Herne is a part of it. To be sure, he leaves the category of excelsior very far behind and approaches very nearly to the best grade of curled hair, but, in spite of all this, he is simply a sort of social filling.

Mr. Browne, on the other hand, is a very different personage. Of medium height, closely knit, with the latent activity and grace of the cat flowing through every movement and even stagnating in his pose, he is a man that the first casual gaze instantly returns to with sharpened focus. You have seen gymnasts whose normal movements were slowly performed springs, just as rust is a slow combustion and fire the same thing in less time. Well, Clinton

Browne strongly suggested that sort of athlete. Add to this a regularly formed, clearly cut, and all-but-beautiful face, with a pair of wonderfully piercing, albeit somewhat shifty, black eyes, and one need not marvel that men as well as women stared at him. I have spoken of his gaze as "somewhat shifty," yet am not altogether sure that in that term I accurately describe it. What first fastened my attention was this vague, unfocussed, roving, quasi-introspective vision flashing with panther-like suddenness into a directness that seemed to burn and pierce one like the thrust of a hot stiletto, His face was clean-shaven, save for a mere thumb-mark of black hair directly under the centre of his lower lip. This Iago-like tab and the almost fierce brilliancy of his concentrated gaze gave to his countenance at times a sinister, Machiavellian expression that was irresistible and which, to my thinking, seriously marred an otherwise fine face. Of course due allowance must be made for the strong prejudice I have against any form of beard. However, I'd wager a box of my best liver-pills against any landscape Browne ever painted, – I don't care if it's as big as a cyclorama, – that if he had known how completely Gwen shared my views, – how she disliked the appearance of be-whiskered men, – that delicately nurtured little imperial would soon have been reduced to a tender memory, – that is to say, if a physician can diagnose a case of love from such symptoms as devouring glances and an attentiveness so marked that it quite disgusted Maitland, who repeatedly measured his rival with the apparent cold precision of a mathematician, albeit there was warmth enough underneath.

This singular self-poise is one of Maitland's most noticeable characteristics and is, I think, rather remarkable in a man of such strong emotional tendencies and lightning-like rapidity of thought. No doubt some small portion of it is the result of acquirement, for life can hardly fail to teach us all something of this sort; still I cannot but think that the larger part of it is native to him. Born of well-to-do parents, he had never had the splendid tuition of early poverty. As soon as he had left college he had studied law, and had been admitted to the bar. This he had done more to gratify the wishes of his father than to further any desires of his own, but he had soon found the profession, so distasteful to him that he practically abandoned it in favour of scientific research. True, he still occasionally took a legal case when it turned upon scientific points which interested him, but, as he once confessed to me, he swallowed, at such times, the bitter pill of the law for the sugar coating of science which enshrouded it. This legal training could, therefore, it seems to me, have made no deep or radical change in his character, which leads me to think that the self-control he exhibited, despite the angry disgust with which I know Browne's so apparent attentions to Gwen inspired him, must, for the most part, have been native to him rather than acquired.

Nothing worthy of record occurred until evening; at least nothing which at the time impressed me as of import, though I afterward remembered that Darrow's behaviour was somewhat strange. He appeared singularly preoccupied, and on one occasion started nervously when I coughed behind him.

He explained that a disagreeable dream had deprived him of his sleep the previous night and left his nerves somewhat unstrung, and I thought no more of it.

When the light failed we were all invited into the parlour to listen to a song by Miss Darrow. The house, as you are perhaps aware, overlooks Dorchester Bay. The afternoon had been very hot, but at dusk a cold east wind had sprung up, which, as it was still early in the season, was not altogether agreeable to our host, sitting as he was, back to, though fully eight feet from, an open window looking to the east. Maitland, with his usual quick observation, noticed his discomfort and asked if he should not close the window. The old gentleman did not seem to hear the question until it was repeated, when, starting as if from a reverie, he said: "If it will not be too warm for the rest of you, I would like to have it partly closed, say to within six inches, for the wind is cold"; and he seemed to relapse again into his reverie. Maitland was obliged to use considerable strength to force the window down, as it stuck in the casing, and when it finally gave way it closed with a loud shrieking sound ending in the bang of the counterweights. At the noise Darrow sprang to his feet, exclaiming: "Again! The same sound! I knew I could not mistake it!" but by this time Gwen was at his side, pressing him gently back into his seat, as she said to him in an undertone audible to all of us: "What is it, father?" The old gentleman only pressed her closer by way of reply, while he said to us apologetically: "You must excuse me, gentlemen. I have a certain dream which haunts me, – the dream of someone striking me out of the darkness. Last night I had the same dream for the seventh time and awoke to hear that window opened. There is no mistaking the sound I heard just now; it is identical with that I heard last night. I sprang out of bed, took a light, and rushed down here, for I am not afraid to meet anything I can see, but the window was closed and locked, as I had left it! What do you think, Doctor," he said, turning to me, "are dreams ever prophetic?"

"I have never," I replied, anxious to quiet him, "had any personal experience justifying such a conclusion." I did not tell him of certain things which had happened to friends of mine, and so my reply reassured him.

Maitland, who had been startled by the old gentleman's conduct, now returned to the window and opened it about six inches. There was no other window open in the room, and yet so fresh was the air that we were not uncomfortable. Darrow, with ill-concealed pride, then asked his daughter to sing, and she left him and went to the piano. "Shall I not light the lamp?" I asked. "I think we shall not need it," the old gentleman replied, "music is always better in the gloaming."

In order that you may understand what follows, it will be necessary for me to describe to you our several positions in the room. The apartment is large, nearly square, and occupies the southeast corner of the house. The eastern side of the room has one window, that which had been left open about six inches, and on the southern side of the room there were two windows, both of which were securely fastened and the blinds of which had been closed by the painters who, that morning, had primed the eastern and southern sides of the house, preparatory to giving it a thorough repainting. On the north side of the room, but much nearer to the western than the eastern end, are folding doors. These on this occasion were closed and fastened. On the western side of the room is the piano, and to the left of it, near the southwest corner, is a door leading to the hallway. This door was closed. As I have already told you, Darrow sat in a high-backed easy-chair facing the piano and almost in the centre of the room. The partly opened window on the east side was directly behind him and fully eight feet away. Herne and Browne sat upon Darrow's right and a little in front of him against the folding doors, while Maitland and I were upon his left, between him and the hall door. Gwen was at the piano. There are no closets, draperies, or niches in the room. I think you will now be able to understand the situation fully.

Whether the gloom of the scene suggested it to her, or whether it was merely a coincidence, I do not know, but Miss Darrow began to sing "In the Gloaming" in a deep, rich contralto voice which seemed fraught with a weird, melancholy power. When I say that her voice was ineffably sympathetic I would not have you confound this quality either with the sepulchral or the aspirated tone which usually is made to do duty for sympathy, especially in contralto voices. Every note was as distinct, as brilliantly resonant, as a cello in a master's hand. So clear, so full the notes rang out that I could plainly feel the chair vibrate beneath me.

"In the gloaming, O my darling!
When the lights are dim and low,
And the quiet shadows falling
Softly come and softly go.
When the winds are sobbing faintly
With a gentle unknown woe,
Will you think of me and love me
As you did once, long ago?

"In the gloaming, O my darling!
Think not bitterly of me,
Though I passed away in silence,
Left you lonely, set you free.
For my heart was crushed with longing.
What had been could never be:
It was best to leave you thus, dear,
Best for you and best – "

But the line was never finished. With a wild cry, more of fear than of pain, Darrow sprang from his chair. "Gentlemen, I have been stabbed!" was all he said, and fell back heavily into his seat. Gwen was kneeling before him in an instant, even before I could assist him. His right hand was pressed to his throat and his eyes seemed starting from their sockets as he shouted hoarsely: "A light, a light! For God's sake, don't let him strike me again in the dark!" Maitland was already lighting the gas and Herne and Browne, so Browne afterward told me, were preparing to seize the assailant. I remembered, after it all was over, a quick movement Browne had made toward the darkest corner of the room.

The apartment was now flooded with light, and

I looked for the assassin. He was not to be found! The room contained only Gwen, Darrow, and his four invited guests! The doors were closed; the windows had not been touched. No one could possibly have entered or left the room, and yet the assassin was not there. But one solution remained; Darrow was labouring under a delusion, and Gwen's voice would restore him. As she was about to speak I stepped back to note the effect of her words upon him. "Do not fear, father," she said in a low voice as she laid her face against his cheek, "there is nothing here to hurt you. You are ill, – I will get you a glass of cordial and you will be yourself again in a moment." She was about to rise when her father seized her frantically by the arm, exclaiming in a hoarse whisper: "Don't leave me! Can't you see? Don't leave me!" and for the first time he removed his hand from his throat, and taking her head between his palms, gazed wistfully into her face. He tried to speak again, but could not, and glanced up at us with a helpless expression which I shall never forget. Maitland, his eyes riveted upon the old gentleman, whose thoughts he seemed to divine, hurriedly produced a pencil and note-book and held them toward him, but he did not see them, for he had drawn Gwen's face down to him and was kissing her passionately. The next instant he was on his feet and from the swollen veins that stood out like cords upon his neck and forehead, we could see the terrible effort he was making to speak. At last the words came, – came as if they were torn hissing from his throat, for he took a full breath between each one of them. "Gwen – I – knew – it! Good-bye! Remember – your – promise!" – and he fell a limp mass into his chair, overcome, I felt sure, by the fearful struggle he had made. Maitland seized a glass of water and threw it in his face. I loosened the clothing about his neck and, in doing so, his head fell backward and his face was turned upward toward me. The features were drawn, – the eyes were glazed and set. I felt of his heart; he was dead!

CHAPTER II

Silence is the only tender Death can make to Mystery.

The look of pain and astonishment upon my face said plainly enough to Gwen:

"Your father is dead." I could not speak. In the presence of her great affliction we all stood silent, and with bowed heads. I had thought Darrow's attack the result of an overwrought mental condition which would speedily readjust itself, and had so counted upon his daughter's influence as all but certain to immediately result in a temporary cure. When, therefore, I found him dead without any apparent cause, I was, for the time being, too dazed to think, much less to act, and I think the other gentlemen were quite as much incapacitated as I. My first thought, when I recovered so that I could think, was of Gwen. I felt sure her reason must give way under the strain, and I thought of going nearer to her in case she should fall, but refrained when I noticed that Maitland had noiselessly glided within easy reach of her. To move seemed impossible to me. Such a sudden transition from warm, vigorous life to cold, impassive death seems to chill the dynamic rivers of being into a horrible winter, static and eternal. Though death puts all things in the past tense, even we physicians cannot but be strangely moved when the soul thus hastily deserts the body without the usual farewell of an illness.

Contrary to my expectations Gwen did not faint. For a long time, – it may not have been more than twenty minutes, but it seemed, under the peculiar circumstances, at least an hour, – she remained perfectly impassive. She neither changed colour nor exhibited any other sign of emotion. She stood gazing quietly, tenderly, at her father's body as if he were asleep and she were watching for some indication of his awakening. Then a puzzled expression came over her countenance. There was no trace of sorrow in it, only the look of perplexity. I decided to break the gruesome silence, but the thought of how my own voice would sound in that awe-inspired stillness frightened me. Gwen herself was the first to speak. She looked up with the same impassive countenance, from which now the perplexed look had fled, and said simply:

"Gentlemen, what is to be done?" Her voice was firm and sane, – that it was pitched lower than usual and had a suggestion of intensity in it, was perfectly natural. I thought she did not realise her loss and said: "He has gone past recall." "Yes," she replied, "I know that, but should we not send for an officer?" "An officer!" I exclaimed. "Is it possible you entertain a doubt that your father's death resulted from natural causes?" She looked at me a moment fixedly, and then said deliberately: "My father was murdered!" I was so surprised and pained that, for a moment, I could not reply, and no one else sought to break the silence.

Maitland, as if Gwen's last remark had given rise to a sudden determination, glided to the body. He examined the throat, raised the right hand and looked at the fingers: then he stepped back a little and wrote something in his note-book. This done, he tried the folding doors and found them locked on the inside; then the two windows on the south side of the room, which he also found fastened. He opened the hall door slightly and the hinges creaked noisily, of all of which he made a note. Then taking a rule from his pocket he went to the east window, and measured the opening, and then the distance between this window and the chair in which the old gentleman had sat, recording his results as before. His next act astonished me not a little and had the effect of recalling me to my senses. With his penknife he cut a circle in the carpet around each leg of the chair on which the body rested. He continued his examinations with quiet thoroughness, but I ceased now to follow him closely, since I had begun to feel the necessity of convincing Gwen of her error, and was casting about for the best way to do so.

"My dear Miss Darrow," I said at length; "you attach too much importance to the last words of your father, who, it is clear, was not in his right mind. You must know that he has, for some months, had periods of temporary aberration, and that all his delusions have been of a sanguinary nature. Try to think calmly," I said, perceiving from her expression that I had not shaken her conviction in the least. "Your father said he had been stabbed. You must see that such a thing is physically impossible. Had all the doors and windows been open, no object so large as a man could possibly have entered or left the room without our observing him; but the windows were closed and fastened, with the exception of the east window, which, as you may see for yourself, is open some six inches or so, in which position it is secured by the spring fastening. The folding doors are locked on the inside and the only possible means of entrance, therefore, would have been by the hall door. Directly in front of that, between it and your father, sat Mr. Maitland and myself. You see by my chair that I was less than two feet from the door. It is inconceivable that, in that half-light, anyone could have used that entrance and escaped observation. Do you not see how untenable your idea is? Had your father been stabbed he would have bled, but I am as certain as though I had made a thorough examination that there is not so much as a scratch anywhere upon his body." Gwen heard me through in silence and then said wearily, in a voice which had now neither intensity nor elasticity, "I understand fully the apparent absurdity of my position, yet I know my father was murdered. The wound which caused his death has escaped your notice, but – "

"My dear Miss Darrow," I interrupted, "there is no wound, you may be sure of that!" For the first time since Darrow's death Maitland spoke. "If you will look at the throat a little more closely, you will see what may be a wound," he said, and went on quietly with his examinations. He was right; there was a minute abrasion visible. The girl's quick observation had detected what had escaped me, convinced as I was that there was nothing to be found by a scrutiny however close.

Gwen now transferred her attention to Maitland, and asked: "Had not one of us better go for an officer?" Maitland, whose power of concentration is so remarkable as on some occasions to render him utterly oblivious of his surroundings, did not notice the question and Browne replied to it for him. "I should be only too happy to fetch an officer for you, if you wish," he said. Have you ever noticed how acute the mind is for trifles and slight incongruities when under the severe tension of such a shock as we had experienced? Such attacks, threatening to invade and forever subjugate our happiness, seem to have the effect of so completely manning the ramparts of our intellect the nothing, however trivial, escapes observation. Gwen's father, her only near relative, lay cold before her, – his death, from her standpoint, the most painful of mysteries, – and yet the incongruity of Browne's "only too happy " did not escape her, as was evident by the quick glance and sudden relaxation of the mouth into the faintest semblance of a smile. All this was momentary and, I doubt not, half unconscious. She replied gravely:

"I would indeed be obliged if you would do so."

Maitland, who had now finished his examination, noticed that Browne was about to depart. When the artist would have passed him on his way to the hall door, he placed his hand upon that gentleman's shoulder, saying: "Pardon me, sir, but I would strongly urge that you do not leave the room!"

Browne paused. Both men stood like excited animals at gaze.

CHAPTER III

Nothing is so full of possibilities as the seemingly impossible.

Maitland's request that Browne should not leave the room seemed to us all a veritable thunderbolt. It impressed me at the time as being a thinly veneered command, and I remember fearing lest the artist should be injudicious enough to disregard it. If he could have seen his own face for the next few moments, he would have had a lesson in expression which years of portrait work may fail to teach him. At length the rapidly changing kaleidoscope of his mind seemed to settle, to group its varied imaginings about a definite idea, – the idea that he had been all but openly accused, in the presence of Miss Darrow, of being instrumental in her father's death. For a moment, as he faced Maitland, whom he instinctively felt to be a rival, he looked so dark and sinister that one could easily have believed him capable of almost any crime.

Gwen was no less surprised than the rest of us at Maitland's interference, but she did not permit it to show in her voice as she said quietly: "Mr. Browne has consented to go for an officer." As I felt sure she must have thought Maitland already knew this, as anyone else must have heard what had passed, I looked upon her remark as a polite way of saying:

"I am mistress here."

Maitland apparently so regarded it, for he replied quickly: "I hope you will not think me officious, or unmindful of your right to dictate in a matter so peculiarly your own affair. My only desire is to help you. Mr. Browne's departure would still further complicate a case already far to difficult of solution. My legal training has given me some little experience in these matters, and I only wish that you may have the benefit thereof. It is now nearly three-quarters of an hour since your father's death, and, I assure you, time at this particular juncture may be of the utmost importance. Not a moment should be wasted in needless discussion. If you will consent to despatch a servant to the police station I will, in due time, explain to you why I have taken the liberty of being so insistent on this point."

He had hardly ceased speaking before Gwen rang for a servant. She hurriedly told him what had transpired and sent him to the nearest police station. As this was but a few rods away and the messenger was fleet of foot, an officer was soon upon the scene. "We were able," he said to us generally as he entered the room, "to catch Medical Examiner Ferris by 'phone at his home in F – Street, and he will be here directly. In the meantime I have been sent along merely to see that the body is not moved before his examination and that everything in the room remains exactly as it was at the time of the old gentleman's death. Did I not understand," he said to Maitland in an undertone, "that there is a suspicion of foul play?"

"Yes," replied George, "that is one explanation which certainly will have to be considered."

"I thought I heard the Cap'n say 'murder' when he 'phoned in town for some specials. They're for detective work on this case, I reckon. Hello! That sounds like the Doctor's rig."

A moment later the bell rang and Dr. Ferris entered the room.

"Ah, Doctor," he said extending his hand to me, "what have we here?"

Before I could answer he had noticed Maitland and advanced to shake hands with him.

"Is this indeed so serious as I have been told?" he asked, after his greeting.

"It seems to me likely," replied Maitland slowly, "to develop into the darkest mystery I have ever known."

"Hum!" replied the Examiner. "Has the body been moved or the disposition of its members altered?"

"Not since I arrived," replied Officer Barker.

"And before?" queried Dr. Ferris, turning to Maitland.

"Everything is absolutely intact. I have made a few notes and measurements, but I have disturbed nothing," replied Maitland.

"Good," said the Examiner. "May I see those notes before I go? You were on that Parker case and you have, you know, something of a reputation for thoroughness. Perhaps you may have noted something that would escape me."

"The notes, Doctor, are at your service," George

replied.

Dr. Ferris' examination of the body was very thorough, yet, since it was made with the rapid precision which comes from extended practice, it was soon over. Short as it was, however, it was still an ordeal under which Gwen suffered keenly, to judge from her manner.

The Examiner then took Maitland aside, looked at his notes, and conversed earnestly with him in an undertone for several minutes. I do not know what passed between them. When he left, a few moments later, Officer Barker accompanied him.

As soon as the door closed behind them Gwen turned to Maitland.

"Did he give you his opinion?" she asked with a degree of interest which surprised me.

"He will report death as having resulted from causes at present unknown," rejoined Maitland.

Gwen seemed greatly relieved by this answer, though I confess I was utterly at a loss to see why she should be.

Observing this change in her manner Maitland approached her, saying:

"Will you now permit me to explain my seeming rudeness in interfering with your plan to make Mr. Browne your messenger, and at the same time allow me to justify myself in the making of yet another request?"

Gwen bowed assent and he proceeded to state

the following case as coolly and accurately as if it were a problem in geometry.

"Mr. Darrow," he began, "has just died under peculiar circumstances. Three possible views of the case at once suggest themselves. First: his death may have been due to natural causes and his last expressions the result of an hallucination under which he was labouring. Second: he may have committed suicide, as the result, perhaps, of a mania which in that case would also serve to explain his last words and acts; or, – you will pardon me, Miss Darrow, – these last appearances may have been intentionally assumed with a view to deceiving us. The officers you have summoned will not be slow in looking for motives for such a deception, and several possible ones cannot fail at once to suggest themselves to them. Third: your father may have been murdered and his last expressions a more or less accurate description of the real facts of the case. It seems to me that these three theories exhaust the possibilities of the case. Can anyone suggest anything further?" And he paused for a reply.

"It is clear," replied Mr. Herne with portly deliberation, "that all deaths must be either natural or unnatural; and equally clear that when unnatural the agent, if human, must be either the victim himself, or some person external to him."

"Precisely so," continued Maitland. "Now our friend, the Doctor, believes that Mr. Darrow's death resulted from natural causes. The official authorities will at first, in all probability, agree with him, but it is impossible to tell what theory they will ultimately adopt. If sufficient motive for the act can be found, some are almost certain to adopt the suicide theory. Miss Darrow has expressed her conviction that we are dealing with a case of murder. Mr. Browne and Mr. Herne have expressed no opinion on the subject, so far as I am aware."

At this point Gwen, with an eagerness she had not before displayed, – or possibly it was nervousness, – exclaimed: "And your own view of the case?" "I believe," Maitland replied deliberately, "that your father's death resulted from poison injected into the blood; but this is a matter so easily settled that I prefer not to theorise upon it. There are several poisons which might have produced the effects we have observed. If, however, I am able to prove this conjecture correct I have still only eliminated one of the three hypotheses and resolved the matter to a choice between the suicide and murder theories, yet that is something gained. It is because I believe it can be shown death did not result from natural causes that I have so strongly urged Mr. Browne not to leave the room."

"Pardon me, sir!" ejaculated Browne, growing very dark and threatening. "You mean to insinuate – " "Nothing," continued Maitland, finishing his sentence for him, and then quietly ignoring the interruption. "As I have already said, I am somewhat familiar with the usual methods of ferreting out crime. As a lawyer, and also as a chemical expert, I have listened to a great deal of evidence in criminal cases, and in this and other ways, learned the lines upon which detectives may confidently be expected to act, when once they have set up an hypothesis.

The means by which they arrive at their hypotheses occasionally surpass all understanding, and we have, therefore, no assurance as to the view they will take of this case. The first thing they will do will be to make what they will call a 'thorough examination' of the premises; but a study of chemistry gives to the word 'thorough' a significance of which they have no conception. It is to shorten this examination as much as possible, – to prevent it from being more tiresome to you than is absolutely necessary," he said to Gwen, "that I have taken the liberty of ascertaining and recording most of the data the officers will require."

"Believe me," Gwen said to him in an undertone not intended for the rest of us, though we heard it, "I am duly grateful for your consideration and shall find a fitting time to thank you."

With no other reply than a deprecating gesture, Maitland continued:

"Now let us look at the matter from the stand-point of the officers. They must first determine in their own minds how Mr. Darrow met his death. This will constitute the basis of their first hypothesis. I say 'first' because they are liable to change it at any moment it seems to them untenable. If they conclude that death resulted from natural causes, I shall doubtless be able to induce them to waive that view of the case until I have been given time to prove it untenable – if I can – and to act for the present upon one of the other two possible theories. It appears, from our present knowledge of the case, that, which-ever one of these they choose, the same difficulty will confront them."

Gwen looked at him inquiringly and he continued, answering the question in her eyes:

"This is what I mean. Your father, whether he committed suicide or was murdered, in all probability met his death through that almost imperceptible wound under his chin. This wound, so far as I have yet been able to examine it without a glass, was made with a somewhat blunt instrument, able, apparently, to little more than puncture the skin and draw a drop or so of blood. Of course, on such a theory, death must have resulted from poisoning. The essential point is: Where is the instrument that inflicted the wound?"

"Might it not be buried in the flesh?" Gwen asked.

"Possibly, but as I have not been able to find it I cannot believe it very likely, though closer search may reveal it," replied Maitland. "Your father's right forefinger," he continued, "is slightly stained with blood, but the wound is of a nature which could not have been caused by a finger nail previously poisoned. Since we know he pressed his hand to his throat this blood-stain makes no more strongly toward the truth of the suicide theory than it does toward that of the murder hypothesis. Suppose now, for we must look at all sides of the question, the officers begin to act upon the assumption that murder has been committed. What will they then do? They will satisfy themselves that the east window was opened six and three-quarters inches and securely fastened in that position; that the two south windows were closed and fastened and that the blinds thereof were also closed. They will ascertain the time when death occurred, – we can easily tell them, – and this will show them that neither of the blinds on the south side could have been opened without so increasing the light in the room as to be sure to attract our attention. They will learn also that the folding doors were locked, as they are now, on this side and that these two gentlemen [indicating Browne and Herne] sat against them. They will then turn to the hall door as the only possible means of entrance and I shall tell them that the Doctor and I sat directly in front of this door and between it and Mr. Darrow. I have taken the liberty to cut the carpet to mark the positions of our chairs. In view of all these facts what must they conclude? Simply this: no one entered the room, did the deed, and then left it, at least not without being observed." "But surely," I ventured to suggest, "you do not think they will presume to question the testimony of all of us that no one was observed."

"That is all negative evidence," he replied, "and does not conclusively prove that another might not have observed what we failed to detect. However, it is all so self-evident that they will not question it. I know so well their methods of reasoning that I am already prepared to refute their conclusions at every point, without, I regret to say, being myself able to solve the mystery, though I may say in passing that I purposely am refraining from formulating any theory whatever until I have ascertained everything which it is possible to learn in the matter. In this way I hope to avoid the error into which the detective is so prone to fall. Once you set up an hypothesis you unconsciously, and in spite of yourself, accentuate unduly the importance of all data making toward that hypothesis, while, on the other hand you either utterly neglect, misconstrue, or fail to fully appreciate, the evidence oppugnant to your theory. In chemical research I gather the material for an entire series of experiments before performing any, so that the first few shall not, either by satisfying or discouraging me, cause me to leave the bush half beaten.

"Let us see how, from the officers' standpoint, the murder hypothesis now stands. No assassin, it will be clear to them, could have entered or left this room unobserved. If, therefore, a man did enter the room and kill our friend, we, all of us, must be his accomplices." This remark drew some sort of exclamatory protest from every other person in the room save Browne.

"Ah, that is probably the true solution," said the artist with ill-concealed disgust.

This remark and the tone in which it was uttered would have been discourteous under any circumstances; at this particular time and in the painful situation in which we all found ourselves it was boorish almost beyond endurance.

There was nothing in Maitland's manner to indicate that he had heard Browne's remark, as he quietly continued:

"You see this cold-blooded view, the mere statement of which causes you all to shudder, – the more so because one of our number is the daughter of the dead man, – is not to be entertained a moment and is only mentioned to show the logical chain which will force the officers into the certain conviction that no assassin did enter or leave this room. What, then, remains of their theory? Two possibilities. First, the murderer may have done the deed without entering. If so, it is clear that he must have made use of the partly-opened window. This seems so likely that they will seize upon it with avidity. At first they will suggest that the assassin reached in at the window and struck his victim as he sat by it. This, they will urge, accounts for our not finding the weapon, and they will be so sure that this is the correct solution of the problem that I shall probably have to point out to them its patent absurdity. This illustrates the danger of forming an hypothesis from imperfect data. Remind them that Mr. Darrow did not sit by the window, but eight feet three and one-half inches from it, in almost the exact centre of the room, and their theory falls to the ground, only to be hastily replaced, as a drowning man catches at a straw, by a slightly varied theory. If the victim sat that distance from the window, they will inform us, it is clear the murderous implement must have been thrown or shot at him by the assassin."

"Indeed," said Mr. Herne, "though I had not thought of that theory it seems to me so plausible, now that you mention it, that I think the officers will show rare acumen if they adopt it. Very properly may they hold that some projectile might have been shot through the partly opened window and none of us have detected the act."

"Ah, yes," rejoined Maitland; "but when I ask them where this implement is under this assumption, and remind them of what I shall already have told them, viz., that Mr. Darrow sat back to the window as well as over eight feet from it, and sat in a chair, the solid back of which extended, like a protecting shield, fully six inches above the top of his head, they will find it difficult to show how, unless projectiles travel in sharp curves or angles, a man in this position could thus receive a wound directly beneath his chin, a wound so slight as not to penetrate the thyroid cartilage immediately under it.

"The abandonment of this hypothesis will force them to relinquish the idea that the murder was committed from without. What then remains? Only the second alternative. They must either give up altogether the idea of murder, or have recourse to what is known as the theory of exclusive opportunity."

"Theory of exclusive opportunity," repeated Gwen, as a puzzled look overspread her countenance. "I – I fear I do not quite understand what you mean."

"Pardon me, Miss Darrow, for not making my meaning clearer to you," said Maitland with a deferential inclination of the head. "The theory of exclusive opportunity, to state it plainly in this case, means simply this: if Mr. Darrow were murdered, some one of us five, we being the only ones having an opportunity to do the deed, must be the assassin. Whether this view be taken, or that of suicide, it becomes of paramount importance to find the weapon. Do you not now see why I objected to having anyone leave the room? If, as appears likely from my search, the weapon is not to be found, and if, as I feel reasonably certain, either the suicide or the murder theory be substantiated, then, anyone who left the room before official search was made would be held to have taken the weapon with him and disposed of it, because his would have been the exclusive opportunity of so doing. Someone must have disposed of it, and no one else had a chance to do so; that would be the way it would be stated. But, since no one of us has left the room, a thorough search both of it and of our persons, must convince the officers that we, at least, are not responsible for the fact that the weapon is not forthcoming."

Maitland paused and looked at Browne as if he expected him to speak, but that gentleman only shut his square jaws the more firmly together and held his peace, – at least in so far as words were concerned. If looks, like actions, "speak louder than words," this black visage with its two points of fire made eloquent discourse. I charged all this display of malice to jealousy. It is not altogether pleasant to be placed at a disadvantage before the one being whose good opinion one prizes above all things else, – that is to say, I have read that such is the case. I do not consider my own views upon such matters expert testimony. In all affairs of the heart my opinions cease to have weight at exactly the point where that organ ceases to be a pump.

Even Gwen, I think, noticed Browne's determined silence, for she said to Maitland:

"I am very grateful that your forethought prevented me from causing Mr. Browne even temporary annoyance by making him my messenger."

She paused a moment and then continued:

"You were speaking of the officers' theories. When they have convinced themselves that no one of us has removed the weapon, what then?"

"In my opinion," said Maitland, "they will ultimately fall back upon the suicide theory, but they must find the weapon here before they can substantiate it; for if it be not here someone must have taken it away and that someone could have only been the one who used it – the assassin, in short – but here are the officers. Let each one of us insist upon being searched. They can send to the station for a woman to search you," he said in an undertone to Gwen and then added: "I trust you will pardon my suggesting a course which, in your case, seems so utterly unnecessary, but, believe me, there are urgent reasons for it which I can explain later. If we would hope to solve this mystery, everything depends upon absolute thoroughness at this juncture."

"I should evince but poor appreciation," Gwen replied, "of the ability you have already shown should I fail to follow your slightest suggestion. It is all I can offer you by way of thanks for the kind interest you have taken."

The return of Officer Barker, accompanied by three other men, now changed the tide of conversation. Maitland advanced and shook hands with one whom he introduced as Mr. Osborne, and this gentleman in turn introduced his brother officer, a Mr. Allen, and M. Godin, a special detective.

Osborne impressed me as a man of only mediocre ability, thoroughly imbued with the idea that he is exceptionally clever. He spoke loudly and, I thought, a bit ostentatiously, yet withal in a manner so frank and hearty that I could not help liking the fellow.

M. Godin, on the contrary, seemed retiring almost to the point of self-abnegation. He said but little, apparently preferring to keep in the background, where he could record his own observations in his note-book without too frequent interruption. His manner was polished in the extreme, and so frank withal that he seemed to me like a man of glass through whom every thought shone unhindered. I wondered how one who seemed powerless to conceal his own emotions should possess a detective's ability to thread his way through the dark and hidden duplicity of crime. When he spoke it was in a low, velvety, and soothing voice, that fell upon the ear with an irresistible charm. When Osborne would make some thoughtless remark fraught with bitterness for Gwen, such an expression of pain would flit across M. Godin's fine face as one occasionally sees in those highly organised and sympathetic natures, --usually found among women if a doctor's experience may be trusted, - which catch the throb of another's hurt, even as adjacent strings strive to sing each other's songs.

M. Godin seemed to me more priest than detective. His clean-shaven face, its beautifully chiselled features suffused with that peculiar pallor which borrows the transparency of marble; the large, limpid brown eyes and the delicate, kindly mouth – all these, combined with a faultless manner and a carriage suggestive of power in reserve, so fascinated me that I found myself watching him continually. I remember saying to myself: "What a rival he would make in a woman's affections!"

At just that time he was looking at Gwen with tender, solicitous sympathy written in every feature, and that doubtless suggested my thought.

Mr. Allen was even more ordinary than Mr. Osborne in manner and appearance. I do not presume to judge his real merits, for I did not notice him sufficiently to properly portray him to you, even if I had the gift of description, which I think you will admit I have not. He lives in my memory only as a something tall, spare, coarse of texture, red, hairy, and redolent of poor tobacco.

How different men are! (Of course women are all alike!) While Osborne, like a good-natured bumble-bee, was buzzing noisily about, as though all the world were his clover-blossom; and Allen, so far as I know, was doing nothing; M. Godin, alert and keen despite his gentleness and a modesty which kept him for the most part unobtrusively in the shadow of his chosen corner, was writing rapidly in a notebook and speaking no word. It seemed as if nothing escaped him. Clearly he was there to enlighten himself rather than others. At length, pausing to make a measurement, he noticed my gaze and said to me in an undertone, as he glanced solicitously at Gwen lest she should hear:

"Pardon me, but did any of you observe anything, at or about the time of Mr. Darrow's death, which impressed you as singular, – any noise, any shadow, any draught or change of temperature, say a rushing or I might say swishing sound, – anything, in fact, that would seem to you as at all unusual?"

"Nothing whatever," I replied. "Everything seemed perfectly normal and commonplace."

"Hum! Strange!" he said, and returned to his notes.

I felt sure M. Godin had had a theory and that my testimony had not strengthened it, but he did not volunteer any information, neither did he take part in the conversation of his companions, and so my curiosity remained ungratified. It was clear that M. Godin's methods were very different from those of Osborne and Allen.

I need not weary you by further narrating what occurred at this official examination. Suffice it to say that, with one or two minor exceptions, Osborne and Allen followed the precise course of reasoning prophesied by Maitland, and, as for M. Godin, he courteously, but firmly, held his peace. The two officers did not, however, lean as strongly to the theory that death resulted from natural causes as Maitland had anticipated, and, I think, this surprised him. He had already told them that he expected to be able to show death to have resulted from poison hypodermically applied, and, as I overheard a remark made by Osborne to Allen, I readily understood their speedy abandonment of their natural-death theory. They were engaged in verifying Maitland's measurement of the east side of the room when Osborne said softly to his companion: "He has figured in several of my cases as a chemical expert, and when he expresses an opinion on a matter it's about the same as proved. He's not the kind that jumps in the dark. He's a lawyer as well as chemist and knows what's evidence, so I reckon we'd better see if we can make anything out of the suicide and murder theories."

Maitland had asked them to send to the station for a woman to search Gwen and she had just arrived. We all requested that a most thorough examination should now be made to assure the officers that no one of us possessed the missing weapon. This done, the officers and departed for the night, assuring Gwen that there was nothing further to be done till morning, and Osborne, doubtless with a view to consoling her, said: "It may be a relief to you, miss, to know that there is scarcely a doubt that your father took his own life." This had an effect upon Gwen very different from that which had been intended. Her face contracted, and it was plain to see she was beginning to think everyone was determined to force a falsehood upon her. Herne and Browne also prepared to take their leave. A glance from Maitland told me he wished me to remain with him a moment after the others had departed, and I accordingly did so.

When we were alone with Gwen he said to her: "I think I understand your feeling with regard to Mr. Osborne's remark, as well as your conviction that it does not represent the truth. I foresaw they would come to this conclusion, and know very well the pains they will take to prove their hypothesis." "Can nothing be done?" she asked beseechingly. "It is that of which I wish to speak," he replied. "If you have sufficient confidence in me to place the case in my hands, I will do everything in my power to establish the truth, – on one condition," and he glanced at her face, now pale and rigid from her long-continued effort of self-control. "And that condition is?" she said quickly. "That you follow my directions and permit me to order your movements in all things, so long as the case remains in my hands; if at any time I seek to abuse your faith, you are as free to discharge me as if I were a paid detective." Gwen looked searchingly at him; then, extending her hand to him, she said impulsively: "You are very kind; I accept the condition. What shall I do?"

I tried to catch Maitland's eye to tell him what he should counsel her, but a man with his ability to observe conditions and grasp situations can very well do without prompting. "First," he said, "you must return home with the Doctor and spend the rest of the night with his sister; I shall stay here until morning; and second, I desire that you use your utmost endeavour to keep the incidents of this evening out of your mind. You cannot, of course, forget your loss, unless you sleep," – and he gave me a look which said: "I depend on you to see to that," – "but you must not continually re-enact the scene in imagination, In the morning the Doctor will come here to bring me my camera, microscope, and a few things I shall require " – and he passed me a list he had written. "If you have slept well you can be of considerable service, and may accompany him – if not, you must remain quietly at his house." With this he turned to me, and said: "She is making a condenser of herself, Doctor, and will soon break through the insulation. Sparks will be dangerous – you must secure the brush effect." He spoke quickly, and used electrical terms, that she might not understand him, but either he failed of his purpose, or the observation she immediately made was a strange coincidence. I believe she understood, for, while young women educated by their mothers are usually ignorant upon all the more masculine subjects, those who have long been their father's companions are ever prone to startle one with the most unexpected flashes of intelligence. "I am in rather a high state of tension now," she said, turning calmly to Maitland; "but when alone the expression which has been denied me here will afford relief." Maitland glanced at her quickly, and then at me, and I knew he was wondering if she had understood. Then he said: "It is getting late. I shall expect you to sleep well and to come in the morning. Please say to the servants as you go that I shall stay here all night, and that no one must enter without permission. Good-night." She held out her hand to him, but made no reply; then she fervently kissed her father's lips, and together we left the chamber of death.

CHAPTER IV

Death speaks with the tongue of Memory, and his ashen hand reaches out of the great unknown to seize and hold fast our plighted souls.

What Maitland's reason was for spending the night with the dead body of Darrow, or how he busied himself until morning, I do not know. Perhaps he desired to make sure that everything remained untouched, or, it may be, that he chose this method of preventing Gwen from performing a vigil by the body. I thought this latter view very probable at the time, as I had been singularly impressed with the remarkable foresight my friend had displayed in so quickly and adroitly getting Gwen away from everything connected with her father's sad and mysterious death.

Arriving at my house my sister took an early opportunity to urge upon Gwen a glass of wine, in which I had placed a generous sedative. The terrible tension soon began to relax, and in less than half an hour she was sleeping quietly. I dreaded the moment when she should awake and the memory of all that had happened should descend like an avalanche upon her. I told my sister that this would be a critical moment, cautioning her to stay by Gwen and to give her, immediately upon her arising, a draught I had prepared for the purpose of somewhat deadening her sensibilities. I arose early, and went to Maitland's laboratory to collect the things he desired. When I returned Gwen was awake, and to my intense gratification in even a better condition than I had dared to hope.

It was quite late when we reached her house, and Maitland had evidently been at work several hours. He looked sharply at Gwen when she entered, and seemed much pleased at her condition. "You have obeyed my instructions, I see, and slept," he said, as he gave her his hand. "Yes," she replied, "I was very tired, and the doctor's cordial quite overcame me;" and she cast an inquiring glance at the network of white string which Maitland had stretched across the carpet, dividing it into squares like an immense checker-board. In reply to her questioning look, he said: "French detectives are the most thorough in the world, and I am about to make use of their method of instituting an exhaustive search. Each one of the squares formed by these intersecting strings is numbered, and represents one square foot of carpet, the numbers running from one to two hundred and eighty-eight. Every inch of every one of these squares I shall examine under a microscope, and anything found which can be of any possible interest will be carefully preserved, and its exact location accurately marked upon this chart I have prepared, which, as you will see, has the same number of squares as the room, the area of each square being reduced from one square foot to one square inch. You will note that I have already marked the location of all doors, windows, and furniture. The weapon, if there be one, may be very minute, but if it be on the floor we may be assured the microscope will find it. The walls of the room, especially any shelving projections, and the furniture, I shall examine with equal thoroughness, though I have now some additional reasons for believing the weapon is not here."

"Have you discovered anything new?" Gwen exclaimed, unable to control the excitement caused by this last remark. "You must pardon me," Maitland rejoined, "if I ask you and the Doctor a question before replying." She nodded assent, and he continued: "I wish to know if you agree with me that we shall be more likely to arrive at a solution of the problem before us if we keep our own counsel than if we take the officers of the law, or, for that matter, anyone else, into our confidence. You undoubtedly noticed how carefully M. Godin kept his own counsel. Official methods, and the hasty generalisations which form a part thereof – to say nothing of the petty rivalries and the passion for notoriety – can do much to hinder our own work, and, I believe, nothing to help it. What say you?" "That we keep our work to ourselves," Gwen quickly rejoined, and I signified that I was of the same opinion. "Then," Maitland continued, "I may say this in answer to your question. I have ascertained something which may bear upon the case in hand. You will remember that part of the gravel for redressing the croquet ground was dumped under the east window there. The painters, I learn, finished painting that side of the house yesterday forenoon before the gravel was removed and placed upon the ground, so that any footprints they may have made in it while about their work were obliterated. As you see, there was loose gravel left under the window to the depth of about two inches. I carefully examined this gravel this morning – there were no footprints."

I glanced at Gwen; her face had a set expression, and she was deathly pale. "There were, however," he continued, "places where the gravel had been tamped down as if by the pressure of a rectangular board. I examined these minutely and, by careful measurement and close scrutiny of some peculiar markings suggestive of the grain of wood, satisfied myself that the depressions in the gravel were made by two, and not, as I had at first thought, by one small piece of wood. I found further that these two boards had always borne certain relative relations to each other, and that when one had been turned around the other had undergone a similar rotation. This last is, in my mind, a most important point, for, when coupled with the fact that between any two impressions of the same board the distance was sensibly constant, and was that of a short stride, there could be no reasonable doubt but these boards had been worn upon some person's feet. They could not have been thrown down merely to be stepped upon, for, in that case, they would not have borne fixed relations to each other – probably would not have been turned end for end at all – and certainly, both would not always have happened to get turned at the same time. I procured a board of the combined area of the two supposed to have made the impressions in the gravel, and weighted it down until, as nearly as I could measure, it impacted the soil to the same extent the others had. The weight was one hundred and thirty-five pounds, which is about right for a man five feet five inches tall. The position of the depressions in the gravel indicated a stride just about right for a man of that height.

"There was one other most important discovery which I made after I had divided the impressions into two classes – according as they were produced by the right or left board – which was that when the right foot was thrown forward the stride was from three to four inches longer than when the left foot led. Directly under the window there was a deep impression in the sand. I took a plaster cast of it, and here it is," he said, producing an excellent facsimile of a closed hand. "There can be little doubt," he continued, "from the position occupied by the depression, of which this is a reverse copy, that it was either accidentally made by someone who, stooping before the east window to avoid obstructing its light, suddenly lost his balance and regained his equilibrium by thus thrusting out his hand, or – and this seems far more likely to me – that the hand was deliberately placed in the gravel in order to steady its possessor while he performed some peculiar operation."

At this point I ventured to ask why he regarded the latter view as so much more tenable than the former. "There are several reasons," he replied, "which render the view I prefer to take all but certain. First, the impression was made by the left hand. Second, it is the impression of a closed hand, with the upper joints of the fingers undermost. Did you ever know one to save himself from falling by thrusting out a closed hand? Certainly not. There is a certain amount of fear, however slight, invariably associated with losing one's balance. This sentiment, so far as the hand is concerned, is expressed by opening it and spreading the fingers. This he would instinctively have done, if falling. Then there is the position of the impression relative to the window and some slight testimony upon the sill and glass, for the thorough investigation of which I have been obliged to await my microscope. I have worked diligently, but that is all I have been able to accomplish."

"All!" exclaimed Gwen, regarding him with ill-concealed admiration. "It seems to me a very great deal. The thoroughness, the minuteness of it all, overwhelms me; but, tell me, have your discoveries led you to any conclusion?" "No," he replied, "nothing definite yet; I must not allow myself to become wedded to any theory, so long as there is anything further to be learned. If I were to hazard a few idle guesses, I should say your father was murdered in some mysterious way – by a person about five feet five inches tall, weighing, say, one hundred and thirty-five pounds, and having a lame leg, or, perhaps, one limb shorter than the other, – at all events having some deformity or ailment causing a variation in the length of the strides. I should guess also that this person's feet had some marked peculiarity, since such pains had been taken to conceal the footprints. Then the cast of the hand here encourages speculation. Fingers long, slim, and delicate, save at the nails, where, with the exception of the little finger, are to be found unmistakable signs of the habit of biting the nails, – see, here are the hang-nails, – but, strange to say, the nail of the little finger has been spared, and suffered to grow to an unusual length. I ask myself why this particular nail has been so favoured, and can only answer, 'because it has some peculiar use.' It is clear this is not the hand of a manual labourer; the joints are too small, the fingers too delicate, the texture of the skin, which is clearly visible, much too fine – in short, wouldn't it pass anywhere for a woman's hand? Say a woman who bit her nails. If it were really such there would be a pair of feminine feet also to be concealed, and boards would do it very nicely – but this is all guesswork, and must not be allowed to affect any subsequent conclusions. If you will excuse me a few minutes I will use the microscope a little on the sill of the east window before we are interrupted by our friends the officers, who will be sure to be here soon."

While Maitland was thus engaged I did all in my power to distract Gwen's attention, as much as possible, from her father's body. Whenever she regarded it, the same intense and set expression overspread her countenance as that which at first had alarmed me. I was glad when Maitland returned from the window and began mixing some of the chemicals I had brought him, for Gwen invariably followed all his movements, as if her very existence depended upon her letting nothing escape her. Maitland, who had asked me for a prescription blank, now dipped it in the chemicals he had mixed and, this accomplished, put the paper in his microscope box to dry.

"I have something here," he said, "which I desire to photograph quite as much as this room and some of its larger objects," and he pinned a tiny, crumpled mass against the wall, and made an exposure of it in that condition. "Do you know what this is?" he said, as he carefully smoothed it out for another picture. "I haven't the slightest idea," I said. "It is plain enough under the microscope," he continued, placing it upon the slide, and adjusting the focus. "Would you like to examine it, Miss Darrow?" Gwen had scarcely put her eye to the instrument before she exclaimed: "Why, it's a piece of thin outside bark from a twig of alder." Maitland's face was a study. . . "Would you mind telling me," he said deliberately, "how you found that out so quickly?" She hesitated a moment, and then said methodically, pointing toward the water, "I know the alder well – our boat is moored near a clump of them." "You are a keen observer," he replied, as he took the prepared paper from his box and spread the film of bark upon it to take a blue print of it. "There is one other object upon the sill which, unfortunately, I cannot take away with me," he continued, "but shall have to content myself with photographing. I refer to a sinuous line made in the paint, while green, and looking as if a short piece of rope, or, more properly, rubber tubing, since there is no rope-like texture visible, had been dropped upon it, and hastily removed – but see, here are Osborne and Allen looking for all the world as if they were prepared to demonstrate a fourth dimension of space. Now we shall see the suicide theory proved – to their own satisfaction, at least. But, whatever they say, don't forget we are to keep our own work to ourselves."

The two officers were alone. M. Godin had apparently decided to work by himself. This did not in the least surprise me, since I could easily see that he had nothing to gain by working with these two officers.

"We've solved the matter," was the first thing Osborne said after passing the time of day. "Indeed?" replied Maitland in a tone which was decidedly ambiguous; "you make it suicide, I suppose?" "That's just what we make it," returned the other. "We hadn't much doubt of it last night, but there were some things, such as the motive, for example, not quite clear to us; but it is all as plain as daylight now."

"And what says M. Godin?" asked Maitland.

Mr. Osborne burst into a loud guffaw.

"Oho, but that's good! What says M. Godin? I say, Allen, Maitland wants to know what 'Frenchy' says," and the pair laughed boisterously. "It's plain enough you don't know," he continued, addressing Maitland. "He's tighter 'n any champagne bottle you ever saw. The corkscrew ain't invented that'll draw a word out of M. Godin. You saw him making notes here last night. Well, the chances are that if this were a murder case, which it isn't, you'd see no more of M. Godin till he bobbed up some day, perhaps on the other side of the earth, with a pair of twisters on the culprit. He's a 'wiz,' is M. Godin. What does he think? He knows what he thinks, and he's the only individual on the planet that enjoys that distinction. I say, Allen, do you pump 'Frenchy' for the gentleman's enlightenment," and again the pair laughed long and heartily.

"Well, then," said Maitland, 'since we can't have M. Godin's views we shall have to content ourselves with those of your more confiding selves. Let's hear all about the suicide theory."

"I think," said Osborne in an undertone, "you had better ask Miss Darrow to withdraw for a few moments, as there are some details likely to pain her." This suggestion was intended only for Maitland, but the officer, used to talking in the open air, spoke so loudly that we all overheard him. "I thank you for your consideration," Gwen said to him, "but I would much prefer to remain. There can be nothing connected with this matter which I cannot bear to hear, or should not know. Pray proceed."

Osborne, anxious to narrate his triumph, needed no further urging. "We felt sure," he began, "that it was a case of suicide, but were perplexed to know why Mr. Darrow should wish to make it appear a murder. Of course, we thought he might wish to spare his daughter the shame such an act would visit upon her, but when this was exchanged for the horrible notoriety of murder, the motive didn't seem quite sufficient, so we looked for a stronger one – and found it." "Ah! you are getting interesting," Maitland observed.

Osborne cast a furtive glance at Gwen, and then continued: "We learned on inquiry that certain recent investments of Mr. Darrow's had turned out badly. In addition to this he had been dealing somewhat extensively in certain electric and sugar stocks, and when the recent financial crash came, he found himself unable to cover his margins, and was so swept clean of everything. Nor is this all; he had lost a considerable sum of money in yet another way – just how my informant would not disclose – and all of these losses combined made his speedy failure inevitable. Under such conditions many another man has committed suicide, unable to face financial ruin. But this man had a daughter to consider, and, as I have already said, he would wish to spare her the disgrace which the taking of his own life would visit upon her, and, more than all, would desire that she should not be left penniless. The creditors would make away with his estate, and his daughter be left a beggar. We could see but one way of his preventing this, and that was to insure his life in his daughter's favour. We instituted inquiries at the insurance offices, and found that less than a month ago he had taken out policies in various companies aggregating nearly fifty thousand dollars, whereas, up to that time, he had been carrying only two thousand dollars insurance. Why this sudden and tremendous increase? Clearly to provide for his daughter after his act should have deprived her of his own watchful care. And now we can plainly see why he wished his suicide to pass for murder. He had been insured but a month, and immediate ruin stared him in the face. His death must be consummated at once, and yet, by our law, a man who takes his life before the payment of his second annual insurance premium relieves the company issuing his policy of all liability thereunder, and robs his beneficiary of the fund intended for her. Here, then, is a sufficient motive, and nothing more is required to make the whole case perfectly clear. Of course, it would be a little more complete if we could find the weapon, but even without it, there can be no doubt, in the light of our work, that John Darrow took his own life with the intentions, and for the purposes, I have already set forth."

"Upon my soul, gentlemen," exclaimed Maitland, "you have reasoned that out well! Did you carefully read the copies of the various policies when

interrogating the companies insuring Mr. Darrow?"
"Hardly," Osborne replied. "We learned from the officials all we needed to know, and didn't waste any time in gratifying idle curiosity." A long-drawn "hm-m" was the only reply Maitland vouchsafed to this. "We regret," said Osborne, addressing Gwen, "that our duty, which has compelled us to establish the truth in this matter, has been the means of depriving you of the insurance money which your father intended for you." Gwen bowed, and a slight enigmatical smile played for a moment about her lips, but she made no other reply, and, as neither Maitland nor I encouraged conversation, the two officers wished us a good-morning, and left the house without further remark.

"I wish to ask you a few questions," Maitland said to Gwen as soon as the door had closed behind Osborne and his companion, "and I beg you will remember that in doing so, however personal my inquiries may seem, they have but one object in view – the solution of this mystery." "I have already had good proof of your singleness of purpose," she replied. "Only too gladly will I give you any information in my possession. Until this assassin is found, and my father's good name freed from the obloquy which has been cast upon it, my existence will be but a blank, – yes, worse, it will be an unceasing torment; for I know my father's spirit – if the dead have power to return to this earth – can never rest with this weight of shame upon it." As she spoke these words the depth of grief she had hitherto so well concealed became visible for a moment, and her whole frame shook as the expression of her emotion reacted upon her. The next instant she regained her old composure, and said calmly:

"You see I have every reason to shed whatever light I can upon this dark subject."

"Please, then, to answer my questions methodically, and do not permit yourself to reason why I have asked them. What was your father's age?"

"Sixty-two."

"Did he drink?"

"No."

"Did he play cards?"

"Yes."

"Poker?"

"Yes, and several other games."

"Was he as fond of them as of croquet?"

"No; nothing pleased him as croquet did – nothing, unless it were chess."

"Hum! Do you play chess?"

"Yes; I played a good deal with father."

"What kind of a game did he play?"

"I do not understand you. He played a good game; my father did not enjoy doing anything that he could not do well."

"I mean to ask if his positions were steadily sustained – or if, on the other hand, his manoeuvres were swift, and what you might call brilliant."

"I think you would call them brilliant."

"Hum! How old are you?"

"Twenty-two."

"Tell me your relations with your father."

"We were most constant companions. My mother – she and my father – they were not altogether companionable – in short, they were ill-mated, and, being wise enough to find it out, and having no desire to longer embitter each other's lives, they agreed to separate when I was only four. They parted without the slightest ill-feeling, and I remained with father. He was very fond of me, and would permit no one else to teach me. At seven I was drawing and painting under his guidance. At eight the violin was put into my hands and my studies in voice began. In the meantime father was most careful not to neglect my physical training; he taught me the use of Indian clubs, and how to walk easily. At eight I could walk four miles an hour without fatigue. The neighbours used to urge that I be put to school, but my father would reply – many a time I have heard him say it – 'a child's brain is like a flower that blossoms in perceptions and goes to seed in abstractions. Correct concepts are the raw material of reason. Every desk in your school is an intellectual loom which is expected to weave a sound fabric out of rotten raw material. While your children are wasting their fibre in memorising the antique errors of classical thought my child is being fitted to perceive new truths for herself.' It is needless to say his friends considered these views altogether too radical. But for all that I was never sent to school. My father's library was always at my disposal, and I was taught how to use it. We were constantly together, and grew so into each other's lives that " – but her voice failed her, and her eyes moistened. Maitland, though he apparently did not notice her emotion, so busy was he in making notes, quickly put a question which diverted her attention.

"Your father seemed last night to have a presentiment of some impending calamity. Was this a common experience?"

"Of late, yes. He has told me some six or seven times of dreaming the same dreams – a dream in which some assassin struck him out of the darkness." "Did you at any of these times notice anything which might now lead you to believe this fancied repetition was the result of any mental malady?"

"No."

"Was his description of the dreams always the same?"

"No; never were they twice alike, save in the one particular of the unseen assassin."

"Hum!, Did the impression of these dreams remain long with him?"

"He never recovered from it, and each dream only accentuated his assurance that the experience was prophetic. When once I tried to dissuade him from this view, he said to me: 'Gwen, it is useless; I am making no mistake. When I am gone you will know why I am now so sure – I cannot tell you now, it would only ' – here he stopped short, and, turning abruptly to me, said with a fierceness entirely alien to his disposition: 'Hatred is foreign to my nature, but I hate that man with a perfect hell of loathing! Have I been a kind father to you, Gwen? If so, promise me ' – and he seized me by the wrist – ' promise me if I'm murdered – I may as well say when I'm murdered – you will look upon the man who brings my assassin to justice – the thought that he may escape is damning – as your dearest friend on earth! You will deny him nothing. You will learn later that I have taken care to reward him. My child, you will owe this man a debt you can never repay, for he will have enabled your father's soul to find repose. I dreamed last night that I came back from the dead, and heard my avenger ask you to be his wife. You refused, and at your ingratitude my restless soul returned to torment everlasting. Swear to me, Gwen, that you'll deny him nothing, nothing, nothing!' I promised him, and he seemed much reassured. 'I am satisfied,' he said, 'and now can die in peace, for you are an anomaly, Gwen, – a woman who fully knows the nature of a covenant,' and he put his arm about me, and drew me to him. His fierceness had subsided as quickly as it had appeared, and he was now all tenderness."

Maitland, who appeared somewhat agitated by her recital, said to her: "After the exaction of such a promise you have, of course, no doubt that your father was the victim of a mental malady – at least, at such times as those of which you speak?"

Gwen replied deliberately: "Indeed, I have grave doubts. My father was possessed by a strange conviction, but I never saw anything which impressed me as indicating an unsound mind. I am, of course, scarcely fitted to judge in such matters."

Maitland's face darkened as he asked: "You would not have me infer that you would consider your promise in any sense binding?"

"And why not?" she ejaculated in astonishment.

"Because," he continued, "the request is so unnatural as to be in itself sufficient evidence that it was not made by a man in his right mind."

"I cannot agree with you as to my father's condition," Gwen replied firmly; "yet you may be right; I only know that I, at least, was in my right mind, and that I promised. If it cost me my life to keep that pledge, I shall not hesitate a moment. Have you forgotten that my father's last words were, 'remember your promise'?" She glanced up at Maitland as she said this, and started a little as she saw the expression of pain upon his face. "I seem to you foolishly deluded," she said apologetically; "and you are displeased to see that my purpose is not shaken. Think of all my father was to me, and then ask yourself if I could betray his faith. The contemplation of the subject is painful at best; its realisation may, from the standpoint of a sensitive woman, be fraught with unspeakable horror, – I dare not think of it! May we not change the subject?"

For a long time Maitland did not speak, and I forbore to break the silence. At last he said: "Let us hope, if the supposed assassin be taken, the discovery may be made by someone worthy the name of man – someone who will not permit you to sacrifice either yourself or your money." Gwen glanced at him quickly, for his voice was strangely heavy and inelastic, and an unmistakable gloom had settled upon him. I thought she was a little startled, and I was considering if I had not better call her aside and explain that he was subject to these moods, when he continued, apparently unaware of the impression he had made: "Do you realise how strong a case of suicide the authorities have made out? Like all of their work it has weak places. We must search these in order to overthrow their conclusion. The insurance policies they were 'too busy' to read we must peruse. Then, judging from your story, there seems little doubt that your father has left some explanation of affairs hitherto not confided to you – some document which he has reserved for your perusal after his death. No time should be lost in settling this question. The papers may be here, or in the hands of his attorney. Let us search here first."

"His private papers," Gwen said, rising to lead the way, "are in his desk in the study."

"One moment, please," Maitland interrupted, calling her back, "I have something I have been trying to ask you for the last hour, but have repeatedly put off. I believe your father's death to have resulted from poisoning. You know the result of the post-mortem inquest. It is necessary to make an analysis of the poison, if there be any, and an absolutely thorough microscopic examination of the wound. I – I regret to pain you – but to do this properly it will be necessary to cut away the wounded portion. Have we your permission to do so?"

For a moment Gwen did not answer. She fell upon her knees before her father's body, and kissed the cold face passionately. For the first time since the tragedy she found relief in tears. When she arose a great change had come over her. She was very pale and seized a chair for support as she replied to Maitland's question between the convulsive sobs which she seemed powerless to check: "I – I have bidden him good-bye. We shall but obey his command in sparing no pains to reach the assassin. You – you have my permission to do anything – everything – that may be – necessary to that end. I – I know you will be as gentle – " But she could not finish her sentence. The futility of gentleness – the realisation that her father was forever past all need of tenderness, fell like a shroud about her soul. The awakening I had dreaded had come. Her hand fell from the chair, she staggered, and would have fallen to the floor had not Maitland caught her in his arms.

THE EPISODE OF THE SEALED DOCU-MENT

CHAPTER I

*Father of all surveyors, Time drags his chain of
rust through every life, and only Love – unag-
ing God of the Ages – immeasurable, keeps his
untarnished youth.*

Maitland carried the unconscious girl into the
study, and for some time we busied ourselves in
bringing her to herself. When this task was accomplished we did not feel like immediately putting any
further tax upon her strength. Maitland insisted that
she should rest while he and I ransacked the desk,
and, ever mindful of her promise to obey his instructions, she yielded without remonstrance. Our search
revealed the insurance policies, and a sealed envelope bearing the inscription: "To Miss Gwen Darrow,
to be opened after the death of John Darrow," and
three newspapers with articles marked in blue pencil. I read the first aloud. It ran as follows:

I have reason to believe an attempt will sooner
or later be made upon my life, and that the utmost
cunning will be employed to lead the authorities
astray. The search for the assassin will be long, ex-
pensive, and discouraging – just such a task as is
never successfully completed without some strong
personal incentive. This I propose to supply in ad-
vance. My death will place in my daughter's hands
a fund of fifty thousand dollars, to be held in trust by
her, and delivered, in the event of my being murdered, to such person or persons as shall secure evi-

dence leading to the conviction of the murderer. (Signed) JOHN HINTON DARROW.

I glanced at the other two papers – the marked article was the same in each. "I wonder what your friend Osborne would say to that," I said to Maitland.

"How old are the papers?" he replied.

"March 15th, – only a little over a month," I answered.

"Let me see them, please," he said. "Hum! All of the same date, and each in the paid part of the paper! It is clear Mr. Darrow inserted these singular notices himself. I will tell you what Osborne will say when he learns of these articles. He will say they strengthen his theory; that no sane man would publish such a thing, except as a weak attempt to deceive the insurance companies. As for the money all being paid to the discoverer of the assassin, instead of to his daughter, he will simply dispose of that by saying: 'No assassin, no reward, and the fund remains intact.' If now, the other papers permit Miss Darrow to use the interest of this fund while holding the principal in trust, we do not at present know enough of this matter to successfully refute Osborne's reasoning. This mystery seems to grow darker rather than lighter. The one thing upon which we seem continually to get evidence is the question of sanity. If Mr. Darrow's suspicions were directed against no one in particular, then it is clear his dreams, and all the rest of his fears for that matter, had a purely subjective origin, which is to say that upon this one subject, at least, he was of unsound mind. '

"I cannot think so," Gwen interrupted. "He was so rational in everything else."

"That is quite possible," I replied. "I have known people to be monomaniacs upon the subject of water, and to go nowhere without a glass of it in their hands. There is also a well-authenticated case of a man who was as sane as you or I until he heard the words 'real estate.' One day while quietly carving the meat at a dinner to which he had invited several guests, a gentleman opposite him inadvertently spoke the fatal words, when, without a word of warning, he sprang at him across the table, using the carving-knife with all the fury of the most violent maniac; and yet, under all other conditions, he was perfectly rational."

"If, on the other hand," said Maitland, continuing his remarks as if unaware of our interruption, "Mr. Darrow's suspicions had any foundation in fact, it is almost certain they must have been directed against some specific person or persons. If so, why did he not name them? – but, stay – how do we know that he did not? Let us proceed with our examination of the papers," and he began perusing the insurance policies. Neither Gwen nor I spoke till he had finished and thrown them down, when we both turned expectantly toward him.

"All in Osborne's favour so far," he said. "Principal to be held in trust by Miss Darrow under the terms of a will which we have yet to find; the income, until the discharge of the trust, to go to Miss Darrow. Now for this," and he passed Gwen the sealed envelope addressed to her.

She broke the seal with much agitation. "Shall I read it aloud?" she asked.

We signified our desire to hear it, and she read as follows:

MY DEAR GWEN:

My forebodings have seemed to you strange and uncalled for, but when this comes to your hand you will know whether or not they were groundless. Of one episode in my career which shook the structure of my being to its foundation stone, you have been carefully kept in ignorance. It is necessary that you should know it when I am gone, and I have accordingly committed it to this paper, which will then fall into your hands. My early life, until two years after I married your mother, was spent in India, the adult portion thereof being devoted to the service of the East India Company. I had charge of a department in their depot at Bombay. You have seen Naples. Add to the beauties of that city the interesting and motley population of Cairo and you can form some idea of the attractions of Bombay. I was very happy there until the occurrence of the event I am about to narrate.

One morning, my duties calling me to one of the wharves, my attention was attracted by a young girl dancing upon the flags by the water's edge. The ordinary bayadere is so common an object in India as to attract but little notice from anyone of refined tastes, but this girl, judging from the chaste beauty of her movements, was of a very different type. As my curiosity drew me nearer to her she turned her face toward me, and in that instant I knew my hour had come.

Though many years her senior she was still my first love, – the one great passion of my life.

I do not attempt to describe her ineffable loveliness, for, like the beauty of a flower, it was incapable of analysis. Nothing that I could write would give you any adequate idea of this girl's seraphic face, for she was like unto no one you have ever seen in this cold Western world. I watched in a wild, nervous transport, I know not how long – time and space had no part in this new ecstasy of mine! I could think of nothing, do nothing – only feel, – feel the hot blood deluge my brain only to fall back in scalding torrents upon my heart with a pain that was exquisite pleasure.

Suddenly she changed her step and executed a quick backward movement toward the water, stopping just as her heels touched the curb at the edge of the wharf; then forward, and again a quick return to the backward movement, but this time she mistook the distance, her heels struck the curb forcibly, and she was precipitated backward into the water. For a moment I stood as one petrified, unable to reason, much less to act; then the excited voices of the crowd recalled me. They had thrown a rope into the water and were waiting for her to come to the surface and grasp it. The wall from which she had fallen must have been at least fifteen feet above the water, which was littered with broken spars, pieces of timber, and other odd bits of wood. It seemed as if she would never come to the surface, and when at length she did, she did not attempt to seize the rope thrown to her, but sank without a movement. The truth flashed upon me in an instant. She had struck her head against some of the floating drift and was unconscious! Something must be done at once. I seized the rope and sprang in after her, taking good care to avoid obstructions, and although, as you know, I never learned to swim, I succeeded in reaching her, and we were drawn up together. I bore her in my arms into one of the storerooms close by, and, laying her upon a bale of cotton, used such restoratives as could be quickly procured.

I was kneeling by her, my arm under her neck, in the act of raising her head, when she opened her eyes, and fastened them, full of wonderment, upon my face. A moment more, her memory returning to her, she made a little movement, as if to free herself. I was too excited then to heed it, and continued to support her head. She did not repeat the movement, but half closed her eyes and leaned back resignedly against my arm. If, I thought, these few minutes could be expanded into an eternity, it would be my idea of heaven. She was recovering rapidly now and soon raised herself into a sitting posture, saying, in very good English, "I think I can stand now, Sahib." I gave her my arm and assisted her to her feet. Her hand closed upon my sleeve as if to see how wet it was, and glancing at my dripping garments, she said simply: "You have been in the water, Sahib, and it is to you I owe my life. I shall never forget your kindness." She raised her eyes to my face and met my gaze for a moment, as she spoke. We are told that the eye is incapable of any expression save that lent it by the lids and brow, – that the eyeball itself, apart from its direction, and the changes of the pupil resulting from variations in the intensity of light, can carry no message whatsoever. This may be so, but, without any noticeable movement of the eyes that met mine, I learned with ineffable delight that this young girl's soul and mine were threaded upon the same cord of destiny. My emotion so overpowered me that I could not speak, and when my self-possession returned the young girl had vanished.

From the height of bliss I now plunged into the abyss of despair. I had let her go without a word. I did not even know her name. I had caught her to myself from the ocean only to suffer her to drown herself among the half-million inhabitants of Bombay. What must she think of me? I asked the wharfinger if he knew her, but he had never seen her before. All my other inquiries proved equally fruitless. I wondered if she knew that I loved her, but hardly dared to hope she had been able to correctly interpret my boorish conduct. I could think of but one thing to do. If I did not know her name, neither did she know mine, and so if she desired a further acquaintance, she, like myself, must rely upon a chance meeting. If she had detected my admiration for her she must know that I too would strive to meet her again. Where would she be most likely to expect me to look for her? Clearly at the same place we had met before, and at the same time of day. She might naturally think my duties called me there daily at that hour. I determined to be there at the same time the next day.

I arrived to find her there before me, anxiously peering at the passers-by. She was certainly looking for me, – there was ecstasy in the thought!

It is not necessary, my dear child, that I should describe the details of our love-making, for my present purpose is not merely to interest you, but rather to acquaint you with certain occurrences which I now deem it wise you should know. Time only intensified our love for each other, and for several months all went well. One serious obstacle to our union presented itself, – that of caste. Her people, Lona said, would never permit her to marry outside her own station in life, besides which there was another ground upon which we might be equally sure of their opposition. They had already chosen for her and she was betrothed to Rama Ragobah. It is of this man that I have chiefly to speak. By birth he was of the same Vaisya caste as Lona. Early in life his lot had fallen among fakirs and he had acquired all their secrets. This did not satisfy his ambitions, for he wished to be numbered among the rishis or adepts, and subjected himself to the most horrible asceticism to qualify himself for adeptship. His indifference to physical pain was truly marvellous. He had rolled his naked body to the Ganges over hundreds of miles of burning sands! He had held his hands clinched until the nails had worn through the palm and out at the back of the hand. He had at one time maintained for weeks a slow fire upon the top of his head, keeping the skin burned to the skull.

When he came wooing Lona, his rigid asceticism had much relaxed, but he would still seek to amuse her by driving knives into his body until she would sicken at the blood, a condition of affairs which, she said, afforded him great enjoyment.

Ragobah was a man of gigantic build and immense physical strength. His features were heavy and forbidding. You are familiar with pictures of Nana Sahib. If I had not known this fiend to have died while beset in a swamp, I should have mistaken Ragobah for him. It was to such a being that Lona was betrothed in spite of the loathing her parents knew she felt for him. She told me all this one night at our accustomed tryst on Malabar Hill. We had chosen to meet here on account of the beauty of the place and the seclusion it offered. There, on bright moonlit nights, with the sea and the city below me, the "Tower of Silence" in the Parsees' burial plot ablaze with reflected glory, the majestic banyan over me rustling gently in the soft sea breeze, while Lona nestled close beside me, – the exquisite perfume of the luxuriant garden less welcome than the delicious fragrance of her breath, – hours fraught with years of bliss would pass as if but pulse-beats. In the world of love the heart is the only true timepiece. On one or two occasions Lona had thought she had been followed when coming to meet me, and she began to conceive a strange dislike for a little cavelike recess in the rocks just back of the tree by which we sat. I tried on one occasion to reassure her by telling her it was so shallow that, with the moonlight streaming into it, I could see clear to the back wall, and arose to enter it to convince her there was no one there, but she clung to me in terror, saying: "Don't go! Don't leave me! I was foolish to mention it. I cannot account for my fear, – and yet, do you know," she continued in a low, frightened tone, "there is a shaft at the back of the cave that has, they say, no bottom, but goes down, – down, – down, – -hundreds of feet to the sea?" It is useless, as you know only too well, to strive to reason down a presentiment, and so, instead, I sought to make use of her fear in the accomplishment of my dearest wish. "Why need we," I urged, "come here; why longer continue these clandestine meetings? Let us be brave, darling, in our loves. Your people have chosen another husband for you, – my people another wife for me; but we are both quite able to choose for ourselves. We have done so, and it is our most sacred duty to adhere to and consummate that choice. Let us, I beseech you, do so without further delay. Dearest, meet me here to-morrow night prepared for a journey. We will take the late train for Matheron Station, where I have friends who can be trusted. We will be married immediately upon our arrival, and can communicate by post with our respective families, remaining away from them until they are glad to welcome us with open arms."

She raised some few objections to my plan and expressed some misgivings, but she loved me and I was able to reason away the one and kiss away the other, and with our souls upon our lips we parted for the night. The last thing I had said to her, – I remember it as if it all happened yesterday, – was: "Think of it, dear heart, there will be no more such partings between us after to-night!" and she had replied by silently nestling closer to me and twining her arms about my neck. And so we parted on that never-to-be-forgotten night more than a score of years ago.

The twenty-four hours intervening between this parting and our next meeting may be passed over in silence, as nothing occurred during that time at all essential to the purpose this narrative subserves. The longed-for time came at last and, with a depth of happiness I had never known before – a peace passing all understanding – I set out for Malabar Hill. The night was perfect and the moonlight so bright I could distinctly see the air-roots of our trysting tree when more than a quarter of a mile away. I thought at the time how this tree, with its crown of luxuriant foliage and its writhing roots, might well pass for some gigantic Medusa-head with its streaming serpent-hair. As I neared the tree Lona stepped from behind it and awaited my approach. She was even more impatient than I, I thought, and my heart beat more wildly than ever. "Sweet saint, have I kept you waiting?" I asked, as I came within speaking distance of her. She stood motionless against the tree and apparently did not hear me. I waited till I was within ten feet of her and repeated the question, but, although she fixed her unfathomable eyes full upon mine, she made no reply, and gave no evidence of having heard me. I stood as if petrified. A nameless dread was settling upon me, paralysing my faculties. She had always before sprung forward at sight of me and thrown herself with a bewitching little pirouette into my arms, now she stood coldly aloof, silent and motionless, on this, our wedding night! I waited for some word of explanation, but none came. The suspense became unbearable – I could endure it no longer!

"For God's sake, what has happened?" I cried, rushing forward to seize her in my arms. She raised her right hand above her head and, as I had almost reached her, threw something full in my face! Instinctively I struck at it with my walking-stick, and it fell in the grass at my feet, – it was a young Indian cobra – Naja tripudians – a serpent of the deadliest sort. I did not pause to reason how this sweet angel had been so quickly changed into a venomous fiend, although the thought that somehow she had been led to think me false to her, and that this act was the swift vengeance of her hot Eastern blood, flashed momentarily through my mind, – all that could be explained as soon as I had her nestling in my arms. I reached forward to embrace her, but she struck me in the face and fled! For an instant my heart stood still. It seemed to me it would never start, but it soon began to throb again like a thing of lead, and the blood it pumped was cold, for the winter had closed in upon it. The elasticity of my life, that ineffable resiliency of the soul which makes us more than beasts of burden, was gone forever. An automaton, informed only with the material life, remained, – the spirit followed that fleeting figure down the hill. More than twenty years have passed and still the unrewarded chase continues!

But it is to facts I have to call your attention, rather than to their effects. A flutter of white muslin in the moonlit distance was all that was visible of the retreating girl when I started mechanically, and without any particular purpose in view, in pursuit of her. My path lay by the banyan tree under which we had so often sat, but every air-root seemed changed to a writhing serpent. As I threaded my way among them, a man stepped from behind the trunk and disputed my passage. His gigantic form was silhouetted against the mass of rock forming the entrance to the little cave. The bright moonlight did what it could to illumine that sinister face. It was Rama Ragobah! For fully a minute we stood silently face to face, each expecting the assault of the other. It was Ragobah who spoke first. "She is mine, body and soul; and the English cur may find a mate in his own kennel!" He bent toward me and hissed these words in my very face. His hot breath seemed to poison me. It made me beside myself. I knew he meant to take advantage of his physical superiority and attack me, by the narrow watch he kept upon the heavy walking-stick I still carried in my right hand. He had expected I would attempt to strike with this, but my constant practice at boxing had made my fists the more natural weapon. I was so enraged I did not notice he was too close to use my stick to advantage. I simply acted without any thought whatever. His attitude was such, as he hissed his venom into my face, as to enable me to give him a powerful "upper cut" under the jaw. This, as I was so much lighter than he, was the most effective blow I could deliver; yet, although it took him off his feet, it did not disable him. I had not succeeded in placing it as I had intended, and it had only the effect of rendering him demoniacal. In an instant he was again upon his feet, and unsheathing a long knife. I knew it meant death for me if he were able to close with me. It was useless for me to call for help, for in those days this part of Malabar Hill was as deserted as a wilderness. Now, the very spot on which we stood is highly cultivated, and forms a part of the garden of the Blasehek villa. There, early in the eighties, as the guest of the hospitable Herr Blasehek, Professor

Ernst Haeckel botanised a week, on his way to Ceylon. Now, in response to a cry from his intended victim, an assassin might be frustrated by assistance from a dozen bungalows, but at the time of which I write, the victim, if he were wise, saved his breath for the struggle which he knew he must make unaided.

Ragobah paused, and coolly bared his right arm to the elbow. There was a studied deliberation in his movements, which said only too plainly: "There is no hurry in killing you, for you cannot escape." I grasped my stick firmly as my only hope, and awaited his onslaught. My early military drill now stood me in good stead, and to it I owe my life. Without the knowledge which I had derived from the use of the broadsword, I should have been all but certain to have attempted to strike him a downward blow upon the head. This is just what he was expecting, and it would have cost me my life. He would have had only to throw up his left arm to catch the blow, while with his right hand he plunged the knife into my heart. My experience had taught me how much easier it is to protect one's self from a cutting blow than from a thrust, and I determined to adopt this latter means of assault. Ragobah advanced upon me slowly, much as a cat steals upon an unsuspecting bird. I raised my stick as if to strike him, and he instinctively threw up his left arm, and advanced upon me. My opportunity had come; I lowered the point of my cane to the level of his face, and made a vigorous lunge forward, throwing my whole weight upon the thrust. As nearly as I could tell, the point of my stick caught him in the socket of the left eye, just as he sprang forward, and hurled him backward, blinded and stupefied. Before he had recovered sufficiently to protect himself, I dealt him a blow upon the head that brought him quickly to the earth. Without stopping to ascertain whether or not I had killed him, I fled precipitately to my lodgings, hastily packed my belongings, and set out for Matheron Station by the same train I had so fondly believed would convey Lona and me to our nuptial altar. Words cannot describe the suffering I endured upon that journey. For the first time since my terrible desertion I had an opportunity to think, and I did think, if the pulse of an overwhelming pain, perpetually recurring like the beat of a loaded wheel, can be called thought. Although there is no insanity in our family nearer than a great-uncle, I marvel that I retained my wits under this terrible blow. I seriously contemplated suicide, and probably should have taken my life had not my mental condition gradually undergone a change. I was no longer conscious of suffering, nor of a desire to end my life. I was simply indifferent. It was all one to me whether I lived or died. The power of loving or caring for anything or anybody had entirely left me, and when I would reflect how utterly indifferent I was even to my own father and mother, I would regard myself as an unnatural monster. I tried to conceal my lack of affection by a greater attention to their wishes, and it was in this way that I yielded, without remonstrance, to those same views regarding my marriage, to which, but a little while before, I had made such strenuous objections as to quite enrage my father. I was an only child, and (as often happens in such cases) my father never could be brought to realise that I had many years since attained my majority. It had been his wish, ever since my boyhood, that I should marry your mother, and he made use, when I was nearly forty, of the selfsame insistent and coercive methods with which he had sought to subdue my will when I was but twenty, and at last he attained his end. I had learned from friends in Bombay that not only had Rama Ragobah recovered from the blows I had given him, but that, shortly after my encounter with him, he had married Lona, she whom I had loved, God only knows how madly! It was all one to me now whether I was married or single, living or dead. So it was all arranged. I myself told the lady that, so far as I then understood my feelings, I had no affection for any person on earth; but it seemed only to pique her, and I think she determined then and there to make herself an exception to this universal rule. This is how I came to marry your mother. There was not the slightest community of thought, sentiment, or interest between us. The things I liked did not interest her; what she liked bored me; yet she was pre-eminently a sensible woman, and when she learned the real state of affairs was the first to suggest a separation, which was effected. We parted with the kindliest feelings, and, as you know, remained fast friends up to her death.

It was nearly a year after the affair on Malabar Hill before I had the heart to return with your mother to Bombay. I had thought all emotion forever dead within me, but, ah! how little do we understand ourselves. Twelve months had not passed, and already I was conscious of a vague ache – a feeling that something, I scarcely knew what, had gone wrong, so terribly wrong! I told myself that I was now married, and had a duty both to my wife and society, and I tried hard to ignore the ache, on the one hand, and not to permit myself to define and analyse it on the other. But a man does not have to understand anatomy in order to break his heart, and so my longing defined itself even by itself. The old fire, built on a virgin hearth, was far from out. Society had heaped a mouthful of conventional ashes upon it, but they had served only to preserve it. From the fiat of the human heart there is no court of appeal.

One night, to my utter amazement, I received a letter from Lona which you will find filed away among my other valuable documents.

It was addressed in her own quaint little hand, and I trembled violently as I opened the envelope. It was but a brief note, and ran as follows:

"I am dying, and have much to explain before I go. Be generous, and do not think too harshly of me. Suspend your judgment until I have spoken. You must come by stealth, or you will not be permitted to see me. Follow my directions carefully and you will have no trouble in reaching me. Go at once to the cave on Malabar Hill, whistle thrice, and one will appear who will conduct you safely to me. Follow him, and whatever happens, make no noise. Do not delay – I can last but little longer. "LONA."

I did not even pause to re-read the letter, or to ask why it was necessary to follow such singular directions in order to be led to her. I simply knew she had written to me; that she was dying; that she wanted me; that was all, but it was enough. Dazed, filled with a strange mixture of dread and yearning, I hurried to the cave. It was already night when I reached it – just such a moonlit night as that on which, nearly a year before, Lona and I had planned our elopement; and now that heart, which then had beaten so wildly against mine, was slowly throbbing itself into eternal silence, – and I – I had been more than dead ever since.

I looked about on all sides, but no human being was visible. I whistled thrice, but no sound came in response. Again I whistled, with the same result. Where was my guide? Perhaps he was in the cave and had not heard me. I entered it to see, but had barely passed the narrow portal when a voice said close behind me: "Did you whistle, Sahib?" The suddenness, the strangeness of this uncanny appearance, so close to me that I felt the breath of the words upon my neck, sent a chill over me. I shall never forget that feeling! Many times since then have I dreamt of a hand that struck me from out the darkness, while the same unspeakable dread froze up my life, until, by repetition, it has sunk deep into my soul with the weight of a positive conviction. I know, as I now write, that this will be my end, and his will be the hand that strikes. The fibre of our lives is twisted in a certain way, and each has its own fixed mode of unravelling, – this will be mine.

When I had recovered from the first momentary shock I turned and looked behind me. There, close upon me, with his huge form blocking the narrow entrance, stood Rama Ragobah, my rival, his face hideous with malignant triumph! I was trapped, and that, too, by a man whom my hatred, could it have worked its will, would have plunged into the uttermost hell of torment. I felt sure my hour had come, but my assassin should not have the satisfaction of thinking I feared him. I did not permit myself to betray the slightest concern as to my position – indeed, after the shock of the first surprise, I did not care so very much what fate awaited me. Why should I? Had I not seriously thought of taking my own life? Was it not clear now that Lona, whose own handwriting had decoyed me, had most basely betrayed me into her husband's hands? If I had wished to end my own life before, surely now, death, at the hands of another, was no very terrible thing. Could I have dragged that other down with me, I would have rejoiced at the prospect!

Ragobah broke the silence. "You have left your stick this time, I see," he said, as he unsheathed the long knife I had once before escaped, and ostentatiously felt its edge as if he were about to shave with it.

"You were in haste, Sahib, when you left me last time, or I should not now have the pleasure of this interview. Be assured I shall do my work more thoroughly this time. Behind you there is a hole partly filled with water. If you drop a stone into this well, it is several seconds before you hear the splash, and there is a saying hereabouts that it is bottomless. I am curious to know if this be true, and I am going to send you to see. Of course, if the story is well founded, I shall not expect you to come back. That would be unreasonable, Sahib."

All this was said with a refined sarcasm which maddened me, and, as he concluded, he began to edge stealthily toward me. So strong is the instinct of self-preservation within us that I doubt not a would-be suicide, caught in the act of hanging himself, would struggle madly for his life were someone else to forcibly adjust the noose about his neck. At all events, I found myself unwilling, at the last moment, to have someone else launch me into eternity and, as I wished to gain time to think what I should do to escape, I said to him:

"Why do you bear me such malice? Can you not see that any injury I may have done you was purely in self-defence? You sought the quarrel, and I took the only means at hand to protect myself. I did not, as you know, seek to kill you, a thing I could easily have done, but was content merely to make good my escape. I – "

"Bah!" he said, interrupting me savagely. "That has nothing to do with it. Had you only pounded my head you might live, but you have pounded my heart! It is for that I hate you, and for that you die!"

"What have I done?" I asked.

"What have you done?" he roared, furious with rage. "I will tell you. You have by magic possessed the mind of my wife. Your name, your cursed name is ever upon her lips! My entreaties, my supplications are answered by nothing else. Even in her sleep she starts up and calls for you. You have cast a spell upon her. Day by day she droops and withers like a lotus-flower whose root is severed; yet ever and always, is your cursed name upon her lips, goading me to madness, until at last I have registered a sacred oath to kill you, and remove the accursed spell you have thrown upon her."

Had he advanced upon me at this moment he would have found me as helpless as a child, so overcome was I by the sudden joy which seized upon me, and seemed to turn my melancholy inside out. Those words of hatred had been as a torch illumining the gloom of my despair, for they had shown me that my existence was not altogether barren and unproductive. The life which has known the heaven of true love cannot be called a failure. There is no wall so high, no distance so great, no separation so complete as to defy the ineffable commerce of two loving hearts! Lona, then, was still mine, despite all obstacles. What a change this knowledge made! In an instant life became an inexpressible benefaction, for it permitted me to realise I was beloved, – and death was dowered with a new horror – the fear that I should cease to know it.

I was roughly aroused from my reflections by Rama Ragobah.

"Come, Sahib," he said, as his thick lips curled sneeringly, "suppose you try your spells upon me? You will never have a better chance than now to show your power," and again he made a slight movement toward me with the gleaming knife. The moon, low down upon the horizon, sent a broad beam of light into the entrance of the cave and over the head and shoulders of the Indian. Its cold light shimmered along the blade which was now held threateningly toward me. The crisis had been reached.

In times of such great urgency one has frequently an inspiration – instantaneous, discon-
nected, unbidden – which no amount of quiet, peace-
ful thought would suggest. Such extraordinary
flashes are the result of reasoning too rapid for consciousness to note. The Indian had already laid bare
his right arm to the elbow before I had determined
upon the desperate course I would pursue, and upon
which I must hazard all. As he advanced upon me I
seized the large, white sola hat from my head, and
hurled it full in his face. It was a schoolboy trick, yet
upon its success depended my life. Instinctively, and
in spite of himself, Ragobah dodged, closed his eyes,
and raised his right hand, knife and all, to shield his
face. I sprang upon him at the same instant I threw
my hat, and so was able to reach him before he
opened his eyes. I had well calculated his movements, and had made no mistake. As I reached him
his head was bent downward and forward to let the
hat pass over him. His position could not have been
better for my purpose. I "swung on him," as we used
to say at the gymnasium, catching him under his
protruded jaw, not far from the region of the carotid
artery. The blow was well placed, and desperation
lent me phenomenal strength. It raised him bodily
off his feet, and hurled him backward out of the
cave, where he lay motionless. He was now in my
power. I seized his knife and bent over him. Words
cannot express the hatred, the loathing I felt for him
then and always. Between me and the light of my
happiness he had ever stood, an impenetrable black
mass. Twice had he sought my life, yet now, when

he was in my power, I could not plunge his weapon into his heart. Would it not be just, I thought, to drag him into the cave, and hurl him down the abyss he had intended for me? Yes; he certainly merited it; yet I could not do that either. I wished the snake a thousand times dead, yet I could not stamp it into the earth.

He was beginning to slightly move now, and something must be done. It was useless to run, for the way was long, and he could easily overtake me. You may wonder why I did not take to the thicket, but if you had ever had any experience with Indian jungles you would know that, without the use of fire and axe, they are practically impenetrable. Professor Haeckel, botanising near that same spot, spent an hour in an endeavour to force his way into one of these jungles, but only succeeded in advancing a few steps into the thicket, when, stung by mosquitoes, bitten by ants, his clothing torn from his bleeding arms and legs, wounded by the thousands of sharp thorns of the calamus, hibiscus, euphorbias, lantanas, and myriad other jungle plants, he was obliged, utterly discomfited, to desist. If this were the result of his efforts, made in broad daylight, and with deliberation, what might I expect rushing into the thicket at night, as a refuge from a pursuer far my superior in physical strength and fleetness of foot, and who, moreover, had known the jungle from his boyhood? Once overtaken by my enemy, the long knife in my hands would be of no avail against a stick in his. I saw all this clearly, and realised that he must be prevented from following me.

There was no time to be lost, for he was rapidly

recovering possession of his powers. I seized a large rock and hurled it with all the force I could command upon his left foot and ankle. Notwithstanding his immense strength his hands and feet were scarcely larger than a woman's, and the small bones cracked like pipe-stems. Though I had not the will to kill him, my own safety demanded that I should maim him as the only other means of making good my escape. As the rock crushed his foot the pain seemed to bring him immediately into full possession of his faculties, and he roared like an enraged bull. I turned and looked back as I beat a hasty retreat down the hill. He had seized one of the airroots of the banyan tree, and raised himself upon his right leg. The expression of his face as the moonlight fell upon it was something never to be forgotten. It riveted me to the spot with the fascination of horror. He shook his fist at me fiercely, as he shrieked from the back of his throat:

"You infidel cur! You may as well try to brush away the Himalyas with a silk handkerchief as to escape the wrath of Rama Ragobah. Go! Bury yourself in seclusion at the farthermost corner of the earth, and on one night Ragobah and the darkness shall be with you!"

These were the last words this fiend incarnate ever spoke to me, but I know they are prophetic, and that he will keep his oath.

The next day I learned that Lona was dead. She had died with my name upon her lips, and her secret – the explanation of her strange conduct on that night – died with her. I shall never know it. Bitterly did I repent my inability to reach her. The thought that she had waited in vain for me, that with her last breath she had called upon me, and I had answered not, was unendurable torture, and I fled India and came to America in the futile endeavour to forget it all. Out of my black past there shone but one bright star – her love! All these long years have I oriented my soul by that sweet, unforgettable radiance, prizing it above a galaxy of lesser joys.

There is little more to be said. I shall meet death as I have stated – I am sure of it – and no man will see the blow given. Remember, as I loved that Indian maiden with a passion which death has not chilled, so I loathe my rival with a hatred infinite and all-consuming; for, somehow, I know that demon crushed out the life of my fragile lotus-flower. He will work his will upon me, but if his cunning enable him to escape the gallows, my soul, if there be a conscious hereafter, will never rest in peace. Remember this, my dear child, and your promise, that God may bless you even as I bless you.

It was some time after Gwen had finished this interesting document before any of us spoke. The narrative, and the peculiar circumstances under which it had been read, deeply impressed us. At length Maitland said in a subdued voice, as if he feared to break some spell:

"The Indian girl's letter; let us find that, and also the will."

Gwen went to the drawer in which her father kept his private papers, and soon produced them both. Maitland glanced hastily at the letter, and said:

"You have already heard its contents"; then turning to Gwen, he said: "I will keep it with your permission. Now for the will." It was handed to him, and his face fell as he read it. In a moment he turned to us, and said: "The interest on the insurance money is to go to Miss Darrow, the entire principal to be held in trust and paid to the person bringing the assassin to justice, unless said person shall wed Miss Darrow, in which case half of the fund shall go to the husband, and the other half to the wife in her own right. The balance of the estate, which, by the way, is considerable, despite the reports given to Osborne, is to go to Miss Darrow. This is all the will contains having any bearing upon the case in hand. Let us proceed with the rest of the papers." We made a long and diligent search, but nothing of importance came to light. When we had finished Maitland said:

"Our friend Osborne would say the document we have just perused made strongly for his theory, and was simply another fabrication to blind the eyes of the insurance company. That's what comes of wedding one's self to a theory founded on imperfect data."

"And what do you think?" Gwen inquired.

"That Rama Ragobah has small hands and feet," he replied. "That his left foot has met with an injury, and is probably deformed; that most likely he is lame in the left leg; that he had the motive for which we have been looking; that he may or may not have the habit of biting his nails; that he is crafty, and that if he were to do murder it is almost certain his methods would be novel and surprising, as well as extremely difficult to fathom – in short, that suspicion points unmistakably to Rama Ragobah. That is easily said, but to bring the deed home to him is quite another thing. I shall analyse the poison of the wound and microscopically examine the nature of the abrasion this afternoon. To-night I take the midnight train for New York. To-morrow I shall sail for Bombay, via London and the Continent. I will keep you informed of my address. While I am away I would ask that you close the house here, leaving everything just as it is now dismiss the servants, and take up your abode with the Doctor and his sister." He rose to go as he said this, and then continued, as he turned to me: "I shall depend upon you to look after Miss Darrow's immediate interests in my absence." I knew this meant that I was to guard her health, not permitting her to be much by herself, and I readily acquiesced.

The look of amazement which had at first overspread Gwen's face at the mention of this precipitate departure gave place to one of modest concern, as she said softly to Maitland: "Is it necessary that you should encounter the dangers of such a journey, to say nothing, of the time and inconvenience it will cost?" He looked down at her quickly, and then said reassuringly: "Do you know one is, by actual statistics, safer in an English railway carriage than when walking the crowded streets of London? I am daily subjecting myself to laboratory dangers which, I believe, are graver than any I am likely to meet between here and Bombay, or, for that matter, even at Bombay in the presence of our recent acquaintance Ragobah."

"I deeply appreciate," she replied, "the generous sacrifice you would make in my interests – but Bombay is such a long way – and – "

"If suspicion directed me to the North Pole," he interrupted, "I should start with equal alacrity," and he held out his hand to her to bid her farewell. She took it in a way that bespoke a world of gratitude, if nothing more. He retained the small hand, while he said: "Have you forgotten, my friend, your promise to your father? Do you not see in what terrible relations it may place you? How important, then, that no effort should be spared to prevent you from becoming indebted to one unmanly enough to take advantage of your position. I shall use every means within my power to myself discover your father's murderer, and you may comfort yourself with the assurance that, if successful, I shall make no demand of any kind whatsoever upon your gratitude. I think you understand me."

As he said this Gwen looked him full in the face. A little nervous tremor seized the corners of her mouth, and the tears sprang to her eyes. "Good-bye" was all she could say before she was compelled to turn aside to conceal her emotion.

Maitland, observing her agitation, said to her tenderly: "Your gratitude for the little that I have already done is reward, more than ample, for all I shall ever be able to do. Good-bye,' and he left the room.

Oh, man with your microscope! How is it that you find the smallest speck of dust, yet miss the mountain? Does the time seem too short? It would not if you realised that events, not clocks, were the real measure thereof.

THE EPISODE OF RAMA RAGOBAH

CHAPTER I

Life is but a poor accountant when it leaves the Future to balance its entries long years after the parties to the transactions are but a handful of insolvent dust. When, in such wise, the chiefest item of one side of the sheet fails to explain itself to the other, the tragic is attained.

On the day following Maitland's departure for New York, Mr. Darrow was buried. The Osborne theory seemed to be universally accepted, and many women who had never seen Mr. Darrow during his life attended his funeral, curious to see what sort of a person this suicide might be. Gwen bore the ordeal with a fortitude which spoke volumes for her strength of character, and I took good care, when it was all over, that she should not be left alone. In compliance with Maitland's request, whose will, since her promise to him, was law to her, she prepared to close the house and take up her abode with us.

It was on the night of the funeral, just after the lamps were lighted, that an event occurred which made a deep impression upon Gwen, though neither she nor I fully appreciated its significance till weeks afterward.

Gwen, who was to close the house on the morrow, was going from room to room collecting such little things as she wished to take with her. The servants had been dismissed and she was entirely alone in the house. She had gathered the things she had collected in a little heap upon the sitting-room table, preparatory to doing them up. She could think of but one thing more which she must take – a cabinet photograph of her father. This was upon the top of the piano in the room where he had met his death. She knew its exact location and could have put her hand right upon it had it been perfectly dark, which it was not. She arose, therefore, and, without taking a light with her, went into the parlour. A faint afterglow illumined the windows and suffused the room with an uncertain, dim, ghostly light which lent to all its objects that vague flatness from which the imagination carves what shapes it lists. As Gwen reached for the picture, a sudden conviction possessed her that her father stood just behind her in the exact spot where he had met his death, – that if she turned she would see him again with his hand clutching his throat and his eyes starting from their sockets with that never-to-be-forgotten look of frenzied helplessness.

It would be difficult to find a woman upon whom superstition has so slight a hold as it has upon Gwen Darrow, yet, for all that, it required an effort for her to turn and gaze toward the centre of the room. A dim, ill-defined stain of light fell momentarily upon the chair in which the dead man had sat, and then flickered unsteadily across the room and, as it seemed to her, out through its western side, the while a faint, rustling sound caught her ear. She was plainly conscious, too, of a something swishing by her, as if a strong draught had just fallen upon her. She was not naturally superstitious, as I have said before, yet there was something in the gloom, the deserted house, and this fatal room with its untold story of death which, added to her weird perceptions and that indescribable conviction of an unseen presence, caused even Gwen to press her hand convulsively upon her throbbing heart. For the first time in her life the awful possibilities of darkness were fully borne in upon her and she knew just how her father had felt.

In a moment, however, she had recovered from her first shock and had begun to reason. Might not the sound she had heard, and the movement she had felt, both be explained by an open window? She knew she had closed and locked all the windows of the room when she had finished airing it after the funeral, and she was not aware that anyone had been there since, yet she said to herself that perhaps one of the servants had come in and opened a window without her knowledge. She turned and looked. The lower sash of the eastern window – the one through which she felt sure death had approached her father – was raised to its utmost.

"How fortunate," she murmured, "that I discovered this before leaving."

She was all but fully reassured now, as she stepped to the window to close it. Remembering how the sash stuck in the casing she raised both hands to forcibly lower it. As she did so a strong arm caught the sash from the outer side, and a stalwart masculine form arose directly in front of her. His great height brought his head almost to a level with her own, despite the fact that he was standing upon the ground outside. He was so near that she could feel his breath upon her face. His eyes, like two great coals of fire, blazed into hers with a sinister and threatening light. His countenance seemed to utterly surpass any personal malignancy and to exhibit itself as a type of all the hatreds that ever poisoned human hearts.

Only a moment before Gwen had felt a creepy, sickening sensation stealing over her as the result of an ill-defined and apparently causeless dread. Now an actual, imminent, and fearful peril confronted her. Under such circumstances most women would have fainted, and, indeed, if Gwen had herself been asked how she would have acted under such a supreme test, she would have prophesied the same maidenly course as her own, yet, in the real exigency – how little do we know of ourselves, save what actual experience has taught us! – this is precisely what she did not do. When the horrible apparition first rose in her very face, as it were, a momentary weakness caught her and she clung to the sash for support. Then the wonderful fire of the malignant eyes, green, serpentine, opalescent, with the wave-like flux of a glowworm's light seen under a glass, riveted her attention. She had ceased to tremble. Our fear of death varies with our desire for life. Dulled by a great grief, she did not so very much care what became of her. The future's burden was heavy, and if it were necessary she now put it down, there would still be a sense of relief. As this thought passed like a shadow over her consciousness she felt herself irresistibly attracted to the awful face before her. Her assailant's gaze seemed to have wound itself about her own till she could not disentangle it. She was dimly conscious that she was falling under a spell and summoned all her remaining strength to break it. Quick as the uncoiling of a released spring, and without the slightest movement of warning, she threw her entire weight upon the sash in a last endeavour to close the window, but the man's upraised arm held both her weight and it, as if its muscles had been rods of steel. Gwen saw a long knife in his free hand, – saw the light shimmer along its blade, saw him raise it aloft to plunge it into her bosom, yet made no movement to withdraw beyond his reach and uttered no cry for help. It seemed to her that all this was happening to another and that she herself was only a fascinated spectator. She was wondering whether or not the victim would try to defend herself when the knife began its descent. It seemed ages in its downward passage, – so long, indeed, that it gave her time to think of most of the main experiences of her life. At last it paused irresolutely within an inch of her bosom. She wondered that the victim made no attempt to escape, uttered no cry for help. Suddenly she felt something whirling and buzzing in her brain, while a wild fluttering filled both her ears; then the swirling, fluttering torment rose in a swift and awful crescendo which seemed to involve all creation in its vortex; then a pang like a lightning-thrust and a crash like the thunder that goes with it, and she saw a tall man striding rapidly from the window. She was still sure it was no personal concern of hers, yet an idle curiosity noted his great height, his dark, mulatto-like skin, and a slight halt in his walk as he passed through a narrow beam of light and off into the engulfing darkness.

It was many minutes before Gwen regained any considerable command of her faculties, and she afterwards told me that she was even then more than half inclined to consider the whole thing as a weird dream of an overwrought mind. At length, however, she realised that she had had an actual experience, and that it was of sufficient importance to make it known at once. She accordingly hastened to lay the whole matter before me, and I, in my turn, notified the police, who, at once instituted as thorough a search as Gwen's description made possible. She had told me that her assailant was dark-skinned, yet with straight hair, and a cast of features that gave no hint of any Ethiopian taint. This, and his halting gait and great stature, were all the police had in the way of description, and I may as well add that the information was insufficient, for they never found any trace of Gwen's assailant.

I had had some hopes of this clue, but they were doomed to disappointment. It seemed evident to us that if anything were ever done in bringing Mr. Darrow's assassin to justice, Maitland would have to do it, unless, indeed, M. Godin solved the problem. Osborne, Allen, and their associates were simply out of the question.

We debated for some time as to whether or not we should write Maitland about Gwen's strange experience, and finally decided that the knowledge would be a constant source of worriment without being of the least assistance to him while he was so far away. We, therefore, decided to keep our own counsel, for the present at least.

Maitland had written us a few lines from New York telling us the result of his analysis, and ended by saying:

There is no doubt that Mr. Darrow died of poison injected into the blood through the slight wound in the throat. This wound was not deep, and seemed to have been torn rather than cut in the flesh. What sort of weapon or projectile produced that wound is a question of the utmost importance, shrouded in the deepest of mysteries. Once this point is settled, however, its very uniqueness will be greatly in our favour. I have an idea our friend Ragobah might be able to throw some light upon this subject, therefore I am starting on my way to visit him this afternoon, and shall write you en route whenever occasion offers. My kindest regards to Miss Darrow.

Yours sincerely, GEORGE MAITLAND.

P. S. I shall have leisure now on shipboard to set tie that question of atomic pitches, which is still a thorn in my intellectual flesh.

I handed this letter to Gwen, and, after she had read it through very carefully, she questioned me about this new theory of Maitland's. I went through the form of telling her, after the usual practice of amiable men discoursing to women, feeling sure she would be no wiser when I had finished, and was dumfounded when she replied: "It looks very reasonable. Professor Bjerknes, if I remember the name, has produced all the phenomena of magnetic attraction, repulsion, and polarisation, by air vibrations corresponding, I suppose, to certain fixed musical notes. Why might not something similar to this be true of atomic, as well as of larger, bodies?"

If the roof of my house had fallen in, I should not have been more surprised than at this quiet remark. How many times had I said: "You can always count on a young woman, however much she flutter over the surface of things, being ignorant of all the great underlying verities of existence"? I promptly decided, on all future occasions, to add to that – "When not brought up by her father." I was convinced that of the attainments of a girl educated by her father absolutely nothing could be definitely predicted.

We had a short note from Maitland written at Trieste. He excused its brevity by saying he had been obliged to travel night and day in order to reach this port in time to catch the Austrian Lloyd steamer Helois, bound for Aden, Bombay, Ceylon, Singapore, and Hong Kong. From Aden I received the following:

MY DEAR DOCTOR:

We have just been through the Red Sea, and I know now the real origin of the Calvinistic hell. Imagine it! A cloudless sky; the sun beating down with an intolerable fierceness; not a breath stirring, and the thermometer registering 120 degrees F. in the shade! It seemed as though reason must desert us. The constant motion of the punkas in the saloons, and an unlimited supply of ice-water was all that saved us. Sleep was hardly to be thought of, for at no time during the night did the mercury drop below 100 deg. F. Apart from the oppressive heat referred to, the entire voyage has been exceedingly pleasant. I have not solved the atomic-pitch problems, as attendance at meals has left me little time for anything else. They seem to eat all the time on these boats. At 8 A. M. coffee and bread; at ten a hearty breakfast of meat, eggs, curry and rice, vegetables and fruit; at 1 P. M. a luncheon, called "tiffin," of cold meats, bread and butter, potatoes, and tea; at five o'clock a regular dinner of soups, meats with relishes, farinaceous dishes, dessert, fruits, and coffee, and lastly, at 8 P. M., the evening meal of tea, bread and butter, and other light dishes. Five meals a day, and there are some English people who fill up the gaps between them by constantly munching nuts and sweets! Verily, if specialisation of function means anything, some of these people will soon become huge gastric balloons with a little wart on top representing the atrophied brain structure. They run their engines of digestion wholly on the high-pressure system.

After eight days' voyage on the Indian Ocean we shall be in Bombay. I must close now, for there is really nothing to say, and, besides, I am wanted on deck. My engagement is with a Rev. Mr. Barrows, who is bound as missionary to Hong Kong. This worthy Methodist gentleman is very much exercised because I insist that potentiality is necessity and rebut his arguments on free-will. He got quite excited yesterday, and said to me severely: "Do you mean to say, young man, that I can't do as I please?" I must say I don't think his warmth was much allayed by my replying: "I certainly mean to say you can't please as you please. You may eat sugar because you prefer it to vinegar, but you can't prefer it just because you will to do so." He has probably got some new arguments now and is anxious to try their effect, so, with kind regards to Miss Darrow – I trust she is well – I remain, Cordially your friend, GEORGE MAITLAND.

P. S. (Like a woman I always write a postscript.) You shall hear again from me as soon as I reach Bombay.

This last promise was religiously kept, though his letter was short and merely announced his safe arrival early that morning. He closed by saying: "I have not yet breakfasted, preferring to do so on land, and I feel that I can do justice to whatever is set before me. I intend, as soon as I have taken the edge off my appetite, to set out immediately for Malabar Hill, as I believe that to be our proper starting-point. I inclose a little sketch I made of Bombay as we came up its harbour, thinking it may interest Miss Darrow. Kindly give it to her with my regards. You will note that there are two tongues of land in the picture. On the eastern side is the suburb of Calaba, and on the western our Malabar Hill. Good-bye until I have something of interest to report."

I gave the sketch to Gwen, and she seemed greatly pleased with it.

"Are you aware," she said to me, "that Mr. Maitland draws with rare precision?"

"I am fully persuaded," I rejoined, "that he does not do anything which he cannot do well."

"I believe there is nothing," she continued, "which so conduces to the habit of thoroughness as the experiments of chemistry. When one learns that even a grain of dust will, in some cases, vitiate everything, he acquires a new conception of the term 'clean' and is likely to be thorough in washing his apparatus. From this the habit grows upon him and widens its application until it embraces all his actions."

This remark did not surprise me as it would have a few weeks before, for I had come to learn that Gwen was liable at any time to suddenly evince a very unfeminine depth of observation and firmness of philosophical grasp.

Maitland had been gone just six weeks to a day when we received from him the first news having any particular bearing upon the matter which had taken him abroad. I give this communication in his own words, omitting only a few personal observations which I do not feel justified in disclosing, and which, moreover, are not necessary to the completeness of this narrative:

MY DEAR DOCTOR:

I have at last something to report bearing upon the case that brought me here, and perhaps I can best relate it by simply telling you what my movements have been since my arrival. My first errand was to Malabar Hill. I thought it wise to possess myself, so far as possible, of facts proving the authenticity of Mr. Darrow's narrative. I found without difficulty the banyan tree which had been the trysting-place, and close by it the little cave with its mysterious well, – everything in fact precisely as related, even to the "Farsees'" garden or cemetery, with its 'Tower of Silence," or "Dakhma," as it is called by the natives.

The cave and the banyan are among the many attractions of what is now Herr Blaschek's villa. This gentleman, with true German hospitality, asked me to spend a few days with him, and I was only too glad to accept his invitation, as I believed his knowledge of Bombay might be of great service to me. In this I did not mistake. I told him I wished to ascertain the whereabouts of a Rama Ragobah, who had been something between a rishi and a fakir, and he directed me at once to a fakir named Parinama who, he said, would be able to locate my man, if he were still alive and in Bombay.

You can imagine how agreeably surprised I was to find that Parinama knew Ragobah well. I had anticipated some considerable difficulty in learning the latter's whereabouts, and here was a man who could – for a sufficient consideration – tell me much, if not all, about him. I secured an interpreter, paid Parinama my money, and proceeded to catechise him. I give you my questions and his answers just as I jotted them down in my notebook:

Q. What is Ragobah's full name?

A. Rama Ragobah.

Q. How long have you known him?

A. Thirty-five year.

Q. Has he always lived in Bombay?

A. No, Sahib,

Q. Where else?

A. For a good many year he have travel all the time.

Q. Is he in Bombay now?

A. No, Sahib.

Q. Where is he?

A. Over the sea, Sahib.

Q. Do you know where?

A. He sail for America; New York.

Q. When?

A. About eleven week ago.

Q. Do you know for what he undertook this journey?

A. Some personal affair of long time ago which he wish to settle – the same which make him so many year travel through India.

Q. Was he in search of someone?

A. Yes, Sahib.

Q. Some Indian woman?

A. No, Sahib.

Q. Some other woman, then?

A. No, Sahib.

Q. A man, then; an Englishman,

A. Yes, Sahib.

Q. What kind of a man is this Ragobah?

A. He very big man.

Q. What is his disposition? Is he generally liked?

A. No. His temper bad. He cruel, revengeful,

overbearing, and selfish. He most hated by those who best know him.

Q. He is a friend of yours, you say?

A. I say no such thing! Do you think I sell secret of friend? I have great reason for hating him, or I not now be earning your money.

Q. Ah! I see. What did you say he wanted of this Englishman?

A. I no say, Sahib.

Q. You said some personal affair of long standing, I believe.

A. Yes, Sahib.

Q. Do you know its nature?

A. No; I not know it, but I have not much doubt about it, Sahib.

Q. What do you think, then?

A. I think there but one passion strong enough in Ragobah to make plain his hunt like dog for last twenty year. Such persevere mean strong motive, and as I have good reason to remember how quick he forget a kindness, I know he not moved by friendship, Sahib.

Q. His motive then is –

A. Revenge.

Q. Have you any idea why he cherishes this malice?

A. I think it because some old love affair; some rival in his wife's love.

Q. Indeed! Then he has been married?

A. Yes, Sahib.

Q. Where shall I find his wife?

A. All that is left of her is in the bottomless well in the cave on Malabar Hill.

Q. Did Ragobah kill her?

A. No; that is, not with his own hand.

Q. How long ago did she die?

A. More than twenty year, Sahib.

Q. Are any of her relatives living?

A. Her husband, Sahib, and a cousin, that is all.

Q. Is there anyone else who could tell me of this woman?

A. Moro Scindia could, but he not do it.

Q. Why? Is he Ragobah's friend?

A. Ragobah has no friends, Sahib.

Q. Why, then?

A. He under oath to tell what was told him only to one person. He has keep his secret out of every year for more as twenty year, and can no be expect to tell to you, Sahib.

Q. Can you bring this man to me? You will both be well paid for your time, of course.

A. I bring him, Sahib, but I not make him speak.

Q. Let me see you both, then, to-night at eight, at

Herr Blaschek's villa on Malabar Hill. Ask for Mr. Maitland.

A. We be there. Anything more, Sahib?

Q. Yes. When is Ragobah expected to return?

A. He write that he think he return on the Dalmatia. She due next day after to-morrow.

Q. Has Ragobah any physical peculiarities?

A. His hands and feet they very small for man so big and strong.

Q. Anything else?

A. His left leg been hurt. The foot very bad shape, and the whole leg some bad, and, – what you call – halt when he walk.

Q. Has he the habit of biting his finger nails?

A. I not know he has, Sahib.

This completed the list of questions which I had desired to ask him, so, after once more receiving his assurance that he would meet me in the evening with his friend Scindia, I left him. As you know, I am not wont to draw conclusions until all the evidence is in, but I must confess that, looking at the whole matter from start to finish, there seems to have fallen upon Ragobah a net of circumstantial evidence so strong, and with a mesh of detail so minute, that it does not seem possible a mosquito could escape from it. Look at it a moment from this standpoint. Ragobah alone, so far as we know, has a motive for the murder. His victim has related the feud existing between them and foretold, with an air of the utmost assurance, just such an outcome thereof. Add to this that this man leaves India on a mission which those about him do not hesitate to pronounce one of vengeance, at just such a time as would enable him to reach Boston just a little before the commission of the murder; that this mission is the culmination of twenty years of unremitting search for revenge; that this malignity is supposed to be directed against some rival in his wife's affections, and the chain of circumstantial evidence possesses, so far as it extends, no weak link. Then, too, Ragobah has very small hands, a deformed left foot, and a limping gait, – everything almost which we had already predicted of the assassin. So sure am I that Ragobah is the guilty man that I shall ask for his arrest upon his arrival day after to-morrow should he return then, a thing which, I regret to say, does not impress me as altogether likely. Should he not come I shall cable you to institute a search for your end of the line. The next thing in order which I have to relate is my interview with Moro Scindia. I had engaged an interpreter, but was able to dismiss him as my guest spoke English with more ease and fluency than he, being an intelligent and well-to-do member of the Vaisya caste. I thought it wise to see the venerable Scindia alone, and accordingly sent Parinama out of the room with the interpreter. As before; I give you what passed between us as I jotted it down in my notebook.

Q. You are a friend of Rama Ragobah, are you not?

A. No, Sahib; he has no friends.

Q. You speak as if you disliked him.

A. It is not Mono Scindia's habit to play the hypocrite. I have good reason to hate him.

Q. You would not, then, had he committed a crime, assist him to escape justice?

A. I would track him like a bloodhound to the ends of the earth.

Q. You knew Ragobah's wife?

A. She was my cousin, Sahib.

Q. Were your relations friendly?

A. They were more than friendly. I loved her dearly, and would have tried to win her had I not been so much her senior.

Q. Did she live happily with Ragobah?

A. No, Sahib.

Q. Why?

A. I cannot answer. I have sworn to reveal the last experiences of my cousin to but one person.

Q. And that person is?

A. I must decline to answer that also, Sahib.

Q. If I succeed in naming him will you acknowledge it?

A. You will not succeed, Sahib.

Q. But if I should?

A. I will acknowledge it.

Q. The person is John Hinton Darrow.

The old man started as if he had been stabbed, and looked at me in amazement. He seemed at first to think I had read his thoughts and riveted his dark eyes upon me as if, by way of return, he would read my very soul. I think he did so, for his scrutiny seemed to satisfy him. He replied, somewhat reassured: "I can speak only to John Hinton Darrow."

"John Darrow is dead," I said.

"Dead!" he exclaimed, springing to his feet; "Darrow Sahib dead!" and he fell back into his chair, covering his face with his hands. "Ah, my poor Lona!" he muttered feebly; "I have failed to keep my promise. Do not reproach me, for I have done my best. For twenty years have I searched in vain for this man that I might fulfil your last request, and the very first information I receive is the news of his death. I have been no less vigilant than Ragobah, yet I have failed, even as he has failed."

I took this opportunity to again question him.

Q. Are you sure Ragobah failed?

A. Yes; had he found Darrow Sahib he would have killed him. His mission was one of revenge; mine one of love and justice; both have failed utterly since their object is dead. My pledge is broken!

Q. In its letter, yes; but the chance is still left you to keep the spirit of your covenant.

A. I do not understand you, Sahib.

Q. I will explain. Lona Ragobah confided to you certain facts in explanation of her conduct toward John Darrow. She loved him passionately, and it was her desire to stand acquitted in his sight. Were she alive now, any wish he had expressed during his life would be fulfilled by her as a sacred and pleasurable duty. This, then, as one who lovingly performs her will, should be your attitude also. John Darrow was the only man she ever loved, and, were she living, every drop of her loyal blood would rise against anyone who had done him injury. Do I not speak the truth?

A. Yes; she was loyal unto death and so shall I be. My hand has ever been against all who have done her harm; Ragobah knows that full well.

Q. Were she alive, you certainly would aid her in bringing to justice one who has done her the most cruel of wrongs and, at the same time, fulfilling the dying request of the man who to her was more than life.

A. I should do her bidding, Sahib.

Q. How much more need, then, now that the poor woman is dead, that you should act for her as she would, were she here.

A. You have not told me all; speak your mind freely, Sahib. You may depend upon my doing whatever I believe Lona would do were she here.

Q. I ask nothing more, and am now prepared to fully confide in you. As you doubtless know, Rama Ragobah left Bombay for New York about eleven weeks ago. He went, I have been told, on an errand of revenge. Six weeks ago John Darrow was murdered. He left behind him a written statement describing his wooing of Lona Scindia and his experiences with Rama Ragobah. He asserted, furthermore, his belief that he would die by Ragobah's hand, – the hand which twice before had attempted his life. Even as he loved your cousin, so he hated her husband, and, confident that he would ultimately be killed by him, he was haunted by the fear that he would escape the just penalty for his crime. He bound his heir by the most solemn of promises to use, in the event of his murder, every possible means to bring the assassin to justice. There can, of course, be little doubt that the assassin and Rama Ragobah are one and the same person. The last request John Darrow ever made – it was after he had been attacked by the assassin – had for its object the punishment of his murderer. Were your cousin living, do you think she would be deaf to that entreaty?

A. No. She would make its fulfilment the one object of her life, and, acting in her stead, I shall do all in my power to see justice done. If I can render you any aid in that direction you may command me, Sahib.

Q. You can assist me by telling me all you know of your cousin's married life, and, more especially, the message she confided to you.

A. In doing this I shall break the letter of my oath, but, were I not to do it, I should break the spirit thereof, therefore listen:

You have, I suppose, already learned from the statement of Darrow Sahib what occurred at his last meeting with my cousin on Malabar Hill. Her act, in throwing a venomous serpent in his face, was one which doubtless led him to believe she wished to kill him, although it must have puzzled him to assign any reason for such a desire. Not long after this incident my cousin married Ragobah, a man for whom she had always cherished an ill-concealed hatred. I saw but little of her at this time, yet, for all that, I could not but observe that she was greatly changed. But one solution suggested itself to me, and that was that she had discovered her lover false to her and had, out of spite as it is called, hastily married Ragobah. I confess that when this conclusion forced itself home upon me, I felt much dissatisfied with Lona, for I thought such a course unworthy of her. As I saw more of her I noted still greater changes in her character. As I had known her from childhood, she had been most uniform in her temper and her conduct; now all this was changed. To-day, perhaps, she would be like her old self, – only weaker and more fragile, – to-morrow a new being entirely, stronger and more restless, with a demoniac light in her eyes, and a sort of feverish malignancy dominating her whole personality. When I noticed this I studied to avoid her. If the Lona I had known were merely an ideal of which no actual prototype existed, I wished to be allowed to cherish that ideal rather than to have it cruelly shattered to make room for the real Lona. I had not seen her for many weeks when one day, to my surprise, I received a note from her. It was short, and so impressed me that I can remember every word of it.

"My DEAR COUSIN:

"I send this note to you by Kandia that you may

get it before it is too late for you to do what I wish. I am a caged bird in my husband's house. My every movement is watched, and they would not let you come to me were my husband at home, so, I beseech you, come at once lest he should return before I have had time to intrust to you my last request. I am dying, Moro, and it is within your power to say whether my spirit shall rest in peace, or be torn forever and ever by the fangs of a horrible regret. My secret is as lead upon my soul and to you only can I tell it. Come – come at once!

"LONA."

You can imagine the effect of this revelation upon me better than I can describe it. I did not even know she was seriously ill, and with her urgent request for an interview came the sad tidings that she was dying, and the confirmation of my fear – that she had adopted the religion of her English lover. I lost no time in going to her. I found her in a state of feverish expectation, fearful lest I should either not be able to come at all, or her husband would return before my arrival. She was worn to a shadow of her former self, and I realised with a pang that she was indeed dying.

"I knew I could depend upon you, Moro," she said as I entered, "even though you think I have lost all claim upon your regard. I said to myself, 'He will come because of the respect he once had for me,' and I was right. Yes," she continued, noticing my astonishment at the change in her condition, "I am almost gone. I should not have lasted so long, were it not that I could not die till I had spoken. Now I shall be free to go, and the horrible struggle will be over. You have been much among the English, Moro, both here and in England, and know they believe they will meet again in heaven those they have loved on earth."

She sank back exhausted from excitement and effort, as she said this, and I feared for a moment she would be unable to proceed. I told her what I knew about the Christian's hope of heaven, and suggested to her that, as her husband might return at any moment, she had best confide to me at once any trust with which she wished to charge me. For a moment she made no reply, but said at length:

"Yes, you are right. It is not a very long story, and I suppose I had better begin at the beginning. You remember well my being rescued by an English gentleman, a Mr. John Darrow. I afterward became well acquainted, – in fact we were to be married. To this union my parents strongly objected. They had promised me to Rama Ragobah, and were horrified at my seeking to outrage the laws of caste by bestowing my hand not only outside of my station but upon a foreigner and Christian as well. This had only the effect of causing me to meet the Sahib secretly. We chose for our meeting-place the great banyan on the top of Malabar Hill, where I passed the happiest moments I have ever known. Everything went well until the night on which we had planned to run away. We were to meet at the usual place and hour, take the night train for Matheron Station, and there be married.

"My heart bounded with joy as I climbed Malabar Hill on that fatal evening, but my delight was of short duration. In my fear lest I should keep my lover waiting I must have arrived fully fifteen minutes before the appointed time. I was standing with my back against the banyan tree, awaiting the first sound of his approach, when my attention was attracted by what seemed to be two little balls of fire shining from a clump of bushes almost directly in front of me. They seemed to burn with a lurid and wicked glare, and, as my gaze became entangled by them, a tremor ran through my frame and a cold sweat bathed my entire body. Overcome by an unspeakable dread I made one last frantic effort to withdraw my eyes, but could not. Then gradually, by slow degrees, my terror was succeeded by an over-whelming fascination. I felt myself drawn irresistibly toward the thicket. Then came a vague sense of falling, falling, falling, and I knew no more, at least for some little time.

"The next thing I remember is seeing my lover stretch out his arms to me, while I was inspired with an unaccountable hatred of him so bitter that it left me mute and transfixed. Then he sought to embrace me, and I threw a young cobra, which, coiled in a wicker basket, had been placed in my hand, full in his face. I think, also, that I struck him, and then ran down the hill and straight to the house of Ragobah. What happened during the next few months I know not. I seemed to have been in a continual sleep full of dreams. When I awoke I seemed conscious that I had dreamt, but could not tell of what. You can imagine my horror, my despair, when I was first addressed as Ragobah's wife. I denied the relation, but everyone told me the same story – I was Ragobah Sahibah. This shock, coming as it did with the memory of my conduct that terrible night on Malabar Hill, nearly killed me, and was followed by another long period of the dream existence. I began to think I was a sufferer from some terrible brain disease, and to doubt which was my real existence, the dreams or the waking moments.

"One day when, for the first time in several weeks, I was in possession of my normal faculties, Ragobah came into my room and sat down beside me. I arose instantly and fled to the farther corner of the apartment. He pursued me and sought to conquer my all too apparent aversion for him by terms of endearment, but the more he pressed his suit the more my loathing grew until, maddened by references made to Darrow Sahib, I lost all self-control and permitted him to learn my detestation of him. He heard me through in silence, his face growing darker with every word, and when I had finished said with slow and studied malice:

"'You forget that you are my wife and that I can follow my entreaty by command. You spurn my love. You are not yet weaned from that English cur whose life, let me tell you, is in my hands. Fool, can you not see how powerless you are? I have but to will you to kill him and your first cursed failure on Malabar Hill will be washed out with his infidel blood. You will do well to yield peaceably. The thread of your very existence passes through my hands, to cut or tangle it as I list – yield you must!' With this he strode frantically from the room, leaving me more dead than alive. As he disclosed his fiendish secret something about my heart kept tightening with every word till, at length, it seemed as if it must burst, so terrible was the pressure. I could not breathe. My lungs seemed filled with molten lead. How long this agony continued I do not know, for the thread of consciousness broke under its terrible tension and I fell senseless upon the floor.

"When I recovered from my swoon the inexpressible horror of my situation again descended upon my spirit like a snuffer upon a candle. I was Ragobah's wife, his slave, his tool, as powerless to resist his will as if I were one of his limbs. All was now clear. The long sleep, crowded with unremembered dreams, represented the period when I was under Ragobah's control, – the horrible night on Malabar Hill being one of them, – and the waking moments, those periods when my feeble, overridden consciousness flickered back to dimly light for a time the gloom of this intellectual night. There was no hope for me. Already had I been so dominated by his will and inspired by his malice as to attempt the life of my lover. What might I not be made to do in future? As I thought of this, Ragobah's last threat rang with a sinister warning upon my ears till it seemed as if it would drive me into madness. The suspicion grew to be a certainty from which there was but one means of escape – death – and I determined at once to embrace it before I could be made the instrument for the infliction of further injury upon my lover. I seized a little dagger which in my normal moments I always kept concealed about me, and was about to plunge it into my bosom when I was smitten by the thought, – and it cut me as the steel could not have done, – that Darrow Sahib would never know the truth, and that his love for me would be forever buried beneath a mass of black misgivings. The certainty of this conviction paralysed my will, and my arm dropped nervelessly at my side. It would be a simple matter, I thought, to find some way of confiding my story to you and pledging you to explain everything to Darrow Sahib, after which I could die in peace, if not without regret. But it was not so easy to communicate with you as I had expected. Days passed before I had a chance to make the attempt, and the only result of it was to show me how closely I was watched. If Ragobah were absent, there was always someone in his employ who made it his business to acquaint himself with my every movement. I dare not take the time to tell you how I succeeded in obtaining this interview further than to say that I was able to win to my cause the man who bore my message to you – a servant in whom Ragobah has the utmost confidence. When my husband departed this morning Kandia was left in charge of me, and so your visit was made possible.

"You are now acquainted with the trust I would impose upon you: swear to me, Moro, that you will make this explanation for me to John Darrow and to no other human being! Swear it by the love you once said you bore me!" She sank back exhausted and awaited my response. For a moment I dared not trust myself to speak, yet something must be said. As I noted her impatience I replied: "Lona, you have lifted a great weight from my heart and placed a lesser one upon it. Forgive me that I have ever doubted you. Even as you have been true to yourself, I swear by the love I still bear you to deliver your message to Darrow Sahib and to no other human being. I shall commit your words at once to writing that nothing may be lost through the failure of my memory."

She reached her hand out feebly to me, and never shall I forget the look of gratitude which accompanied its tremulous pressure as she murmured: "After John, Moro, you are dearest. I shall not try to thank you. May the ineffable peace which you bring my aching heart return a thousand-fold into your own. Farewell. Ragobah may return at any moment. Let us not needlessly imperil your safety. Once more good-bye. The dew-drop now may freely fall into the shining sea." Poor distraught child! She had tried to adopt her lover's religion without abandoning her own. I bent over and kissed her. It was my first and last kiss and she gave it with a sweet sadness, the memory of which, through all these years, has dwelt in the better part of me, like a fragrance in the vesture of the soul. One long, lingering look and I departed, never to see again this woman I had so fondly, so hopelessly loved.

You now know the exact nature of the covenant I have felt constrained to violate. I have told you her story in her own words. I wrote it out immediately after my interview with her and have read it so many times, during the last twenty years, that I have committed it to memory. The recollection of that last meeting, of her kiss and her grateful look has been throughout all these long, weary years the one verdant spot in the desert of my life.

[Moro Scindia paused here, as one who had reached the end of his narrative, and I continued my interrogations.]

Q. Although you never again saw your cousin you must, I think, have heard something of her fate.

A I learned of it through Nana Kandia, the servant who had secretly embraced Lona's cause, and who had borne her message to me. It seems that, after my interview with her, my cousin was seized with a consuming desire to see her English lover once more before her death; so she devised a plan by which, with Kandia's help, Darrow Sahib was to be secretly conducted to her under cover of night. She wrote a letter asking him, as a last request, to meet her messenger on Malabar Hill, and instructing him how to make himself known. This she gave to Kandia to post early in the morning of the day upon which their plan was to be put into execution. As he was about leaving the house Ragobah called him into his chamber and demanded to know what was taking him forth so early in the morning. Kandia saw at once that the purpose of his errand had been discovered, and determined to meet the issue bravely. "I was going to post a letter, Sahib," he replied quietly. "Let me see it!" Ragobah roared. "I have no right to do so," Kandia replied, springing toward the door. But he was not quick enough for the wary Ragobah, who felled him to the floor with a chair before he had reached the threshold. When he returned to consciousness he found his assailant, who had skilfully opened the letter, standing over him perusing it in malicious glee. When he had finished reading he carefully resealed it and placed it in his pocket. Then he called two of his servants and gave Kandia into their charge with orders to gag him, to bind him hand and foot, and, as they valued their lives, not to permit him to leave the room till he ordered it.

What occurred between that time and the return of Ragobah, wounded and furious, late in the evening, we can only surmise. He doubtless posted the letter, and went himself to meet Darrow Sahib on Malabar Hill. When he returned home he hobbled into his wife's apartment and then ordered Kandia to be sent to him. His left leg was badly crushed and his face, contorted with pain and fiendish malevolence, was horrible to look upon.

"Our trusty friend here," he said, addressing his wife and pointing to Kandia, "could not conveniently post your letter this morning, my dear, so I did it myself." Lona's face turned ashen pale, but she made no reply.

"I thought," he continued in his sweetest accents and with the same demoniac sarcasm, "that you would be anxious to know if the Sahib received it, – our mail service is so lax of late, – so I went tonight to Malabar Hill to see, for I felt certain he would come if he got your note, and, sure enough, he was there even ahead of time. I was obliged to forego the pleasure of bringing him to you on account of two most unfortunate accidents. As you see I hurt my foot, and poor Darrow Sahib slipped and fell headlong into the well in the little cave. As it has no bottom I could not, of course, get the Sahib out, and so was obliged to return, as best I could, alone." As he finished this heartless lie, every word of which he knew was a poisoned dart, Lona fell fainting upon the floor. Kandia raised her gently, expecting to find her dead, but was able at length to revive her. The first words she said were directed to Ragobah in a voice devoid of passion or reproach, – of everything in fact save an unutterable weariness.

"I am ill," she said; "will you permit Nana to get me some medicine which has helped me in similar attacks?" Ragobah's reply was directed to Kandia.

"You may do as the Sahibah bids you," was all he said.

Kandia turned to Lona for instructions and she said to him, "Get me half an ounce of – stay, there are several ingredients – I had better write them down." She wrote upon a little slip of paper, naming aloud the ingredients and quantities as she did so, and then asked Kandia to move her chair to an open window before he left. When he had done so, she passed him the note, saying, "Please get it as quickly as possible." As he took the paper she seized his hand for a moment and pressed it firmly. He noticed this at the time, but its significance did not dawn upon him until he had nearly reached his destination, when, all at once, he realised with a pang that the momentary pressure of the hand and the mute gratitude which shone from the eyes were meant as a farewell. His first impulse was to hurriedly retrace his steps, but before he had acted upon it, the thought occurred to him that she intended to poison herself with the drugs he was about to procure. If this were the case, there was no great need of hurry. Then he began to recall to mind the names of the drugs she had mentioned as she wrote and to reflect that not one of them was poisonous. With this new light all his former uneasiness returned. He strove to reassure himself with the thought that she might, in order to mislead Ragobah, have spoken the name of a harmless drug while she wrote down that of a poisonous one. It was easy to settle this question, and he determined to do so at the next light. He unfolded the paper, expecting to see a prescription, but read instead these words:

"To MORO SCINDIA;

"My Dear Cousin: Death has relieved you of the task I imposed upon you. John Darrow's body is in the well in the cave on Malabar Hill, where, before this reaches you, my body will have also gone to meet it. To this fragment of paper, then, must I confide the debt of gratitude I owe to you and to him who will bear it to you, Nana Kandia. Good-bye. If I had had two hearts, I should have given you one. Do not mourn me, but rather rejoice that my struggle and its agony are over. John has already gone – one tomb shall inclose both our bodies – how could it have been better? "LONA."

No sooner had Kandia grasped the import of this letter than he rushed with all speed to Malabar Hill, but he was too late, for scarcely had he left the house upon Lona's errand before she had sprung out of the window by which he had placed her. Ragobah's wound prevented his following her, and when he had summoned others to pursue her, the darkness had closed about her form and none knew the way she had taken. At the edge of the fatal well Kandia found a piece of paper beneath a stone and on it these words:

"Farewell, Moro and Nana, the only beings on earth I regret to leave! – Lona."

The body was never recovered. The news of his wife's death, and the knowledge that he was the cause of it, produced an effect upon Ragobah from which he never recovered. More than twenty years have passed since then, yet from that day to this he has never been known to smile. Long before his mangled limb had healed it became evident to all who knew him that he had henceforth but one purpose in life, – revenge, and that nothing save death could turn him from his purpose, so long as his rival lived. The knowledge of this made my search for Darrow Sahib more than ever difficult from the fact that it must be prosecuted secretly. I could only learn that he had left Bombay for the interior, nothing more. My inquiries in all the Indian cities proved fruitless, and in many instances, I was informed that Ragobah had instituted a search for the same man. I think, in spite of my precautions, some of my agents ultimately told Ragobah of my efforts, for I found myself so closely watched by men in his interests that I was at length compelled to give up the personal conduct of the search, and to continue it through a deputy, unknown to him. All my endeavours to find the Sahib were, as you are already aware, fruitless, and, until I met you, I had no doubt Ragobah's efforts were equally unproductive. You have now all the information I can offer upon the subject. If I can be of any further service to you, you need not hesitate to command me.

As he said this he rose to depart and I promised to keep him informed of what occurred. I have nothing now to do but to await, with such patience as I can command, the arrival of the Dalmatia. It does not seem to me altogether probable that Ragobah will return upon this boat, but if he should I shall have him arrested the moment he sets foot on shore. If he escape the net that has been woven about him, I shall be a convert to Eastern occultism and no mistake. I trust Miss Darrow is well and hopeful. I know she will religiously keep the promise she made, for she is one of those women who fully understand the nature of a covenant, and I am easier, therefore, than I otherwise could be regarding her condition. Give her my kind regards and tell her that she may expect news of importance by my next communication. It is very late, so good-bye, until the arrival of the Dalmatia.

Your friend, GEORGE MAITLAND.

This letter was delivered one morning when Gwen, my sister Alice, and I were at breakfast. As I broke the seal I noticed that both ladies put down their knives and forks and ceased to eat. A glance at Gwen's eager face convinced me that she had no appetite for anything but my letter, and I accordingly read it aloud. When I came to the last part of it, where Maitland referred to her, a flush of pride I thought at the time, overspread her face, and when I had finished she said with some show of excitement, "If Mr. Maitland succeed in bringing Ragobah to justice I – I shall owe him a debt of gratitude I can never repay! It all seems like a romance, only so frightfully real. We may expect another letter in a few days, may we not? And Mr. Maitland, when may we expect him?"

I replied that I thought we might reasonably expect news of importance within five or six days, and that, so far as Maitland's return was concerned, I did not look for it for as many weeks, as he would doubtless have to cope with the law's delay there, as he would if here, and to comply with many tedious formalities before the government would allow Ragobah to be brought to this country for trial. The only reply Gwen vouchsafed to this statement was a long-drawn unconscious sigh, which I interpreted as meaning, "Will it never end!"

CHAPTER II

*He who shakes the tree of Vengeance but har-
vests apples of Sodom in whose fruit of ashes he
becomes buried, for the wage of the sinner is
death.*

There was no doubt of Ragobah's guilt in any of
our minds, so that action at our end of the line
seemed entirely useless, and nothing was left us but
to quietly await whatever developments Maitland
should disclose. We were not kept long in suspense,
for in less than a week his next letter arrived. I broke
its seal in the presence of Gwen and my sister who, if
possible, were even more excited than I myself. Is it
to be wondered at? Here was the letter which was to
tell us whether or not the murderer of John Darrow
had been caught. We felt that if Ragobah had returned to India, according to his expressed intention,
there could be no doubt upon this point. But had he
so returned? I read as follows:

MY DEAR DOCTOR:

The Dalmatia arrived as expected on Thursday,
and on her came Ragobah. I had him arrested as he
stepped from the boat. When examined he did not
seem in the least disconcerted at the charges I preferred against him. This did not surprise me, however, as I had expected that a man who could roll his
naked body over the burning sands from Mabajan to
the Ganges, and who could rise from the Vaisyan to
the Brahman caste, – albeit he fell again, – would not
be likely to betray his cause by exhibiting either fear
or excitement. He acknowledged his acquaintance
with Mr. Darrow and the ill-feeling existing between

them. When charged with his murder at Dorchester on the night of the 22d of April he coolly asked if I were aware when and how he had left India. I had not neglected to look this matter up and told him he had left on the same steamer which had brought him back – the Dalmatia – which should have arrived at New York on the 21st of April, thus leaving him ample time to get to Boston before the night of the 22d. To this he replied with the utmost assurance. (I give you the exact gist of what he said. Since I was not able to immediately commit his language to writing, you will, of course, hardly expect me to remember those peculiar Oriental idioms which an Indian, however great his command of English, never drops. What I say here is, of course, true of all conversations I put before you except such as I practically reported.) – But to return to our muttons. As I was saying, he replied with the utmost assurance:

"The Sahib is right. I did sail upon the Dalmatia, due at New York on the 21st of April. This steamer, as you are perhaps aware, is propelled by twin screws. On the trip in question she broke one of her propellers in mid-Atlantic and in consequence, arrived in New York on the 24th of April, three days late, without the transference of any of her passengers to other boats. If you will take the trouble to at once verify this statement at the steamship office, you will be able to relieve me of the annoyance of further detention."

All this was said with a rare command of language and a cold, cynical politeness which cut like a knife. I at first thought it was merely a ruse to gain time, but the steamship officials substantiated every word uttered by Ragobah relative to their vessel. The Dalmatia had steamed into New York at eleven o'clock on the morning of the 24th day of April with a broken screw!

Imagine my amazement! The net of circumstantial evidence wound around Ragobah seemed to be such as to leave no possibility of escape, and yet, the very first effort made to draw it tighter about him had resulted in his walking, with the utmost ease, right through its meshes! There is no gainsaying such an alibi, and I am, therefore, forced to acknowledge that Rama Ragobah could not, by any possibility, have murdered John Darrow. That he may have planned the deed and that he may have intended to be present at its execution is quite possible, but we may at once dismiss the idea of his having personally committed the act. You will immediately appreciate that nearly all of the evidence which we secured against Ragobah was directed against him as the assassin, and is of little or no use to prove his complicity in an affair committed by another. In his hatred of Mr. Darrow we have, I believe, a sufficient motive for the act, but what evidence have we to support the theory that the murder was committed by anyone acting in his interests? I must confess my inability to detect, at present writing, the slightest evidence that Ragobah acted through an accomplice. So, here the matter rests.

I may state in closing that Ragobah has requested the "pleasure" (sic) of a private interview with me on Malabar Hill to-morrow night. As there is a bare possibility he may let fall something which may shed some light upon the accomplice hypothesis, I have agreed to meet him at the entrance to the little cave at nine o'clock. He has requested that I come alone and I shall do so, but, lest you fear for my safety, let me assure you that I know very well the unscrupulous nature of the man with whom I am to deal and that I shall take good care not to afford him any opportunity to catch me unawares. You will hear from me again after I meet Ragobah.

Remember me kindly to Miss Darrow. The failure of my enterprise will, I know, be a bitter disappointment to her, and you must temper this acknowledgment of it with such a hope of ultimate success as you may enjoy. Tell her I shall never cease my efforts to solve this mystery so long as I am able to find a clue, however slight, to follow. At present I am all at sea, and it looks as if I should have to go clear back and start all over again. Ragobah, as a point of departure, has not proved a success. With my kind regards to you all, I remain, cordially yours, GEORGE MAITLAND.

I read this through aloud, despite the fact that I knew some parts of it were intended only for my perusal. Gwen did not speak until some minutes after I had finished, and then only to express a fear that, despite his caution, harm might come to Maitland at his interview with Ragobah. She seemed to be far less disappointed at Maitland's failure to convict Ragobah than she was fearful for her friend's personal safety. She was restless and ill at ease for the next two or three days – in fact, until the arrival of Maitland's next letter. This came during my absence on a professional call, and when I returned home she met me with it at the door with an expression of relief upon her countenance so plain as not to be misconstrued. We went into the sitting-room, where my sister was awaiting the news, and I read as follows:

MY DEAR DOCTOR:

I kept my appointment last night with Rama Ragobah and, although nothing transpired at all likely to assist me in locating Mr. Darrow's assassin, yet the interview, though short, was interesting and worth narrating. Promptly at nine o'clock I was at my post by the little cave. I am still staying with Herr Blaschek and, as I had but a few rods to travel, I did not quit the house until within five minutes of the time appointed for our meeting. As I stepped out into the darkness I noticed a tall form glide behind a tree, about a rod away from the door. I could not be sure it was Ragobah, yet I had little doubt of it. I was a trifle taken aback at the moment, and instinctively placed my hand upon my revolver and grasped my cane more firmly. Should occasion require it, I counted upon this cane quite as much as upon my revolver, for, innocent and inoffensive as it looked, it was capable of most deadly execution. I had chosen it in preference to many other more pretentious weapons which had suggested themselves to me. It consisted of a small, flexible steel wire hardly bigger than the blade of a foil, surmounted by a good-sized lead ball, and the whole covered with a closely woven fabric. By grasping the cane by its lower end a tremendously heavy blow could be struck with the ball, and, if an attempt were made to shield the head by throwing up the arm, it was almost certain to fail of its object since the flexibility of the wire permitted it to bend about an obstruction until its loaded end was brought home. You will perhaps think that, since I did not make use of this weapon, I need not have troubled myself to describe it. Perhaps that is so, but, let me assure you, when I saw Ragobah, for it was he, glide behind that tree, and reflected how capable he was of every kind of treachery, I wouldn't have parted with that cane for its weight in gold. The Indian had pledged me to come alone and had promised to do likewise, but I felt any tree might conceal one of his minions, hired to assassinate me while he engaged my attention. All this, of course, did not in the least affect my decision. I had promised to go alone, and Miss Darrow's interests required that I should keep my covenant. I should have done so, even though I had known Ragobah meant to betray me. I may as well, however, tell you at once that my suspicions wronged the fellow. He had evidently taken his station behind a tree to satisfy himself, without exposure, that I meant to keep my promise and come alone.

When I reached the cave I found him awaiting me. How he was able to get there before me passes my comprehension, but there he was. He did not waste time, but addressed me at once, and, as my memory is excellent and our interview was short, I am able to give you an accurate report of what passed between us. I copy it here just as I entered it in my notebook, immediately upon my return to the house.

"You naturally wish to know," Ragobah began, "why I have sought this interview. That is easily explained. You have done me the honour, Sahib, for

I feel it is such, to suspect me of the murder of John Darrow. You have come here from America to fasten the crime upon me, and, from the bottom of my heart, I regret your failure to do so. I would give everything I possess on earth, and would gladly suffer a life of torment, to be able truthfully to say: 'I, Rama Ragobah, killed John Darrow.' But despite all my efforts, I, wretch that I am, am innocent! For more than twenty years I have had but one purpose, – one thought, – and that was to track down and slay John Darrow. This desire consumed me. It led me all over India in vain search for him. For nineteen years I laboured incessantly, without discovering so much as a trace of him. When he fled Bombay his belongings went inland, so I was told. I believed the story and felt sure I should one day find him on Indian soil. Years passed and I did not find him. It was but a few months ago that I discovered his ruse and learned his whereabouts. I could scarcely contain myself for joy. My life-work was at last to be completed. Nothing now remained but to plan his destruction. This, however, was not so easy a thing to do, since, in order to make my revenge complete, I must disclose my identity before killing him. At length I decided upon a plan. I would come upon him at night, when asleep, gag him and bind him to his bed. Then he should learn the name of his doomsman, and the horrible nature of the death that awaited him."

Ragobah paused here as if overcome by his disappointment, and I said, "And how did you intend to kill him?" He gave a throaty chuckle, as he replied: "It was all so very pretty! I had only to saturate the bedclothes with oil and set fire to them. I should have lighted them at his feet and watched the flames creep upward toward his head till safety compelled my retreat. It was for this purpose I went to New York. You already know the fatal delay I incurred. When I landed I made all haste to the home of Darrow Sahib, in Dorchester, only to learn that he had killed himself a few days before my arrival. The morsel for which I had striven and hungered for twenty long years was whipped from my hand, even as I raised it to my mouth. My enemy was dead, beyond the power of injury, and my hands were unstained by his blood.

"I then determined to kill his daughter. It was the night of my enemy's burial. The Sahibah was alone in the house and was intending to leave it that night. I knew she would see that everything was securely fastened before she went away, and so, when I opened one of the windows, I was sure she would come to close it. Crouching down outside I awaited her approach, intending to spring up and stab her while she was pulling the window down. Everything happened as I planned – what ails the Sahib? I did not kill her! No, at the last moment something – never mind what – stayed my arm! The death of an innocent girl did not promise me any lasting satisfaction and I gave up the idea, returned to New York, and re-embarked for Bombay as innocent in act as when I left it. My life had been a failure and I had no desire to prolong it. When you arrested me on the charge of murder, nothing would have given me greater pleasure than to have been able to plead guilty.

"You already know why I so hated Darrow. He robbed me of the only woman I ever loved. Maddened by jealousy, I told her I had thrown him into the well in the cave here. It was a lie, but she believed it, and fled from me, and in a few minutes had thrown herself into that bottomless hole. See, Sahib," he said, entering the cave and pointing down the dark shaft, – "that is the road she took in order that her bones might rest with his, and, after all, they are thousands of miles apart. It's not the triumph I planned, but it's all I have! And this is why I brought you here; that you may take back to my enemy's family the knowledge that in death I am triumphant. Tell them," he said, rising to his full height, "that while the carcass of the English cur rots in a foreign land, Rama Ragobah's bones lie mingled with those of his beautiful Lona!" – My blood was up, and I rushed fiercely at him. With the quickness of a cat he dodged me, spat in my face as I turned, and, with a horrible laugh, sprang headlong into the well. Down deeper and deeper sank the laugh – then it died away – then a faint plash – and all was silent. Rama Ragobah was gone! For fully ten minutes I stood dazed and irresolute and then returned mechanically to the house. I at first thought of informing the authorities of the whole affair, but, when I realised how hard it would be for me to prove my innocence were I charged with Ragobah's murder, I decided to keep the secret of the well.

I shudder when I think of Miss Darrow's narrow escape. Did you suspect who her assailant really was? I wonder you have written me nothing about it, but suppose you thought it would only needlessly alarm me. If you had known it was our friend Rago-bah, you would doubtless have felt it imperative that I should know of it, – so I conclude from your silence that you did not discover his identity.

I need not, of course, tell you, my dear Doctor, that we have reached the end of our Indian clue, and that I deem it wise, all things considered, for me to get out of India just as soon as possible. If this letter is in any way delayed, you need not be surprised if I have the pleasure of relating its contents in person. Remember me to Miss Darrow and tell her how sorry I am that, thus far, I have been unable to be of any real service to her. As I shall see you so soon I need write nothing further. Kind regards to Miss Alice.

Ever yours, GEORGE MAITLAND.

When I had finished reading this letter I looked up at Gwen, expecting to see that its news had depressed her. I must confess, however, that I could not detect any such effect. On the contrary, she seemed to be in much better spirits than when I began reading. "According to this letter, then," she said, addressing me somewhat excitedly, "we may – " but she let fall her eyes and did not complete her sentence. My sister bestowed upon her one of those glances described in the vernacular of woman as "knowing" and then said to me: "We may expect Mr. Maitland at any time, it seems." "Yes," I replied; "he will lose no time in getting here. He undoubtedly feels much chagrined at his failure and will now be more than ever determined to see the affair through to a successful conclusion. He is in the position of a hound that has lost its scent, and is eager to return to its point of departure for a fresh start. I fancy it will be no easy task to discover a new clue, and I shall watch Maitland's work in this direction with a great deal of curiosity." Gwen did not speak, but she listened to our conversation with a nearer approach to a healthy interest than I had known her to display on any other occasion since her father's death. I regarded this as a good omen. Her condition, since that sad occurrence, had worried me a good deal. She seemed to have lost her hold on life and to exist in a state of wearied listlessness. Nothing seemed to impress her and she would at times forget, in the midst of a sentence, what she had intended to say when she began it! Her elasticity was gone and every effort a visible burden to her. I knew the consciousness of her loss was as a dull, heavy weight bearing her down, and I knew, too, that she could not marshal her will to resist it, – that, in fact, she really didn't care, so tired was she of it all. Experience had taught me how the dull, heavy ache of a great loss will press upon the consciousness with the regular, persistent, relentless throb of a loaded wheel and eat out one's life with the slow certainty of a cancer. This I knew to have been Gwen's state since her father's death, and all my attempts to bring about a healthful reaction had hitherto been futile. It is not to be wondered at, therefore, that even the transient interest she had evinced was hailed by me with delight as the beginning of that healthful reaction for which I had so long sought. When a human bark in the full tide of life is suddenly dashed upon the rocks of despair the wreckage is strewn far and wide, and it is with no little difficulty that enough can be rescued to serve in the rebuilding of even the smallest of craft. The thought, therefore, that Gwen's intellectual flotsam was beginning at length to swirl about a definite object in a way to facilitate the rescue of her faculties was to me a decidedly reassuring one, and I noted with pleasure that the state of excited expectancy which she had tried in vain to conceal did not wane, but waxed stronger as the days went by.

THE EPISODE OF THE PARALLEL READERS

CHAPTER I

The events of the present are all strung upon the thread of the past, and in telling over this chronological rosary, it not infrequently happens that strange, unlike beads follow each other between our questioning fingers.

It was nearly a week after his letter before Maitland arrived. He sent us no further word, but walked in one evening as we were talking about him. He came upon us so suddenly that we were all taken aback and, for a moment, I felt somewhat alarmed about Gwen. She had started up quickly when the servant had mentioned Maitland's name and pressed her hand convulsively upon her heart, while her face and neck became of a deep crimson colour. I was saying to myself that this was a common effect of sudden surprise, when I saw her clutch quickly at the back of her chair, as if to steady herself. A moment later she sank into her seat. Her face was now as pale as ashes, and I felt I had good reason to be alarmed. I think she was conscious of my scrutiny, for she turned her face from me and remained motionless. The movement told me she was trying to regain command of her faculties and I forbore to interfere in the struggle, though I watched her with some solicitude. My fears were at once dispelled, however, when Maitland entered, for Gwen was the first to welcome him. She extended her hand with much of her old impulsiveness, saying: "I have so much for which to thank you – " but Maitland interrupted her. "Indeed, I regret to say," he rejoined, "that I have been unable thus far to be of any real service to you. The Ragobah clue was a miserable failure, though we may do ourselves the justice to admit that we had no alternative but to follow it to the end. I confess I have never been more disappointed than in the outcome of this affair." "My dear fellow," I said, "we all have much to be thankful for in your safe return, let us not forget that." Maitland laughed: "That reminds me," he said, "of the man who passed the hat at a coloured camp-meeting. When asked how much he had collected, he replied: 'I didn't get no money, but I'se done got de hat back.' You've got your hat back, and that's about all. However, with Miss Darrow's permission, I shall go back to the starting point and begin all over again."

"You are making me your debtor," Gwen replied slowly, "beyond my power ever to repay you."

"It is in the hope that no payment may ever be demanded of you," he rejoined, "that I am busying myself in your affairs." The colour sprang to Gwen's cheeks, but she only replied by a grateful glance. I knew what was passing through her mind. She was thinking of her promise – of her father's last words, and of the terrible possibilities thereof from which Maitland was seeking to rescue her. She felt that she could safely owe him any debt of gratitude, however great, while he, on his part, took what I fancied, both then and afterward, were unnecessary pains to assure her that, in the event of his finding the assassin, she need have no fear of his making any claim whatsoever upon her. And so the whole affair was dropped for the time being and the rest of the evening devoted to listening to Maitland's account of his experiences while abroad.

The next morning I called upon our detective at his laboratory and asked him what he intended to do next. He replied that he had no plans as yet, but that he wished to review with me all the evidence at hand.

"You see," he said, "the thing that renders the solution of this mystery so difficult is the fact that all our clues, while they would be of the utmost service in the conviction of the assassin had we found him, are almost destitute of any value until he has been located. Add to this that we are now unable to find any motive for the crime and you can see how slight are our hopes of success. If ever we chance to find the man, – for I feel that such a consummation would result more from chance than from anything else, – I think we can convict him.

"Here, for example," he said, taking up a small slip of glass which he had cut from the eastern parlour window of the Darrow house, "is something I have never shown either you or Miss Darrow. It is utterly worthless, so far as assisting us to track the assassin is concerned, but, if ever we suspect the right man, the evidence on that glass would probably convict him, though there were ten thousand other suspects."

I took the glass from him and, examining it with the utmost care, I detected a smutch of yellowish paint upon it, nothing more. "For Heaven's sake, Maitland!" I said in astonishment, "of what possible use can that formless daub of paint be, or is there

something else on the glass that has escaped me?"
He laughed at my excitement as he replied:

"There is nothing there but the paint spot. Regarding that, however, you have come to a very natural though erroneous conclusion. It is not formless"; and he passed me a jeweller's eye-glass to assist me in a closer examination. He was right. The paint lay upon the glass in little irregular furrows which arranged themselves concentrically about a central oval groove somewhat imperfect in shape. "Well," continued. Maitland, as I returned him the magnifying glass, "what do you make of it?" "If you hadn't already attached so much importance to the thing," I said, "I should pronounce it a daub of paint transferred to the glass by somebody's thumb, but, as such a thing would be clearly useless, I am at a loss to know what it is."

"Well," he rejoined, "you've hit the nail on the head, – that's just what it is, but you are entirely wrong in your assumption that the thumb-mark can have no value as evidence. Do you not know that there are no two thumbs in the world which are capable of making indistinguishable marks?" I was not aware of this. "How do you know," I asked, "that this mark was made by the assassin? It seems to me there can hardly be a doubt that one of the painters, while priming the sill, accidentally pressed his thumb against the glass. His hands would naturally have been painty, and this impression would as naturally have resulted."

"What you say," replied Maitland, "is very good, so far as it goes. My reasons for believing this thumb-mark was made by the assassin are easily understood. First: there was another impression of a thumb in the moist paint of the sill directly under that upon the glass. Both marks were made by the same thumb and, in the lower one, the microscope revealed minute traces of gravel dust, not elsewhere discernible upon the sill. The thumb carried the dust there, and was the thumb of the hand pressed into the gravel, – the hand of which I have a cast. You see how this shows how the thumb came to have paint upon it when pressed upon the glass. Second: the two men engaged in priming the house, James Cogan and Charles Rice, were the only persons save the assassin known to have been upon that side of the house the day of the murder. "Here," he said, carefully removing two strips of glass from a box, "are the thumb-marks of Cogan and Rice made with the same paint. You see that neither of these men could, by any possibility, have made the mark upon the glass. So there you are. But we are missing the question before us. What line of procedure can you suggest, Doc? I'm all at sea."

"We must find someone," I said, "who could have had a motive. This someone ought to have a particularly good reason for concealing his footprints, and is evidently lame besides. I can't for the life of me see anything else we have to go by, unless it be the long nail of the little finger, and I don't see how that is going to help us find the assassin – unless we can find out why it was worn long. If we knew that it might assist us. As I have already suggested, a Chinaman might have a long nail on the little finger, but he would also have the other nails long, wouldn't he? Furthermore, he might use the boards to conceal the prints of his telltale foot-gear; but why should he not have put on shoes of the ordinary type? If he had time to prepare the boards, – the whole affair shows premeditation, – clearly he had time to change his boots. The Chinese are usually small, and this might easily account for the smallness of the hand as shown by your cast. These are the pros and cons of the only clue that suggests itself to me. By the way, Maitland, it's a shame we did not try, before it was too late, to track this fellow down with a dog."

"Ah," he replied, "there is another little thing I have not told you. After you had left the house with Miss Darrow on the night of the murder, and all the servants had retired, I locked the parlour securely and quietly slipped out to look about a bit. As you know, the moon was very bright and any object moderately near was plainly visible. I went around to the eastern side of the house where the prints of the hand and boards were found, and examined them with extreme care. What I particularly wished to learn was the direction taken by the assassin as he left the house and the point at which he had removed the boards from his feet. The imprints of the boards were clearly discernible so far as the loose gravel extended, but beyond that nothing could be discovered. I sat down and pondered over the matter. I had about concluded to drive two nails into the heels of my boots to enable me to distinguish my own footprints from any other trail I might intersect, and then, starting with the house as a centre, to describe an involute about it in the hope of being able to detect some one or more points where my course crossed that of the assassin, when I remembered that my friend Burwell, whose Uncle Tom's Cabin Combination recently stranded at Brockton was at home. As you are perhaps aware an Uncle Tom Company consists of a 'Legree,' one or two 'Markses,' one or two 'Topsies,' 'Uncle Tom,' a 'Little Eva,' who should not be over fifty years old, – or at least should not appear to be, – two bloodhounds, and anybody else that happens to be available. It really doesn't make the least difference how many or how few people are in the cast. I have heard that an Uncle Tom manager on a Western circuit, most of whose company deserted him because the 'ghost' never walked, succeeded in cutting and rewriting the piece so as to double 'George Harris' and 'Legree,' ' Marks' and 'Topsy,' 'Uncle Tom' and 'Little Eva.' As for the rest he had it so arranged that he could himself 'get off the door' in time to 'do,' with the aid of the dogs, all the other characters. You see the dogs held the stage while he changed, say, from 'Eliza' to Eva's father. 'George Harris' would look off left second entrance and say that 'Legree' was after him. Then he would discharge a revolver, rush off right first entrance, where he would pass his weapon to 'Eva' and 'Uncle Tom,' and this bisexual individual would discharge it in the wings at the imaginary pursuer, while 'Harris' would put on a wire beard, slouch hat, black melodramatic cape, and, rushing behind the flat, enter left as 'Legree.'

"The hardest thing to manage was the death of 'Little Eva' with 'Uncle Tom' by the bedside, but managerial genius overcame the difficulty after the style of Mantell's 'Corsican Brothers.' You see it is all easy enough when you know how. 'Little Eva' is discovered, sitting up in bed with the curtains drawn back. She says what she has to say to her father and the rest. Then her father has a line in which he informs 'Eva' that she is tired and had better try to sleep. She says she will try, just to please him, and he gently lowers her back upon the pillows and draws the curtains in front of the bed. But instead of utilising this seclusion for a refreshing sleep 'Eva' rolls out at the back side of the bed. 'Legree' snatches off 'Eva's' wig and 'Topsy' deftly removes the white nightdress concealing his – 'Eva's' – 'Uncle Tom' make-up, while the erstwhile little girl hastily blackens his face and hands, puts on a negro wig, and in less than a minute is changed in colour, race, and sex. He 'gets round' left and enters the sick room as 'Uncle Tom' with 'Topsy.' They are both told that 'Little Eva' is asleep, and 'Topsy' peeps cautiously between the curtains and remarks that the child's eyes are open and staring. The father looks in and, overcome by grief, informs the audience that his child is dead. 'Topsy,' tearful and grief-stricken, 'gets off' right and washes up to 'do' 'Little Eva' climbing the golden stair in the last tableau. Meanwhile 'Uncle Tom,' in a paroxysm of grief, throws himself upon the bed and holds the stage till he smells the red fire for the vision; then he staggers down stage, strikes an attitude; the others do likewise; picture of 'Little Eva,' curtain. Talk about doubling 'Marcellus,' 'Polonius,' 'Osric,' and the 'First Grave Digger'! Why, that's nothing to these 'Uncle Tom' productions. But hold on, where did I get side-tracked? Oh, yes, the dogs.

"Well, as I was saying, as soon as I thought of Burwell I made up my mind at once to borrow one of his hounds. It was late when I got to his house. When I knocked at the door both Pompey and Caesar began sub-bass solos of growls, and Burwell was awake in a minute. I told him I wanted a dog for private business and took Caesar off with me. He found the trail with no difficulty, and followed it in a bee-line down to the water, where he raised his big muzzle and howled in dismal impotency. The assassin had taken to the water. I took the dog up and down the shore to see if he had returned to land, but all I found of interest was a clump of alders from which a pole had been cut. I knew by the dog's actions that the assassin had been there, for Caesar immediately took a new trail back to the house. Try as I might I could learn nothing further, and I at once returned the dog. There is no doubt that the murderer made his escape in a boat and took with him the pole he had cut, the boards he had worn, and everything else, I dare say, connected with his crime. One thing seems clear, and that is that we are dealing with no ordinary criminal. I would wager a good deal that this fellow, if ever he is caught, will be found to be a man of brains. I don't place much confidence in the Chinese theory, Doc, but as I have nothing better to offer, let us go see Miss Darrow. If her father has ever had any dealings with Chinamen, we shall probably deem it wise to look the Orientals up a bit."

We immediately acted upon this suggestion, waiting upon Gwen at my house. She said she and her father had spent a year in San Francisco when she was about seven years of age. While there their household was looked after by two Chinese servants, named Wah Sing and Sam Lee. The latter had been discharged by her father because of his refusal to perform certain minor duties which, through oversight, had not been set down as part of his work when he was engaged. So far as she knew no altercation had taken place and there were no hard feelings on either side. Sam Lee had bade her good-bye and had seemed sorry to leave, notwithstanding which, however, he refused, with true Chinese pertinacity, to assume the new duties. She did not think it likely that either of these Chinamen had been instrumental in her father's death, yet she agreed with Maitland that it would be a point gained to be assured of this fact. Maitland accordingly determined to depart at once for San Francisco, and the next day he was off.

We received no letters from him during his absence and were, accordingly, unable to tell when he expected to get back. Since his return from India Gwen had given evidence of a reviving interest in life, but now that he was again away, she relapsed into her old listless condition, from which we found it impossible to arouse her. Alice, who did her utmost to please her, was at her wit's end. She could never tell which of two alternatives Gwen preferred, since that young lady would invariably express herself satisfied with either and did not seem to realise why she should be expected to have any choice in the matter. Alice was quite at a loss to understand this state of affairs, until I told her that Gwen was in a condition of semi-torpor in which even the effort of choice seemed an unwarrantable outlay. She simply did not care what happened. She felt nothing, save a sense of fatigue, and even what she saw was viewed as from afar, – and seemed to her a drama in which she took no other part than that of an idle, tired, and listless spectator. Clearly she was losing her hold on life. I told Alice we must do our utmost to arouse her, to stimulate her will, to awaken her interest, and we tried many things in vain.

Maitland had been gone, I think, about three weeks when my sister and I hit upon a plan which we thought might have the desired effect upon Gwen. Before her father's death she had been one of the most active members of a Young People's Club which devoted every Wednesday evening to the study of Shakespeare. She had attended none of its meetings since her bereavement, but Alice and I soon persuaded her to accompany us on the following week and I succeeded, by a little quiet wire-pulling, in getting her appointed to take charge of the following meeting, which was to be devoted to the study of "Antony and Cleopatra." When informed of the task which had been imposed upon her Gwen was for declining the honour at once, and the most Alice and I were able to do was to get her to promise to think it over a day or so before she refused.

The next morning Maitland walked in upon us. He had found both of Mr. Darrow's former servants and satisfied himself that they were in San Francisco on the night of the murder. So that ended my Chinese clue. While Alice and Gwen were discussing the matter, I took occasion to draw Maitland aside, and told him of Gwen's appointment to take charge of the Cleopatra night, and how necessary it was to her health that she should be aroused from her torpor. It doesn't take long for Maitland to see a thing, and before I had whispered a dozen sentences he had completely grasped the situation. He crossed the room, drew a chair up beside Gwen, and sat down. "Miss Darrow," he began, "I am afraid you will have a poor opinion of me as a detective. This is the second time I have failed. I feel that I should remind you again of our compact, at least, that part of it which permits you to dispense with my services whenever you shall see fit to do so, and, at the same time, to relieve you from your obligation to let me order your actions. I tell you frankly it will be necessary for you to discharge me, if you would be rid of me, for, unless you do so, or I find the assassin, I shall never cease my search so long as I have the strength and means to conduct it. What do you say? Have I not proved my uselessness?" This was said in a tentative, half-jesting tone. Gwen answered it very seriously.

"You have done for me," she said, in the deep, vibrating tones of her rich contralto voice, "all that human intelligence could suggest. You have examined the evidence and conducted the whole affair with a thoroughness which I never could have obtained elsewhere. That your search has been unavailing is due, not to any fault of yours, but rather to the consummate skill of the assassin, who, I think, we may conclude, is no ordinary criminal. I do not know much of the abilities of Messrs. Osborne and Allen, but I understand that M. Godin has the reputation of being the cleverest detective in America. I

cannot learn that he has made any progress whatsoever in the solution of this terrible mystery. I do not
feel, therefore, that you have any right to reproach
yourself. Such hope as I have that my father's murderer may ever be brought to justice rests in your
efforts; else I should feel bound to relieve you of a
task, which, though self-imposed, is, none the less,
onerous and ill-paid. Do not consider me altogether
selfish if I ask that you still continue the search, and
that I – that I still be held to my covenant. I am aware
that I can never fully repay the kindness I am asking
of you, but – "

Maitland did not wait for her to finish. "Let us
not speak of that," he said. "It is enough to know that
you are still satisfied with my, thus far, unsuccessful
efforts in your behalf. There is nothing affords me
keener pleasure than to struggle with and solve an
intricate problem, whether it be in algebra, geometry, or the mathematics of crime; and then – well,
even if I succeed, I shall quit the work your debtor."

He had spoken this last impulsively, and when
he had finished he remained silent, as if surprised
and a bit nettled at his own failure to control himself.
Gwen made no reply, not even raising her eyes; but I
noticed that her fingers at once busied themselves
with the entirely uncalled-for labour of readjusting
the tidy upon the arm of her chair, and I thought
that, if appearances were to be trusted, she was very
happy and contented at the change she had made in
the bit of lacework beneath her hands. With singular
good sense, with which she was always surprising
me, Alice now introduced the subject of the Young
People's Club, and mentioned incidentally that

Gwen was to have charge of the next meeting. Before Gwen had time to inform Maitland that she intended to decline this honour, he congratulated her upon it, and rendered her withdrawal difficult by saying: "I feel that I should thank you, Miss Darrow, for the faithful way in which you fulfil the spirit of your agreement to permit me to order your actions. I know, if you consulted your own desires, you would probably decline the honour conferred upon you, and that in accepting it, you are influenced by the knowledge that you are pursuing just the course I most wish you to follow. Verily, you make my office of tyrant over you a perfect sinecure. I had expected you to chafe a little under restraint, but, instead, I find you voluntarily yielding to my unexpressed desires."

Gwen made no reply, but we heard no more of her resignation. She applied herself at once to the preparation of her paper upon "Antony and Cleopatra." Maitland, who, like all vigorous, healthy, and informed intellects, was an ardent admirer of Shakespeare, found time to call on Gwen and to discuss the play with her. This seemed to please her very much, and I am sure his interest in the play was abnormal. He confessed to me that every morning, as he awoke, the first thing which flashed into his mind, even before he had full possession of his senses, was these words of Antony:

"I am dying, Egypt, dying."

He professed himself utterly unable to account for this, and asked me what I thought was the cause of it. He furthermore suddenly decided that he would ask Gwen to propose his name for membership at the next meeting of the Young People's Club. I hastily indorsed this resolution, for I had a vague sort of feeling that it would please Gwen.

The "Antony and Cleopatra" night at length arrived. We all attended the meeting and listened to a very able paper upon the play. One of the most marked traits of Gwen's character is that whatever she does she does thoroughly, and this was fully exemplified on the night in question. Maitland was very much impressed by some verse Gwen had written for the occasion, and a copy of which he succeeded in procuring from her. I think, from certain remarks he made, that it was the broad and somewhat unfeminine charity expressed in the verse which most astonished and attracted him. but of this, after what I have said, you will, when you have perused it, be as good a judge as I:

CLEOPATRA

In Egypt, where the lotus sips the waters
Of ever-fruitful Nile, and the huge Sphinx
In awful silence, – mystic converse with
The stars, – doth see the pale moon hang her crescent on
The pyramid's sharp peak, – e'en there, well in
The straits of Time's perspective,
Went out, by Caesarean gusts from Rome,
The low-burned candle of the Ptolemies:
Went out without a flicker in full glare
Of noon-day glory. When her flame lacked oil
Too proud was Egypt's queen to be
The snuff of Roman spirits; so she said,

"Good-night," and closed the book of life half read
And little understood; perchance misread
The greater part, – yet, who shall say? Are we
An ermined bench to call her culprit failings up
And make them plead for mercy? Or can we,
Upon whom soon shall fall the awful shadow of
The Judgment Seat, stand in her light and throw
Ourselves that shadow? Rather let fall upon
Her memory the softening gauze of Time,
As mantle of a charity which else
We might not serve. She was a woman,
And as a woman loved! What though the fierce
Simoom blew ever hot within the sail
Of her desire? What if it shifted with
Direction of her breath? Or if the rudder of
Her will did lean as many ways as trampled straws,
And own as little worth? She was a woman still,
And queen. They do best understand themselves
Who trust themselves the least; as they are wisest
Who, for their safety, thank more the open sea
Than pilot will. Oh, Egypt's self-born Isis!
Ought we to fasten in thy memory the fangs
Of unalloyed distrust? We know how little
Better is History's page than leaf whereat the ink
Is thrown. Nor yet should we forget how much
The nearer thou than we didst come to
The rough-hewn corner-stone of Time. We know
Thy practised love enfolded Antony;
And that around the heart of Hercules'
Descendant, threading through and through,
Like the red rivers of its life, in tangled mesh
No circumstance could e'er unravel, thou
Didst coil, – the dreamy, dazzling "Serpent of
The Nile!" Thy sins stick jagged out

From history's page, and bleeding tear
Fair Judgment from thy merits. We perchance
Do wrong thee, Isis; for that coward, History,
Who binds in death his object's jaw and then
Besmuts her name, hath crossed his focus in
Another age, and paled his spreading figment from
Our sight. Thou art so far back toward
The primal autocrat whose wish, hyena-like,
Was his religion, that, appearing as thou dost
On an horizon new flushed in the first
Uncertain ray of Altruism, thou seem'st
More ghost than human. Yet thou lovest, loving
ghost,
And thy fierce parent flame thyself snuffed out
Scarce later than the dark'ning of the fire
Thou gav'st to be eternal vestal of
Thine Antony's spirit. Thou didst love and die
Of love; let, therefore, no light tongue, brazen
In censure, say that nothing in thy life
Became thee like the leaving it. The cloth
From which humanity is cut is woven of
The warp and woof of circumstance, and all
Are much alike. We spring from out the mantle,
Earth,
And hide at last beneath it; in the interim
Our acts are less of us than it. We are
No judge, then, of thy sins, thou ending link
Of Ptolemy's chain. Forsooth, we are too much
O'erfilled with wondering how like to thee
We all had been, inclipt and dressed in thine
Own age and circumstance.

   The exercises of the evening concluded with the
reading of the familiar poem, beginning:

"I am dying, Egypt, dying;
Ebbs the crimson life-tide fast."

It was about noon the next day when Maitland called upon me. "See here, Doc," he began at once, "do you believe in coincidences?" I informed him that his question was not altogether easy to understand. "Wait a moment," he said, "while I explain. For at least two years prior to my recent return from California the name 'Cleopatra' has not entered my mind. You were the first to mention it to me, and from you I learned that Miss Darrow was to have charge of the 'Antony and Cleopatra' night. That is all natural enough. But why should I, on every morning since you first mentioned the subject to me, awake with Antony's words upon my lips? Why should every book or paper I pick up contain some reference to Cleopatra? Why, man, if I were superstitious, it would seem positively spookish. I am getting to believe that I shall be confronted either by Cleopatra's name, or some allusion to her, every time I pick up a book. It's getting to be decidedly interesting."

"I have had," I replied, "similar, though less remarkable, experiences. It is quite a common occurrence to learn of a thing, say, this morning for the first time in one's life, and then to find, in the course of the day's reading, three or four independent references to the same thing. Suppose we step into the library, and pick out a few books haphazard, just to see if we chance upon any reference to Cleopatra."

To this Maitland agreed, and, entering the library, I pushed the Morning Herald across the table to him, saying: "One thing's as good as another; try that." He started a little, but did not touch the paper. "You will have to find something harder than that," he said, pointing to the outspread paper.

I followed the direction of his finger, and read:

"Boston Theatre. Special engagement of Miss Fanny Davenport. For one week. Beginning Monday, the 12th of December, Sardou's Cleopatra.'"

I was indeed surprised, but I said nothing. The next thing I handed him was a copy of Godey's Magazine, several years old. He opened it carelessly, and in a moment read the following line: "I am dying, sweetheart, dying." "Doesn't that sound familiar? It reminds me at once of the poetic alarm clock that wakens me every morning, – 'I am dying, Egypt, dying.' There is no doubt that Higginson's poem suggested this one. Here is the whole of the thing as it is printed here," he said, and read the following:

LOVE'S TWILIGHT

> I am dreaming, loved one, dreaming
> Of the sweet and beauteous past
> When the world was as its seeming,
> Ere the fatal shaft was cast.
>
> I am sobbing, sad-eyed, sobbing,
> At the darkly sullen west,
> Of the smile of ignorance robbing
> The pale face against the breast.
>
> I am smiling, tear-stained, smiling,
> As the sun glints on the crest
> Of the troubled wave, beguiling

Shipwrecked Hope to its long rest.

I am parting, broken, parting,
From a soul that I hold dear,
And the music of whose beauty
Fades a dead strain on my ear.

I am dying, sweetheart, dying,
Drips life's gold through palsied hands, –
See; the dead'ning Sun is sighing
His last note in red'ning bands.

So I'm sighing, sinking, sighing,
Flows life's river to the sea.
Death my throbbing heart is tying
With the strings that ache for thee.

"Yes," I said, when he had finished. "I shall have to admit that immediately suggests Higginson's poem and Cleopatra's name. But here, try this," and I threw an old copy of the Atlantic Monthly upon the table. Maitland opened it and laughed. "This may be mere chance, Doc," he said, "but it is remarkable, none the less. See here!" He held the magazine toward me, and I read: "Cleopatra's Needle. The Historic Significance of Central Park's New Monument. Some of the Difficulties that Attended its Transportation and Erection. By James Theodore Wright, Ph. D." I was dumfounded. Things were indeed getting interesting.

"Magazines and newspapers," I said, "seem to be altogether too much in your line. We'll try a book this time. Here," and I pulled the first one that came to hand, "is a copy of Tennyson's Poems I fancy it will trouble you to find your reference in that." Maitland took it in silence, and, opening it at random, began to read. The result surprised him even more than it did me. He had chanced upon these verses from "A Dream of Fair Women":

> "'We drank the Libyan Sun to sleep, and lit
> Lamps which outburn'd Canopus. O my life
> In Egypt! O the dalliance and the wit,
> The flattery and the strife.

> "'And the wild kiss when fresh from war's alarms,
> My Hercules, my Roman Antony,
> My mailed Bacchus leapt into my arms,
> Contented there to die!

> "'And there he died! And when I heard my name
> Sigh'd forth with life, I would not brook my fear
> Of the other! With a worm I balked his fame.
> What else was left? look here!'

> "With that she tore her robe apart and half
> The polished argent of her breast to sight
> Laid bare. Thereto she pointed with a laugh,
> Showing the aspic's bite."

"There is no doubt about that," I said, as he laid the book upon the table. "I want to try this thing once more. Here is Pascal; if you can find any reference to the 'Serpent of the Nile' in that, you needn't go any farther, I shall be satisfied," and I passed the book to him. He turned the pages over in silence for half a minute, or so, and then said: "I guess this counts as a failure, – no, though, by Jove! Look here!" His face was of almost deathly pallor, and his finger trembled upon the passage it indicated as he held the book toward me. I glanced with some anxiety from his face to the book, and read, as nearly as I now can remember: "If Cleopatra's nose had been shorter, the entire face of the world would have been changed."

It was some minutes before Maitland fully regained his composure, and during that time neither of us spoke. "Well, Doc," he said at length, and his manner was decidedly grave, even for him:

"What do you make of it?" I didn't know what to make of it, and I admitted my ignorance with a frankness at which, considering my profession, I have often since had occasion to marvel. I told him that I could scarcely account for it on the ground of mere coincidence, and I called his attention to that part of "The Mystery of Marie Roget," where Poe figures out the mathematical likelihood of a certain combination of peculiarities of clothing being found to obtain in the case of two young women who were unknown to each other. If the finding of a single reference to Cleopatra had been a thing of so infrequent occurrence as to at once challenge Maitland's attention, what was to be said when, all of a sudden, her name, or some reference to her, seemed to stare at him from every page he read?

"'There is something in this more than natural, If philosophy could find it out,'"

murmured Maitland, more to himself than to me. "Come, what do you say?" and he turned abruptly to me with one of those searching looks so peculiar to him in moments of excitement. "I see," I replied, "that you are determined I shall give my opinion now and here, without a moment's reflection. Very well; you have just quoted 'Hamlet'; I will do likewise:

"'There are more things in Heaven and Earth, Horatio, Than are dreamt of in your philosophy!'

"You seem in some strange way to be dominated by the shade of Cleopatra. Now, if I believed in metempsychosis, I should think you were Mark Antony brought down to date. There, with that present sober air of yours, you'd pass anywhere for such an anachronism. But to be serious, and to give you advice which is positively bilious with gravity, I should say, investigate this thing fully; make a study of this ancient charmer. By the way, why not begin by going to see Davenport in Sardou's 'Cleopatra'? You have never seen her in it, have you?"

In this way, I succeeded in getting him out of his depressed state. We got into an argument concerning the merits of Miss Davenport's work. I know of nothing Maitland would sooner do than argue, and, if attacked on a subject upon which he feels strongly, he is, for the time being, totally oblivious of everything else. For this reason I trapped him into this argument. I abominate what is now known as "realism" just as much as he does, but you don't have much of an argument without some apparent difference of opinion, so, for the nonce, I became a realist of whom Zola himself would have been proud. "Why, man," I said, "realism is truth. You certainly can't have any quarrel with that." I knew this would have the effect of a red rag flaunted in the face of a bull.

"Truth! Bah!" he exclaimed excitedly. "I have no patience with such aesthetic hod-carriers! Truth, indeed! Is there no other truth in art but that coarse verisimilitude, that vulgar trickery, which appeals to the eyes and the ears of the rabble? Are there not psychological truths of immensely greater importance? What sane man imagines for a moment that the pleasure he derives from seeing that greatest of all tragedians, Edwin Booth, in one of Shakespeare's matchless tragedies, is dependent upon his believing that this or that character is actually killed? Why, even the day of the cranberry-juice dagger is long since passed. When Miss Davenport shrieks in 'Fedora,' the shriek is literal – 'real,' you would call it – and you find yourself instinctively saying, 'Don't! – – don't!' and wishing you were out of the house. When Mr. Booth, as 'Shylock' shrieks at 'Tubal's' news, the cry is not real, is not literal, but is suggestive, and you see at once the fiendish glee of which it is the expression. The difference between the two is the difference between vocal cords and grey matter."

"But surely," I rejoined, "one doesn't want untruth; one wants – " but he did not let me finish.

"Always that cry of truth!" he retorted. "Do you not see how absurd it is, as used by your exponents of realism? With a bit of charcoal some Raphael draws a face with five lines, and some photographer snaps a camera at the same face. Which would any sane man choose as the best work of art? The five-line face, of course. Why? Is the work of the camera unreal? Is it not more accurate in drawing, more subtle in gradation than the less mechanical picture? To be sure. What, then, makes the superiority of the few lines of our Raphael? That which makes the superiority of all noble art – its truth,, not on a low, but on a high, plane: its power of interpreting. See!" he said, fairly aglow with excitement. "What does your realist do, even assuming that he has reached that never-to – be-attained perfection which is the lifelong Mecca of his desires? He gives you, by his absolutely realistic goes with you, and interprets its grandeur to you. Stand before his canvas and enjoy it as you would Nature herself if there. Surely, you say, nothing more could be desired, and you clap your hands, and shout, 'Bravo!' But wait a bit; the other side is yet to be heard from. What does the true artist do for you by his picture of Yosemite Valley? He not only gives you a free conveyance to it, but he goes with you, and interprets its grandeur to you. He translates into the language of your consciousness beauties which, without him, you would entirely miss. It is this very capability of seeing more in Nature than is ever perceived by the common throng that constitutes the especial genius of the artist, and a work that is not aglow with its creator's personality – personality, mind you, not coarse realism – can never rank as a masterpiece. But, come, this won't do. Why did you want to get me astride my hobby?"

I thought it advisable to answer this question by asking another, so I said: "But how about Davenport? Will you go?"

"Yes," he replied. "Anything with a Cleopatra to it interests me. I'll go now and see about the tickets," and he left me.

I have related Maitland's aesthetic views as expressed to me upon this occasion, not because they have any particular bearing upon the mystery I am narrating, but because they cast a strong side-light upon the young man's character, and also for the reason that I believe his personality to be sufficiently strong and unique to be of general interest.

We went that same night to see Sardou's "Cleopatra." I asked Maitland how he liked the piece, and the only reply he vouchsafed was: "I have recently read Shakespeare's treatment of the same theme."

CHAPTER II

If events spread themselves out fanwise from the past into the future, then must the occurrences of the present exhibit convergence toward some historical burning-point, – some focal centre whereat the potential was warmed into the kinetic.

It was nearly a week after the events last narrated before I saw Maitland again, and then only by chance. We happened to meet in the Parker House, and, as he had some business pertaining to a case he was on, to transact at the Court House, I walked up Beacon Street with him. There is a book or stationery store, on Somerset Street, just before you turn down toward Pemberton Square. As we were passing this store, Maitland espied a large photographic reproduction of some picture.

"Let us cross over and see what it is," he said. We did so. It was a photograph of L. Alma-Tadema's painting of Antony and Cleopatra. Maitland started a little as he read the title, and then said lightly: "Do you suppose, Doc, that woman's mummy is in existence? I should like to find it. I've an idea she left some hieroglyphic message for me on her mummy-case, and doesn't propose to let me rest easy until I find and translate it. Now, if I believed in transmigration of souls – do you see any mark of Antony about me? Say, though, just imagine the spirit of Marcus Antonius in a rubber apron, making an analysis of oleomargarine! But here we are; good-bye," and he left me without awaiting any reply. He seemed to me to be in decidedly better spirits than formerly, and I was at the time at a loss to account for it. The cause of his levity, however, was soon explained, for that night, as Gwen, my sister, and I were sitting cosily in the study according to our usual custom, Maitland walked in, unannounced. He had come now to be a regular visitor, and I invented not a few subterfuges to get him to call even oftener than he otherwise would, for I perceived that his coming gave pleasure to Gwen. She exhibited less depression when in his presence than at any other time. I had learned that hers was one of those deep natures in which grief crystallises slowly, but with an unconquerable persistence. Instead of her forgetting her bereavement, or the sense thereof waxing weaker by time, she seemed to be drifting toward that ever-present consciousness of loss in which the soul feels itself gradually, but surely, sinking under an insupportable burden – a burden so long borne, so well known, that the mind no longer thinks of it. The heart beats stolidly under its load, and seems to forget the time when it was not so oppressed. No one knows better than we physicians the danger of this autocracy of grief, and I watched Gwen with a solicitude at times almost bordering on despair. But, as I said before, she always seemed to show more interest in affairs when Maitland was present, and, on the night in question, his abrupt and unexpected entrance surprised her into the betrayal of more pleasure than she would have wished us to note, and, indeed, so quickly did she conceal her confusion that I was the only one who noticed it. Maitland was too busy with the news he brought.

"Well, Miss Darrow," he began at once, "at last

your detective has got a clue – not much of a one – but still a clue. I can pick the man for whom we are looking from among a million of his fellows – if I am ever fortunate enough to get the chance."

Somebody has already called attention to the fact that women are more or less curious, and there are well-authenticated cases on record where this inquisitiveness has even extended to things which did not immediately concern themselves; so I have little doubt I shall be believed when I say the women folk were in a fever of expectancy, and besought Maitland with an earnestness quite unnecessary – (it would have required a great deal to have prevented his telling it) – to begin at the beginning, and relate the whole thing. He readily acceded to this request, and began by telling them the experiences which I have just narrated. It was, he said, during the last act of Sardou's "Cleopatra" that the idea had suddenly come to him to change the plan of search from the analytical to the synthetical.

"You see," he continued, "I had from the first been trying to find the assassin without knowing the exact way in which the crime was committed. I now determined to ascertain how, under the same circumstances, I could commit such a crime, and leave behind no other evidences of the deed than those which are in our possession. I began to read detective stories, with all the avidity of a Western Union Telegraph messenger, and, of course, read those by Conan Doyle. The assertion of 'Sherlock Holmes' that there is no novelty in crime; that crimes, like history, repeat themselves; and that criminals read and copy each other's methods, deeply impressed me, and I at once said to myself: 'If our assassin was not original, whom did he copy?'

"It was while reading 'The Sign of the Four,' which I had procured at the Public Library, that I made the first discovery. The crime therein narrated had been committed in such a singular manner that it at once attracted my attention. The victim had apparently been murdered without anyone having either entered or left the room. In this respect it was like the problem we are trying to solve. Might not this book, I said to myself, have suggested to your father's assassin the course he pursued. I concluded to go to the library and ask for a list of the names of persons who had taken out this book for a few months prior to your father's death. I was fully aware that the chance of my learning anything in this way was very slight, In the first place; I reasoned that it was not especially likely your father's murderer had read 'The Sign of the Four,' and, in the second place, even if he had, what assurance had I that he had read this particular copy of it? Notwithstanding this, however, I felt impelled to give my synthetical theory a fair experimental trial. I was informed by the Library attendants that the book had been much read, and given the list of some twenty names of persons who had borrowed the book during the time I had specified. With these twenty-odd names before me, I sat down to think what my next step should be. I went carefully over this chain of reasoning link by link. 'I wish to find a certain murderer, and have adopted this method in the hope that it may help me. If I derive any assistance at all from it, it will be because my man has read this particular copy of this work; therefore, I may as well assume at the start that among these twenty-odd names is that of the man I want. Is there any possibility of this crime having been committed by a woman?' was my next question, and my answer was, 'Yes, a possibility, but it is so decidedly improbable that I may count it out for the time being.' Accordingly, I set aside all the female names, which cut my list down to eighteen. Several of the applicants had only signed the initials of their given names, and the attendant, copying them from the slips, had done likewise; so I was obliged to go to the registration clerk to determine this question of sex, and, while there, I also ascertained the age of each applicant – that is, of all but two. The registrar could give me no information regarding J. Z. Weltz, or B. W. Rizzi. When I told him that one of the clerks had copied the names for me from application slips, he informed me that if I would go back to her I would undoubtedly find she had taken the two last-mentioned names from the green slips used in applying for books for hall use, as neither J. Z. Weltz nor B. W. Rizzi was a card-holder.

"I decided to let these two names rest a while, and to give my attention to the others. After careful deliberation I felt reasonably sure your father's assassin could not fail to be a man of mature judgment and extraordinary cunning, probably a man past middle life – at all events, I could safely say he was over twenty-one years of age. Proceeding upon this assumption my list was reduced to ten names. But how should I further continue this process of exclusion? This was the question which now confronted me. I could think of but one way, apart from personally making the gentlemen's acquaintance, which I did not then wish to do, and that was to ascertain what other books they had borrowed immediately before and after they had read 'The Sign of the Four.' This was the course I determined to pursue.

"If you ask me why I so persistently followed an investigation, a successful outcome of which anyone must recognise would be little short of miraculous, I can only say that I felt impelled to do so. Perhaps the impulse was due to my habit of testing patiently and thoroughly each new theory which impresses me as having any degree of probability, and perhaps it was due to something else – Cleopatra, perhaps, eh, Doctor? – I don't know. I determined, however, to thoroughly satisfy myself regarding these ten men. I made a careful list, with the assistance of an attendant, of ten books taken by each man, five taken just prior to 'The Sign of the Four,' and the other five just following it. I made no deductions until the list was completed, although I began to see certain things of interest as we worked upon it. At length the whole hundred titles were spread before me, and I sat down to see what I could make of them. I purposely reserved consideration of the books borrowed by Weltz and Rizzi until the last, because I had been able to learn nothing of them, and considered, therefore, that they were the most difficult persons in the list about whom to satisfy myself. I found the other eight exhibited no system in their reading. One had read – I think I can remember the books in the order in which they were borrowed – 'Thelma,' 'Under Two Flags,' 'David Copperfield,' 'The Story of an

African Farm,' 'A Study in Scarlet,' 'The Sign of the Four,' 'The Prisoner of Zenda,' 'The Dolly Dialogues,' 'The Yellow Aster,' 'The Superfluous Woman,' and 'Ideala.' This is a fair sample of the other seven. Not so, however, with Messrs. Weltz and Rizzi. The reading of these men at once impressed me as having a purpose behind it.

"I will read you a list of the books taken by Weltz and Rizzi, just to see what you will make out of it:

WELTZ RIZZI

1."Lecons de Toxicologic," 1."Traite de Toxicologic," par M. Orifia. par C. P. Galtier.

2."The Poisons of Asps and 2."The Poisons of Asps and Other Stories," by Florence Other Stories," by Florence Marryat. Marryat.

3."A Practical Essay on 3."A Practical Essay on Cancer," by C. T. Johnson. Cancer," by C. T. Johnson.

4."The Sharper Detected 4."The Sharper Detected and Exposed," by R. Houdin. and Exposed," by R. Houdin.

5."The Sign of the Four," 5."The Sign of the Four," by A. Conan Doyle. by A. Conan Doyle.

6."Cancer, a New Method of 6."Legal Chemistry: A Treatment," by W. H. Guide to the Detection of Broadbent. Poisons, Examinations of Stains, etc., as Applied to Chemical Jurisprudence." From the French of A. Naquet by J. P. Battershall, Nat.Sc.D.

7."Reports of Trials for 7."Traite Pratique des Murder

by Poisoning," Maladies Cancerences," by G. L. Browne and C. par H. Lebert. G. Stewart.

8."A Practical Treatise on 8."A Practical Treatise on Poisons," by O. H. Costill. Poisons," by O. H. Costill.

9."Poisons, Their Effects 9."A Treatise on Poisons in and Detection," by Alexander Relation to Medical Wynter Blyth. Jurisprudence, Physiology, and the Practice of Physic," by R. Christison,M.D., F.R.S.E.

10."Poisons, Their Effects 10."Poisons, Their Effects and Detection," by Alexander and Detection," by Alexander Wynter Blyth. Wynter Blyth.

"There, do you wonder that the perusal of that list excited me? Come, now, before I go any further, tell me what you make of it, Doc," and he passed it to me.

"There seems to me to be a singular unanimity of purpose existing between these two men," I said; "not only as regards the subject-matter of their reading, but in no less than six cases they have both perused the same volume. This never happened by chance. Clearly, they are acquaintances, and are working together toward some common end. I should think it very likely, judging from their interest in cancers and toxicology, that they were medical students. Numbers four and five don't exactly seem to strengthen my medical hypothesis, but they are only two out of the ten. That's about all I can make out of it;" and I returned the list to him.

"Your views in the matter," replied Maitland, "are precisely those which first occurred to me, and I am not sure but I should still hold them, had I been obliged to decide solely from the evidence I have submitted to you. It was clear to my mind from the first that some common purpose actuated both Weltz and Rizzi. With a view to ascertaining where they lived as a preparatory step toward learning more of them, I consulted a Boston directory, only to learn that it contained no such names. I was about to examine some of the directories of neighbouring towns when it occurred to me that the easiest way to find their places of residence would be to consult the green slips upon which they had procured their books, and I accordingly asked the attendant to kindly let me look at them. While she was collecting the slips I re-examined the list of books taken by Weltz and Rizzi, especially those which had been taken by both men. One thing at once struck my attention, and that was that most of these latter were large books which would take a long time to peruse and would require to be borrowed several times for hall use, were they to be examined with any care. I put this fact down for future reference and gave my attention to the green slips, the whole twenty of which the attendant now placed before me. The residence of Weltz was given as No. 15 Staniford Place, Boston, while that of Rizzi was No. 5 Oak Street, Boston. I was about to walk over to Oak Street to see if Rizzi were still there when, in returning the slips to the attendant, I noticed a peculiarity in Weltz's 'z' which I had thought I had seen in Rizzi's signature. I immediately compared the slips. There was the same oddly shaped 'z' in both. It was made like this" – and he handed us a slip of paper with this z* upon it.

"You see," he continued, "it is so unusual a way

of making the letter that it at once attracted my attention, notwithstanding the fact that Rizzi wrote with his left hand. Closer examination revealed other peculiarities, as in the r*'s, common to both hands. Well, to make a long story short, I satisfied myself that the same person wrote the whole twenty slips and was, moreover, ambidextrous. This I considered as a very promising discovery, so much so, indeed, that I gave up an engagement I had for the evening and decided to camp right there until the Library closed. Happily the books I had been consulting were still on the table. I picked out those borrowed under the names of Weltz and Rizzi, and began a most careful examination of them. I had been working about two hours when I discovered something that fairly took my breath away. I was not sure that I was right, but I knew that, if my microscope bore me out, I would be able to stake my life that the murderer of John Darrow had read that book. I was aware, however, that even then I should not be able to name the man who had put his mark upon the book, but I could take oath that the record was made by the same hand that committed the murder.

"I was too excited to do more till this had been settled, so I besought the official in charge to let me take all the books home with me, if only for a day, explaining to him the vital importance of my request. He readily consented and I hastened home with the whole lot. You may imagine with what interest I put the page I wished to examine under my microscope and laid beside it the piece of glass which, you will perhaps remember, I cut from a window of the room in which the murder was committed. I believe I have never yet explained to Miss Darrow why I preserved that bit of glass. There were two reasons for it. The house had been primed that day and there were two smutches of paint upon the glass and two almost identical smutches upon the sill. One was a sinuous line, as if the glass had been struck with a short bit of rope, – or possibly rubber tubing since no rope-like texture was visible, – which had previously been soiled with the paint from the sill. The other mark was that of a human thumb. I had seen at the World's Fair an exhibit of these thumbmarks collected by a Frenchman who has made an exhaustive study of the subject, and had learned there for the first time that no two thumbs in the world can make the same mark. I knew, therefore, that this slip of glass would at any time tell me whether or not a suspected man were guilty. I had not failed to get the thumb-marks of the men who painted the house on that day, as well as those of every other person known to be about the place. The marks upon the glass could not, by any possibility, have been made by any of them. The deduction was inevitable. They were made by the man who stood by the window when the murder was committed.

"You will be surprised when I tell you it was some moments before I could summon up courage to look through my microscope upon the page beneath it. You see, I had been seized by an unaccountable conviction that I had at last found a real clue to the murderer, and I dreaded lest the first glance should show this to have been an idle delusion. At length I looked. The thumb that had pressed the paper was the thumb that had pressed the glass!

There was not a doubt of it. My suspicions were confirmed. Everything now regarding this book was of immense importance. The page upon which the mark was found – well, I think you would open your eyes if I were to read it to you. I will defer this pleasure, however, till I see if my suspicions are correct. The thumb-mark is upon page 469 of 'Poisons, Their Effects and Detection,' by Alexander Wynter Blyth.

"No sooner had I made sure of my discovery than I set out for No. 5 Oak Street, the address given by Rizzi. There was no such person there, nor had there been anyone of that name in the house during the three years of the present tenant's occupancy. I went to 15 Staniford Place with the same result. A young woman about twenty-five years of age came to the door. She informed me that she had been born in the house and had always lived there. She had never known anyone by the name of Weltz. This was just what I had expected. The man for whom we are searching is shrewd almost beyond belief, and if we succeed in finding him it will not, we may be assured, be the result of any bungling on his part.

"I have now told you all I have learned, or rather all that is sufficiently definite to communicate – it is not much, yet it is a clue and may serve to give our hope a new lease of life. What do you think of it, Miss Darrow?"

"I think what you have learned," Gwen replied, "will be of the utmost importance. You have now something definite to guide you. I am most fortunate in having the services of such a detective, – indeed, I am at a loss to know how to thank you for all you have done, – for all you are doing, I – "

"My dear Miss Darrow," Maitland interrupted, "I need no thanks. Be assured I am selfish in all I do. It is a pleasure to me, therefore I do it. You see I deserve no credit. If I am able to free you from the danger of sacrificing yourself, I shall be more than repaid."

Gwen made no reply, but I, sitting as I did close beside her, saw the moisture gather between her drooping lids. Maitland took his leave almost immediately, having, he said, a long evening's work before him; while Gwen, Alice, and I discussed the news he had brought us, until far into the night. I did not see him the next day, which was Tuesday, and I believe not on Wednesday. It was Thursday afternoon, if I do not mistake, that he sent me a note asking me to call on him at his office. I went at once, thinking it might be something very important. I found him alone and waiting for me.

"I wanted," he began as soon as I was seated, "to talk this matter over with you. You see the great difficulty which besets me in this case is that nearly all our evidence, while it is of a nature to enable us to convict our man once we have him, is yet of almost no assistance to us in finding him. What do we know of him up to date; or at least of what do we feel reasonably assured? Let us see. John Darrow was poisoned in some mysterious way by a man who was stationed just outside the partly opened window. The weapon, or whatever was used as such, was taken away by the murderer. Nothing in the nature of a projectile could have been employed, since the wound was upon a part of the victim's throat known to have been turned away from the window and to have been completely shielded upon that side by the high and massive back of the chair in which the victim sat.

"He was fully eight feet from the casement, so that the assassin could not have reached in and struck him. There were no footprints by the window, as the assassin had strapped small boards upon his feet. It is most likely, therefore, that he has some peculiarity about his feet which he thought best to conceal. He is about five feet five inches tall, weighs about one hundred and thirty-five pounds, and steps three or four inches longer when the right foot is thrown forward than he does when the left foot leads. We have a cast of the assassin's hand showing unmistakable evidence of the habit of biting the nails, with the exception of that of the little finger, which nail, by the way, is abnormally long, and could only have been spared for some special reason. The murderer is most likely a foreigner. His handwriting would indicate this even if we did not know, from the books he read, how conversant he is with at least one foreign tongue. Again, he has some decided interest in the subject of cancers and, perhaps, some interest in legerdemain, if we may judge from his perusal of Robert Houdin's book.

"There are one or two other things I have learned, but this, so far as any present effect is concerned, is about all we know, and it doesn't seem to make the conduct of our search a very easy matter. We have clearly to deal with a man who is possessed not merely of low criminal cunning, but, I have reason to believe, with one who has education and culture, and, if anything can be judged from handwriting, rare strength of character as well. If we could only find some motive! No one but a maniac would do such a deed without a motive, yet we can't find one. A maniac! By Jove! I hadn't thought of that. What do you think of the idea? 'Though this be madness, yet there is method in't,' eh?"

I told him that the maniac theory did not appeal to me very strongly. "Madness, to be sure, is often exceedingly cunning," I said, "but it is hardly capable of such sustained masterfulness as our criminal has evinced."

"Look here, Doc," Maitland said, breaking out suddenly, "I've an idea. Might not this fellow's interest in cancers be due to his having one himself? Suppose you make a canvass of the specialists on cancer in Boston and vicinity, and see if any of them remember being consulted by a patient answering the description with which I will provide you. In addition to this I will insert an ad in the papers calling attention to a new method for the cure of cancer, and asking all interested to call at your office for further particulars. The plan does not promise much, still it may bring him. What do you say?"

I expressed my willingness to do all in my power to aid him, and he left me. The next morning's papers contained the advertisement and I had several calls in answer to it. These would have caused me much inconvenience had I not explained the whole ruse in confidence to a medical friend who made a specialty of the treatment of cancers, and persuaded him to come to my office during the hours specified in the advertisement. When a patient would call I would satisfy myself that it was neither the person we were searching for, nor anyone sent by him to make inquiries, and then turn him over to my colleague, Dr. Rhodes. It would never have occurred to me to interest myself in any patient who did not answer the description given me by Maitland, had he not especially cautioned me in this regard.

"We have," he said, "to deal with a man possessed of ability of no common order. We have already seen that he never runs a risk, however slight, which he can avoid. It is more than likely, therefore, if our advertisement meets his eye and interests him, he will inquire into it through some second party. Again, we are by no means certain that his interest in cancers is a purely personal one. Perhaps it is a wife, a sister, or some other relative who is afflicted. In this case we could hardly expect him to come himself. Let me caution you, therefore, to closely scrutinise all applicants and question them until you are satisfied they are in nowise connected with the man for whom we are searching."

I followed this advice most carefully and had no difficulty in convincing myself that none of my callers had any relation whatsoever with the murderer of John Darrow. This order of things was continued for several days with the same result. In the meantime Maitland was working upon a new clue he had discovered. He would tell me all about it, he said, when he had followed it to the end. This was on Tuesday. On Friday he came to the house and informed us that he had met a man who had known a M. Henri Cazot, a Frenchman whose description seemed to tally perfectly with nearly all we knew of Mr. Darrow's murderer.

"It came about in this way," Maitland began in response to Gwen's request that he should tell us all about it: "I determined to thoroughly search every book on the 'Weltz-Rizzi' list, to see if I might not get some additional clue. In the work by Robert Houdin entitled 'The Sharper Detected and Exposed' I found the statement that gamblers often neutralised a cut in a pack of cards by a rapid and dexterous sleight. This, the book went on to say, was accomplished in the following manner: When the cards are cut and left in two packets upon the table, the sharper picks up with his right hand the parcel of cards which was originally at the bottom of the pack. This is brought above the other packet, as in an honest cut, but, just before releasing the cards, the lower parcel is deftly tilted up by inserting the right little finger under it, and the upper packet quickly slid beneath it, leaving the cards in precisely the position they occupied before cutting; For this purpose, the book continued, the nail of the right little finger is worn very long, so as to facilitate its being thrust beneath a packet of cards. Here, I said to myself, is a possible explanation of one of the peculiarities of my plaster cast. The long nail on the left little finger may have served its function at the gaming table. If so, however, it would seem to indicate that our man is left-handed, while, as we have already seen, the writing upon the library slips would indicate that he is ambidextrous. We need not, therefore, I reasoned, be surprised if we find that both little fingers have long nails. I at once acted upon these thoughts and began a search of the gambling resorts of this city. In order not to excite suspicion I played a little in each place, watching my opportunity to engage the proprietor in conversation. In every case I followed the same formula. Did he remember the gentleman who used to come there? Foreigner, – spoke French, a little under medium height; had a sort of halt in his walk; bit his finger nails, etc., etc. I met with no encouragement in the down-town places, though the proprietor of one of the Hayward Place 'dives' had an idea such a man had been there, but only once or twice and he was not sure he could place him. I then went up to the South End and on Decatur Street found a man who promptly responded to my inquiries: 'Gad! that's Henri Cazot fast enough, in all but the height and gait. Dick there, he'll tell you all about him. He owes him a little debt of honour of about a hundred plunks. He gave him his note for it, and Dick carries it around with him, not because he thinks he'll ever get it, but he likes the writing. M. Henri Cazot! eh, Dick?' and he burst into a coarse laugh. I turned to Dick for further information. He had already produced a much-crumpled paper and was smoothing it out upon the table.

"'There's the article,' he said, bringing his hand down emphatically upon it. 'The cuss was hard up. Luck had gone agin him and he had lost every cent he had. Jem Macey was a-dealin' and Cazot didn't seem to grasp that fact, but kept bettin' heavy. You see, young feller, ye ain't over likely to win at cards when yer playin' agin the dealer. Cazot didn't know this and I wouldn't tell him, for he was rather fly with the cards himself when he wan't watched too close. Well, he struck me for a loan; said his little girl was hungry and he hadn't a cent to buy bread. Gad, but he looked wild though! I always thought he was more'n half loony. Well, as I had helped to fleece him I lent him a hundred and took this here note. That's the last I ever see of M. Henri Cazot, and he handed the paper to me. I glanced at the signature. It was the same hand that had written 'Weltz' and 'Rizzi' upon the library slips. There was that unmistakable z and the peculiar r which had just attracted my attention! It required considerable effort on my part to so restrain my feelings as not to appear especially interested in what I had learned. I think, however, I succeeded, as they freely answered my questions regarding Cazot and the daughter of whom he had spoken. They knew nothing further, they said, than what they had told me.

"'It was a year ago come next month that I lent him the money,' my informant continued. He pocketed it, hurried out, and that is the last I have ever seen or heard of him. Shouldn't wonder if he'd blown his brains out long ago. He used to have a mighty desperate look at times. He was one of them Monte Carlo fellers, I reckon.'

"That's all I have been able to learn thus far. It isn't very much, but it shows we are on the right track. By the way, Doc, I'm going to change that ad to-morrow, offering treatment by letter. Perhaps our man is too shy to apply in person. At all events we'll give the other method a trial."

CHAPTER III

When we least expect it the Ideal meets us in the street of the Commonplace and locks arms with us. Nevermore shall we choose our paths uninfluenced. A new leaven has entered our personality to dominate and direct it.

The new advertisement duly appeared and on the next day, which was Wednesday – I remember it because it was my hospital day – I received several written answers, and among them, one in which I felt confident I recognised the peculiar z*'s and r*'s of Weltz and Rizzi.

I took it at once to Maitland. He glanced at it a moment and then impulsively grasped my hand. "By Jove, Doc!" he exclaimed, "if this crafty fox doesn't scent the hound, we shall soon run him to earth. You see he has given no address and signs a new name. We are to write to Carl Cazenove, General Delivery, Boston. Good! we will do so at once, and I will then arrange with the postal authorities to notify me when they deliver the letter. Of course this will necessitate a continuous watch, perhaps for several days, of the general delivery window. It is hardly likely our crafty friend will himself call for the letter, so it will be imperative that someone be constantly on hand to shadow whomsoever he may send as a substitute. May I depend on your assistance in this matter?"

"I will stand by you till we see the thing through," I said, "though I have to live in the Post Office a month."

Well, I wrote and mailed the decoy letter and Maitland explained the situation to the postal authorities, who furnished us a comfortable place inside and near the general delivery window. They promised to notify us when anyone called for our letter. Our vigil was not a very long one. On Thursday afternoon the postal clerk signalled to us that Carl Cazenove's mail had been asked for, and, while he was consuming as much time as possible in finding our letter, Maitland and I quietly stepped out into the corridor. The sight that met our gaze was one for which we had not been at all prepared. There at the window stood a beautiful young girl just on the verge of womanhood. Her frank blue eyes met mine with the utmost candour as I passed by her so that she should be between Maitland and me, and thus unable to elude us, whichever way she turned upon leaving the window. We had previously planned how we should shadow our quarry, one on each side of the street in order not to attract attention, but these tactics seemed to be entirely unnecessary, for the young lady did not have the slightest suspicion that anyone could be in the least interested in her movements. She walked leisurely along, stopping now occasionally to gaze at the shop windows and never once turning to look back. She did not even conceal the letter, but held it in her hand with her porte-monnaie, and I could see that the address was uppermost. A strange sensation came over me as I dogged her steps. I felt as an assassin must feel who tracks his victim into some lonely spot where he may dare to strike him. It was useless for me to tell myself that I was on the side of justice and engaged in an honourable errand. A single glance at the girl's delicate face, as frank and open as the morning light, brought the hot blush of shame to my cheek. In following her I dimly felt that, in some way, I was seeking to associate her with evil, which seemed little less than sacrilege. I could do nothing, however, but keep on, so I followed her through Devonshire Street, to New Washington and thence down Hanover Street almost to the ferry. Here she turned into an alleyway and, waiting for Maitland to come up, we both saw her enter a house at its farther end.

George glanced hastily up at the house and then said, as he seized me impatiently by the arm: "It's a tenement house; come on, the chase is not up yet; we, too, must go in!"

So in we went. The young lady had disappeared, but as we entered we heard a door close on the floor above, and felt sure we knew where she had gone. We mounted the stairs as noiselessly as possible and listened in the hall. We could distinguish a woman's voice and occasionally that of a man, but we could not hear what passed between them. On our right there was a door partly ajar. Maitland pushed it open, and looked in. The room was empty and unfurnished, with the exception of a dilapidated stove which stood against the partition separating this room from the one the young lady had entered. Maitland beckoned to me and I followed him into the room. There was a key on the inside of the door which he noiselessly turned in the lock. He then began to investigate the premises. Three other rooms communicated with the one of which we had taken possession, forming, evidently, a suite which had been let for housekeeping. Everything was in ill-repair, as is the case with most of the cheap tenements in this locality. The previous tenant had not thought it necessary to clean the apartments when quitting them, – for altruism does not flourish at the North End, – but had been content to leave all the dirt for the next occupant.

When we had finished reconnoitering we returned to the room we first entered, which apparently was the kitchen. We could still hear the voices, but not distinctly. "Do you stay here, Doc," whispered Maitland, "while I get into some old clothes and hunt up the landlord of this place. I'm going to rent these rooms long enough to acquaint myself with my neighbours on the other side of the wall. I'll be back soon. Don't let any man leave that room without your knowing where he goes." With this he left me and I soon found a way to busy myself in his absence. In the wall above the stove, where the pipe passed through the partition into our neighbour's apartment, there was a chink large enough to permit me, when mounted upon the stove, to overlook the greater part of the adjacent room. I availed myself of this privilege, though not without those same twinges of conscience which I had felt some minutes before when following the young lady. The apartment was poorly furnished, and yet, despite this scantiness of appointment, there was unmistakable evidence of refinement. Everything visible in the room was scrupulously neat and the few pictures that adorned the walls, while they were inexpensive half-tones, were yet reproductions of masterpieces. In the centre of the room stood a small, deal table, on the opposite side of which sat the man who had answered my letter.

At one end of the table, poised upon the back of a chair, sat a small Capucin monkey of the Weeper or Sai species. He watched the man with that sober, judicial air which is by no means confined exclusively to supreme benches. I, too, observed the man carefully. He was tall and spare. He must have measured nearly six feet in height and could not, I think, have weighed over one hundred and fifty pounds. His face was pinched and careworn, but this effect was more than redeemed by a pair of full, black eyes having a depth and penetration I have never seen equalled, albeit there was, ever and anon, a suggestion of wildness which somewhat marred their deep, contemplative beauty. The brows and the carriage of the head at once bespoke the scholar. While thus I watched him, the young girl came from a corner of the room I could not overlook and laid my letter before him. She stood behind his chair as he opened it, smoothing his hair caressingly and, every now and then, kissing him gently. He paused with the open letter before him, reached up both arms, drew her down to him, kissed her passionately, sighed, and picked up the letter again. I took pains that no act, word, or look should escape me. This show of affection surprised me, and I remember the thought flashed through my mind, "What inconsistent beings we all are! Here is a man apparently capable of a causeless and cold-blooded assassination of a harmless old man. You would say such a murderer must be hopelessly selfish and brutal, amenable to none of the better sentiments of mankind, and yet it needs but a casual glance to see how his whole life is bound up in the young girl before him."

While this was passing through my mind the man had glanced through my letter and thrown it upon the table with an exclamation of disgust. "Bah! he has had the effrontery," he said petulantly, "to send me what he calls a new mode of treatment and it is in every essential that of Broadbent, well known for more than a quarter of a century. New indeed! I shall never find a doctor who has any scientific acumen. I may as well abandon the search now. Mon Dieu! and they call medicine a science! Bah!" and with a frown he dropped his head despondently upon his hand. The young girl passed her hand gently, soothingly, over his forehead and did not speak for nearly a minute.

"You are not feeling well to-night, father," she said at length. "M. Godin has been here during my absence."

"M. Godin!" I exclaimed half aloud, catching at the stovepipe lest I should fall from the stove. "So our rival is hot upon the scent, – probably even ahead of us. How on earth – " But I did not finish the exclamation. My seizure of the pipe upon my side of the partition had produced an audible vibration of that portion extending over the heads of my neighbours. The young girl's quick ear had detected the sound and she had ceased speaking and fastened her eyes suspiciously upon the aperture through which I was gazing. It seemed to me as if she must see me, yet I dared not move. After a little she seemed reassured and continued: "I knew he had been here. You are always this way after his visits. Why, of late, does he always come when I am away?" The question seemed innocent enough, yet the man to whom it was addressed turned crimson and then as pale as ashes. When he spoke the effort his self-control cost him was terribly apparent.

"We have private business, dear," he said, "private business." He hesitated a moment and again his eyes wore the wild look I had first noticed. "I am selling him something," he continued, "very dear to me – as dear as my heart's blood, and I expect to get enough for it to guard you from want."

"And you, father?" the young girl questioned fervently. I thought I noticed a tremor run through his frame, as drawing her face down to his, he said, kissing her, "Me? Never mind me, Puss; this cancer here will take care of me."

She made no reply, but turned away to hide the tears that sprang to her eyes. As she did so she raised her face toward me. I have never been considered particularly sympathetic, – that is, no more than the average, – but there was something in the expression of her face that went to my heart like a knife. I felt as if I were about to sob with her. I do not know what it was that so aroused my sympathies. We are, I fancy, more apt to feel for those whose beauty is like to the ideals we have learned to love, than we are to be moved by the suffering of those whose looks repel us, – and this may have had something to do with my condition, – for the young girl was radiantly beautiful, – yet it could hardly have been the real cause of it.

So rapt was I in the sympathetic contemplation of her that I did not see Maitland's entrance or realise I was observed till he plucked me by the coat and motioned me to get down. I did so and he told me he had rented the rooms, and laid before me the plan he meant to pursue.

As soon as he had ceased speaking I said to him: "George, you are undoubtedly on the right track. The man in there is the one we are looking for, fast enough, but I am afraid we are a bit too late."

"Too late!" he exclaimed in a tone that I feared might be overheard. "What the mischief do you mean?"

"I mean," I replied, "that M. Godin is already upon the scene."

In the next ten seconds Maitland turned all colours and I edged nearer to him, expecting him to fall, but he did not.

"M. Godin!" he ejaculated at length. "How in the name of all the gods at once – Doc, he's all they claim for him, and as fascinating as he is clever;" at which last remark a heavy cloud passed over Maitland's face. "Come," he continued listlessly, "you may as well tell me all you know about it."

I then confided to him what I had heard and ended by asking him what he proposed to do.

"Do?" he replied. "There is but one thing I can do, which makes the choice decidedly easy," and he set his jaws together with a determined expression, the meaning of which I knew full well.

"I shall camp right here," he said, " till I learn all I wish to know of our neighbours yonder. I have already provided myself with instruments which will enable me to note every movement they make, indeed to photograph them, if necessary, and to hear and record every word they utter. You look surprised, but it is easily done. I will place my lenses there at the chink through which you were gazing and bring the image down into my camera obscura by a prism arranged for total internal reflection. As for the hearing, that is easier yet. I will carefully work away the plaster on this side to-night till I get through to the paper covering their wall. This I will leave intact to use as a diaphragm. I have then only to fasten my carbon to it, and, behold, we have a microphone or telephone – whichever you choose to call it. All I have to look out for is that I get it high enough to avoid the danger of the paper being accidentally broken from the other side, and that I work quietly while removing the plaster. I shall, of course, cover it with a bit of black felt to prevent our light from showing, and to deaden any sounds from this side. This will enable us to hear all that goes on in the other room, but this may not be enough. We may need a phonographic record of what transpires.

"The device whereby I secure this at such a distance is an invention of my own which, for patent reasons – I might almost say 'patent patent reasons' – I will ask you to kindly keep to yourself. To the diaphragm there I fasten this bit of burnished silver. Upon this I concentrate a pencil of light which, when reflected, acts photographically upon a sensitised moving tape in this little box, and perfectly registers the minutest movement of the receiving diaphragm. How I develop, etch, and reproduce this record, and transform it into a record of the ordinary type, you will see in due time – and will kindly keep secret for the present. You had better go now and send me the things on this list, as soon as possible,' and he passed me a paper, continuing:

"We will not despair yet. Our clever rival may not be ready to prove his case so quickly as we. At all events, when he comes again I shall be in a condition to ascertain how far he has progressed. I have some things I must settle before I can ask for an arrest, and I am not at all sure that M. Godin is in any better condition in this regard than I am. By Jove! I'd give something to know how that wizard has gotten so far without so much as a single sign to indicate that he had even moved in the matter. I say, Doc, it beats me, blessed if it doesn't! Please say to Miss Darrow that I am at work upon a promising clue-promising for someone, anyway – and may not see her for some time yet."

I did as he requested, and, if I am any judge of feminine indications, my message did not yield Gwen unmixed pleasure; still, she said nothing to warrant such a supposition on my part. I visited Maitland every day to learn what he might wish me to bring him, and also to carry him his mail, for he had determined to remain constantly on the watch at his new quarters.

I have thus far, in the narration of these incidents been perfectly candid both as regards my friends and myself, and, therefore, that I may continue in like manner to the end, I shall suppress certain qualms which are urging me to silence, and confess myself guilty of some things of which you will, perhaps, think I may well be ashamed. Be that as it may, you shall have the whole truth, however it may affect your opinion of me. One reason why I went to Maitland's new quarters so often, and stayed there so long, was because I was always permitted to relieve him of his watch. With a telephone receiver strapped to my right ear, and my eyes fastened upon the screen of the camera obscura, I would sit by the hour prying into the affairs of the two people in the next room. I tried for a number of days to ease my conscience by telling myself that I was labouring in the cause of justice, and was not a common eavesdropper. This permitted me to retain a sort of quasi self-respect for a day or two till my honesty rallied itself, and forced me to realise and to admit that I was, to all intents and purposes, a common Paul Pry, performing a disreputable act for the gratification it gave me. I determined I would at least be honest with myself – and this was my verdict. You will, perhaps, fancy that when I arrived at this decision I at once mended my ways and resigned my seat of observation to Maitland's entirely professional care. This, doubtless, I should have done, if we fallible human beings governed our conduct by our knowledge of what is right and proper. Inasmuch, however, as desires and emotions are the determining factors of human conduct, I did nothing of the sort. I simply watched there day after day, with ever-increasing avidity, until at length I got to be impatient of the duties that took me away, and more than half inclined to neglect them.

I shall gain nothing by attempting to make you believe it was the man in the neighbouring room that interested me, so I shall not essay it. I confess, with a feeling of guilt because I am not more ashamed of it – that it was the young lady who attracted me. You will, I trust, assume I had enough interest in her father to palliate my conduct in a measure. Be generous in your judgment. How do you know you will not be in the same predicament? Think of it! A young woman beautiful beyond my feeble powers of description; her eyes of a heavenly blue; her luxuriant hair like a mass of spun gold; her complexion matched to the tint and transparency of the blush rose – and such a throat! From it came a voice as musical as the unguided waters when Winter rushes down the hills in search of Spring. Never you mind, that's the way I felt about it, and, if you had been in my place, you'd have been just as bad as I; come, now, you know you would. Suppose I was a bachelor, and almost old enough to be her father. Does that help matters any? Is the heart less hungry because it has been starved? Just look at your history. When nuns have relapsed from other-worldliness to this-worldliness how have they been? I'll tell you. They have been just a round baker's dozen times worse than they would have been if they had never undertaken to cheat Nature. Look at the thing fairly. I don't expect to dodge any blame that I deserve, yet I do want all the palliating circumstances duly noted. Many months have passed since then, and yet the thought of that sweet girl sends a thrill all over me. I wonder where she is now? I feel that we shall meet again some time, and perhaps you will see her yourself. If so, you will see that I couldn't be expected to withstand any such temptation.

On these visits Maitland and I talked but very little, and while I was spying nothing of interest occurred – i. e., nothing of interest to him – or, if it did, things of interest to me prevented my observing it. On several occasions he alluded vaguely to things he had learned which he said he should not divulge even to me until the proper time came.

Things went on in this way for about two weeks. I visited Maitland daily, and daily the little lady in the next room wove her spell around me. If, as I am inclined to believe, thinking a great deal of a person is much the same thing as thinking of a person a great deal, I must have adored her.

One night, about a fortnight after Maitland's change of abode, I found Alice in a terrible state of excitement upon my arrival home. She met me at the door, and said Gwen needed my attention at once. I did not stop to hear further particulars, but hastened to the sitting-room, where Gwen lay upon the lounge. She was in a stupor from which it seemed impossible to arouse her. In vain I tried to attract her attention. Her fixed, staring eyes looked through me as if I had been glass. I saw she had received a severe shock, and so, after giving her some medicine, I took Alice aside and asked her what had happened. She said that Gwen and she had been sitting sewing by the window all the afternoon, and talking about Maitland's recent discoveries. At about five o'clock the Evening Herald was brought in as usual. She, Alice, had picked it up to glance over the news, when, in the column headed "Latest," she had seen the heading: "The Darrow Mystery Solved!" This she had read aloud, without thinking of the shock the unexpected announcement might give Gwen, when the sudden pallor that had overspread the young woman's face had brought her to her senses, and she had paused. Her companion, however, had seized the paper when she had hesitated and, in a fever of excitement, had read in a half-audible voice:

John Darrow was murdered. – The assassin's inability to pay a gambling debt the motive for the crime. – Extraordinary work of a French detective! – The net –

But at this juncture the paper had dropped from Gwen's hands, and she had fallen upon the floor before Alice could reach her.

THE EPISODE OF THE TELLTALE THUMB

CHAPTER I

When Disaster is bigger than its victim its bolt o'erlaps the innocent.

It was some time after Gwen had fallen before Alice had succeeded in getting her upon the lounge, and then all her efforts to revive her had failed. She had remained in the same nerveless stupor as that in which I had found her. I asked Alice if she knew why this announcement had produced such an effect upon Gwen, and she returned my question with a look of amazement.

"Have you forgotten Gwen's promise to her father in this matter?" she replied. "Has she not already told you that she should keep that promise, whatever the sacrifice cost her? She is, therefore, entirely at the mercy of this M. Godin, and she is also obliged to advise him of this fact, if she would carry out her father's wishes. Is this nothing for a sensitive nature like hers? If she has any love for anyone else she must crush it out of her heart, for she is M. Godin's now. Surely, Ned, you are not so stupid as your question would indicate."

"We won't discuss that," I rejoined. "Let us go to Gwen and get her to bed."

This done, and the sufferer made easy for the night, I glanced at the article which had so upset her, and read its sensational "scare-head." In full it ran as follows:

THE DARROW MYSTERY SOLVED! JOHN DAR-
ROW WAS MURDERED!

The Assassin's Inability to Pay a Gambling Debt the
Motive for the Crime.

EXTRAORDINARY WORK OF A FRENCH DE-
TECTIVE!

The Net so Completely Woven About the Alleged
Assassin That it is Thought He Will Confess.

The Arrest Entirely Due to the Unassisted Efforts of
M. LOUIS GODIN!

I did not stop to read the article, but seized my
hat and hastened at once to Maitland.

A copy of the Herald lay upon his table, advis-
ing me that he was already acquainted with the
strange turn affairs had taken. He told me that he
had heard the newsboys in the street calling out "The
Darrow Mystery Solved!" and had at once rushed
out and bought a paper.

I informed him of Gwen's condition and he
wished to go to her at once, but I told him he must
wait until the morrow, as she had already retired,
and was, I had reason to hope, fast asleep. I reassured him with the information that a night's sleep
and the medicine I had given her would probably
put Gwen in full possession of her faculties. Having
thus satisfied his fears, I thought it fitting he should
satisfy mine. I asked him what had become of the
young woman in the next room. He did not reply,
but quietly led me into his camera obscura that I
might see for myself. She was sitting at the table in

the centre of the room, with her face buried in her hands. I watched her for a long time, and the only movement I could discern was that occasioned ever and anon by a convulsive catching of her breath. The pet monkey was nowhere to be seen.

"They took her father away early this morning," Maitland said, "and, after the first shock, she sank into this condition. She has not moved since. When I see the despair her father's arrest has occasioned I am almost tempted to rejoice that I had no hand in it, and yet – well, there's no great harm without some small good – no one will say now that John Darrow took his own life, eh? What do you think our friends, Osborne and Allen, will say now? They were so sure their theory was the only tenable one. Ah, well! we should ever hold ourselves in readiness for sur-prises."

"And for emergencies too," I continued; "and this strikes me as being very like one. That young woman needs attention, if I am any judge of appear-ances, and I'm going in there." "No use, Doc," Mait-land replied, "the door is locked, and she either can-not or will not open it. I knocked there for an hour, hoping to be able to comfort her. It's no use for you to try, she won't open the door." "Won't, eh! then I'll go through it!" I exclaimed, in a tone that so amazed Maitland that he seized me by the shoulders and gazed fixedly into my face. "It's all right, George," I said, answering his look. "I'm going in there, and I'm not going to be at all delicate about my entrance either."

He looked at me a little doubtfully, but I could

see that, on the whole, he was pleased with my decision. I went into the hall and knocked loudly on the door. There was no response. I kicked it till I must have been heard all over the house, but still there was no response. It was now clear I should not enter by invitation, so I went up four or five stairs of the flight opposite the door and from that position sprang against it. I am not, if you remember, a heavy man, but momentum is MV and I made up in the 'V' what I lacked in the 'M.' The door opened inwardly, and I tore it from its hinges and precipitated both myself and it into the centre of the apartment. As I look back upon this incident I regard it as the most precipitous thing I ever did in the way of a professional visit. If the young lady started at all, she did so before I had gathered myself together sufficiently to notice it. I spoke to her, but she gave no evidence of hearing me. I raised her head. Her eyes were wide open and stared full at me, yet in such a blank way that I knew she did not hear me. The contraction of the brows, the knotted appearance of the forehead, and the rigor of the face told me she was under an all-but-breaking tension. There were tear-stains from tears which long since had ceased to flow. The fire of fever had dried them up. I regarded her case as far more desperate than Gwen's and determined to lose no time in taking charge of it. It seemed to me so like sacrilege to touch her without an explanation that, though I knew she could not understand me, I said to her, as I took her in my arms. "You are ill, and I must take you away from here."

She was just blossoming into womanhood and her form had that exquisite roundness and grace which it is the particular function of fashion to anni-hilate. If I held her closely, I think all bachelors will agree that it was because this very roundness made her heavy; if I did not put her down immediately I reached Maitland's room, it is because, as a doctor of medicine, I have my own ideas as to how a couch should be fixed before a patient is laid upon it. Mait-land may say what he pleases, but I know how im-portant these things are in sickness, and you know, quick as he is in most things, George has moments when his head is so much in the clouds that he does-n't know what he is doing, and moves as if he were in a dream set to dirge music. He kept telling me to "put her on the couch! – put her on the couch!" To this day, he fondly believes that when I finally did release her, it was as the result of his advice, rather than because he had at last made a suitable bed for her.

I sent Maitland for some medicine, which I knew would relax the tension she was under and make it possible for her to sleep. When I had admin-istered this, Maitland and I talked the matter over and we decided to take her at once to my house, where, with Gwen, she could share the watchful care of my sister Alice. This we did, though I was not without some misgivings as to Gwen's attitude in the matter when she should recover sufficiently to know of it. I expressed my doubts to Maitland and he re-plied: "Give yourself no uneasiness on that score; Miss Darrow is too womanly to visit the sins of a guilty father upon an unoffending daughter, and, besides, this man, – it seems that his real name is Latour, not Cazenove, – has a right to be judged innocent until his guilt is proved."

I found this to be sage counsel, for, when Gwen was able to understand what I had done, she exhibited no antipathy toward the new member of our household, but, on the contrary, became exceedingly interested in her. I was especially glad of this, not only on account of Miss Latour, the suspect's daughter, but also because the one thing Gwen needed above all others was something to challenge her interest. She had again relapsed into the old, state of passive endurance, wherein nothing seemed to reach her consciousness. Her actions appeared to flow more from her nerve-centres than from her mind. She moved like an automaton. There is scarcely any condition of which I am more fearful than this. The patient becomes wax in one's hands. She will do anything without a murmur, or as willingly refrain from anything. She simply is indifferent to life and all that therein is. Is it any wonder, then, that I rejoiced to see Gwen interest herself in poor Jeannette? It was a long time, however, before Jeannette repaid this interest with anything more than a dreamy, far-off gaze, that refused to focus itself upon anything. As time wore on, however, I noticed with relief that there was a faint expression of wonder in her look, and, as this daily grew stronger, I knew she was beginning to realise her novel surroundings and to ask herself if she were still dreaming. Yet she did not speak; she seemed to fear the sound of her own voice and to determine to solve, unaided, the mystery confronting her. I requested that no one question her or make any attempt to induce her to break silence, for I knew the time would come when she would do so of her own free will. As it happened, her first words were spoken to me, and, as my writing this recalls the event, a thrill of pleasurable pain passes through me. You may think this foolish, the more so, indeed, when you learn that nothing was said to warrant such a feeling, but I must urge upon you not to let your satisfied heart set itself up as judge in bachelor regions.

I had been mixing some medicine for her and was holding the cup to her lips that she might drink the draught. She laid her hand upon my wrist and gently put the cup aside, saying, as she gazed thoughtfully at me: "Did you not bring me here?" "Yes," I replied. She reached for the cup, and drinking its contents, sank back upon the pillows with a half-satisfied look upon her face, as if my reply had cleared up one mystery, but left many more to be solved.

From this day Jeannette steadily improved, and within two weeks she and Gwen had come to a very good understanding. It was plainly evident that Alice, too, came in for a very good share of the little French girl's love. They did not exchange confidences to any great degree, for, as Maitland used to say, Alice was one of those rare, sweet women who say but little, but seem to act upon all around them by a sort of catalysis, sweetening the atmosphere by their very presence.

CHAPTER II

Belief, though it be as ample as the ocean, does not always similarly swell in crystallising. It has, however, its point of maximum density, but this, not infrequently, is also ifs point of minimum knowledge.

During all these days Gwen was gaining rapidly. Maitland came to visit us almost every night, and he told Gwen that he did not feel altogether certain that, in arresting M. Latour, the law had secured her father's real assassin. It would be necessary to account for, he told her, some very singular errors in his early calculations if M. Latour was the man.

"When first I took up my abode under the same roof with him," he said, "I had no doubt that we had at last run down our man. Now, although another detective has come to the same conclusion, I myself have many misgivings, and you may be assured, Miss Darrow, that I shall lose no time in getting these doubts answered one way or the other. At present you may say to your friend Jeannette that I am straining every nerve in her father's behalf."

Why all this should so please Gwen I was at a loss to comprehend, but I could not fail to see that it did please her greatly. She had been the most anxious of us all to see her father's murderer brought to justice, and now, when through the efforts of M. Godin, a man stood all but convicted of the crime, she was pleased to hear Maitland, whose efforts to track Latour she had applauded in no equivocal way, say that he should spare no pains to give the suspect every possible chance to prove his innocence. There was certainly a reason, whatever it might have been, for Gwen's attitude in this matter, for that young woman was exceptionally rational in all things. Nothing of especial moment occurred between this time and the beginning of the trial. Maitland, for the most part, kept his own counsel and gave us little information other than a hint that he still thought there was a chance of clearing M. Latour.

With this end in view he had become an associate attorney with Jenkins in order the better to conduct M. Latour's case along the lines which seemed to him the most promising. I asked him on one occasion what led him to entertain a hope that Latour could be cleared and he replied: "A good many things." "Well, then," I rejoined, "what are some of them?" He hesitated a moment and then replied laughingly: "You see I hate to acknowledge the falsity of my theories. I said shortly after the murder was committed that I thought the assassin was short and probably did not weigh over one hundred and thirty-five pounds; that he most likely had some especial reason for concealing his footprints, and that he had a peculiarity in his gait. I felt tolerably sure then of all this, but now it turns out that M. Latour is six feet tall in his stockings, and thin; and that, emaciated as he is, he tips the scales at one hundred and fifty pounds by reason of his large frame. His feet are as commonplace as – as yours, Doc, and his gait as regular as – mine. Is it to be expected that I am going to give up all my pet illusions without a struggle?"

When the hour for the trial arrived Gwen insisted on accompanying us to the court-room. She had a great deal of confidence in George and felt sure that, as he expressed a strong doubt of the prisoner's guilt, he would triumph in proving him innocent. She determined, therefore, to be present at the trial, even before her attendance should be required as a witness.

M. Latour, when he was led into the prisoner's box, seemed to have aged greatly during his incarceration. It was with a marked effort that he arose and straightened himself up as the indictment was read to him. When the words: "Are you guilty or not guilty?" were addressed to him every eye was turned upon him and every ear listened to catch the first sound of his voice, but no sound came. The question was repeated more loudly, "Are you guilty or not guilty?" Like one suddenly awakened from a reverie M. Latour started, turned toward his questioner, and in a full, firm voice replied: "Guilty!" I was so dumfounded that I could offer Gwen no word of comfort to alleviate this sudden shock. Maitland and Godin seemed about the only ones in the court-room who were not taken off their feet, so to speak, by this unexpected plea, and George was at Gwen's side in a moment and whispered something to her which I could not hear, but which I could see had a very beneficial effect upon her. We had all expected a long, complicated trial, and here the whole matter was reduced to a mere formality by M. Latour's simple confession, "Guilty!" Is it any wonder, therefore, that we were taken aback?

While we were recovering from our surprise at this sudden turn of affairs, Maitland was engaged in private conversation with the Judge, with whom, he afterward told me, he had become well acquainted both in his own cases and in those of other lawyers requiring his services as an expert chemist. He never told me what passed between them, nor the substance of any of the brief interviews which followed with the prosecuting attorney, his associate counsel, and other legal functionaries. All I know is that when the case was resumed M. Latour's senior counsel, Jenkins, kept carefully in the background, leaving the practical conduct of the case in Maitland's hands.

If a hazelnut had the shell of a cocoanut, its meat would, in my opinion, sustain about the same relation to its bulk as the gist of the usual legal proceeding sustains to the mass of verbiage in which it is enshrouded. For this reason you will not expect me to give a detailed account of this trial. I couldn't if I would, and I wouldn't if I could. My knowledge of legal procedure is far from profound, albeit I once began the study of law. My memories of Blackstone are such as need prejudice no ambitious aspirant for legal honours. I have a recollection that somewhere Blackstone says something about eavesdropping, – I mean in its literal sense – something about the drippings from A's roof falling on B's estate; but for the life of me I couldn't tell what he says. More distinctly do I remember this learned lawgiver stated that there could be no doubt of the evidence of witchcraft, because the Bible was full of it, and that witches should be punished with death. This made an impression upon me, because it was an instance, rare to me then, but common enough now, of how minds, otherwise exceptionally able, may have a spot so encankered with creed, bigotry, and superstition as to render their judgments respecting certain classes of phenomena erroneous and illogical, puerile and ridiculous.

But to return to those points of the trial which I can remember, and which I think of sufficient interest to put before you. These refer chiefly to Maitland's examination of M. Latour, and of the government's chief witness, M. Godin. Such portions of their testimony as I shall put before you I shall quote exactly as it was given and reported by Maitland's friend, Simonds.

When Maitland began for the defence he said:

"At about half-past seven on the night of the 22d of April, John Darrow met his death at his home in Dorchester. He died in the presence of his daughter, Messrs. Willard, Browne, Herne, and myself. His death was caused by injecting a virulent poison into his system through a slight incision in his neck. That wound the prisoner before you confesses he himself inflicted. I would like to know a little more definitely how he succeeded in doing it without detection, in the presence, not only of his victim, but of five other persons sitting close about him. M. Latour will please take the stand."

As M. Latour stepped into the witness-box, a wave of suppressed excitement ran all over the court-room. Every nerve was strained to its tensest pitch, every ear eager for the slightest syllable he might utter. What could be done for a man who had confessed, and what would be the solution of the crime which had so long defied the authorities? The explanation was now to be made and it is no wonder that the excitement was intense.

I omit all uninteresting formalities.

Q. Have you ever seen me before to-day?

A. Not to my knowledge.

Q. Have you any reason to believe I have ever seen you before to-day?

A. None whatever – er – that is – unless on the night of the murder.

Q. Were you acquainted with John Darrow?

A. Yes.

Q. How long have you known him?

A. About six months – perhaps seven.

Q. What were your relations?

A. I don't understand. – We had gambled together.

Q. Where?

A. In this city – Decatur Street.

Q. What motive led you to kill him?

A. He cheated me at cards, and I swore to be even with him.

Q. Had you any other reason?

A. I owed him twelve hundred and thirty-five dollars which I borrowed of him hoping my luck would change. He won it all back from me by false play, and when I could not meet it he pressed me over hard.

Q. You say this occurred on Decatur Street. What was the date?

A. I do not remember.

Q. What month was it?

A. It was in March. Early in March.

Q. You are sure it was in March?

A. Yes.

Q. Should you say it was between the 1st and 15th of March?

A. Yes. I am positive it was before the 15th of March.

Q. Have you long known that M. Godin was at work upon this case?

A. No.

Q. When did you first become aware of it?

A. Not until my arrest.

Q. When did you first see M. Godin?

A. When I was arrested.

Q. Did he ever call at your rooms?

A. Never – not to my knowledge – I never saw him till the day of my arrest.

Q. With what weapon did you kill Mr. Darrow?

A. I made use of a specially constructed hypodermic syringe.

Half-smothered exclamations of surprise were

heard from every part of the room. Even the Judge gave a start at this astounding bit of testimony. Every person present knew perfectly well that no human being could have entered or left the Darrow parlour without certain discovery, yet here was a man, apparently in his right mind, who soberly asserted that he had used a hypodermic syringe. Maitland and Godin alone seemed cool and collected. Throughout all Latour's testimony, M. Godin watched the witness with a burning concentration. It seemed as if the great detective meant to bore through Latour's gaze down to the most secret depths of his soul. Not for an instant did he take his eyes from Latour. I said to myself at the time that this power of concentration explained, in a great measure, this detective's remarkable success. Nothing was permitted to escape him, and little movements which another man would doubtless never notice, had, for M. Godin, I felt sure, a world of suggestive significance.

Maitland's calm demeanour, so resourceful in its serenity, caused all eyes to turn at length to him as if for explanation. He continued with slow deliberation.

Q. In what particulars was this hypodermic syringe of special construction?

M. Latour seemed nervous and ill at ease. He shifted from side to side as if M. Godin's glance had pierced him like a rapier, and he were trying vainly to wriggle off of it. He seemed unable to disengage himself and at length replied in a wearied and spiritless tone:

A. In two particulars only. In the first place, it was very small, having a capacity of but five or six drops, and, in the second place, it was provided with an internal spring which, when released, worked the plunger and ejected the contents with extreme rapidity.

Q. What operated this spring?

A. Around the needle-like point of the syringe, less than a quarter of an inch from its end, was a tiny, annular bit of metal. This little metallic collar was forced upward by the pressure of the flesh as the sharp point entered it, and this movement released the spring and instantly and forcibly ejected the contents of the cylinder.

Q. Did you use a poison in this syringe?

A. Yes, sir.

Q. What did you use?

M. LATOUR hesitated and shifted helplessly about as if he dreaded to go farther into these particulars, and fondly hoped someone might come to his rescue. His gaze seemed to shift about the room without in the least being able to disentangle itself from that of M. Godin. He remained silent and the question was repeated.

Q. What did you use?

Again the witness hesitated while everyone, save only Maitland and Godin, leaned eagerly forward to catch his reply. At length it came in a voice scarcely above a whisper.

A. Anhydrous hydrocyanic acid.

A long-drawn "Hum!" escaped from Maitland, while M. Godin gave not the slightest indication of surprise. It was quite evident to us all that the astute Frenchman had acquired complete control of the case before he had arrested the assassin. At this juncture the Court said, addressing Maitland:

"This substance is extremely poisonous, I take it."

"Your Honour," Maitland replied, "it is the most fatal of all poisons known to chemists. It is also called cyanhydric, and, more commonly, prussic acid. An insignificant amount, when inhaled or brought into contact with the skin, causes immediate death. If a drop be placed upon the end of a glass rod and brought toward the nose of a live rabbit he will be dead before it reaches him."

A profound silence – the death-like quiet which accompanies an almost breaking tension – reigned in the court-room as Maitland turned again to Latour.

Q. I understand you to say you used anhydrous hydrocyanic or cyanhydric acid.

A. Yes, sir.

Q. Do you sufficiently understand chemistry to use these terms with accuracy? Might you not have used potassium cyanide or prussiate of potash?

A. I am a tolerably good chemist, and have spoken understandingly. Potassium cyanide, KCN, is a white, crystalline compound, and could hardly be used in a hypodermic syringe save in solution, in which condition it would not have been sufficiently poisonous to have served my purpose.

At this reply many of the audience exchanged approving glances. They believed M. Latour had shown himself quite a match for Maitland in not falling easily into what they regarded as a neat little trap which had been set to prove his lack of chemical knowledge. They attributed Maitland's failure to further interrogate Latour upon his understanding of chemistry as evidence that he had met an equal. To be sure, they were not quite clear in their own minds why Latour's counsel should be at such pains to carefully examine a man who had already confessed, but they believed they knew when a lawyer had met his match, and felt sure that this was one such instance. Clinton Browne, who sat in one of the front seats, seemed to find a deal more to amuse him in this incident than was apparent to me. Some men have such a wonderful sense of humour!

Maitland continued:

Q. When Mr. Darrow was murdered he sat in the centre of his parlour, surrounded by his daughter and invited guests. Will you tell the Court how you entered and left this room without detection?

Again the witness hesitated and looked irresolutely, almost tremblingly, about him, but seemed finally to steady himself, as it were, upon Godin's glance. It's a strange thing how the directness and intense earnestness of a strong man will pull the vacillation of a weak one into line with it, even as great ships draw lesser ones into their wakes. The excited audience hung breathlessly upon Latour's utterance. At last they were to know how this miracle of crime had been performed. Every auditor leaned forward in his seat, and those who were a trifle dull of hearing placed their hands to their ears, fearful lest some syllable of the riddle's solution should escape them. M. Latour remained dumb. The Judge regarded him sternly and said:

"Answer the question. How did you enter the Darrow parlour?"

A. I – I did – I did not enter it.

Again a half-suppressed exclamation of surprise traversed the room.

Q. If you did not enter the room how did you plunge the hypodermic syringe into your victim's neck?

It seemed for a moment as if the witness would utterly collapse, but he pulled himself together, as with a mighty effort, and fairly took our breath away with his astounding answer:

A. I – I did not strike Mr. Darrow with the syringe.

The audience literally gasped in open-mouthed amazement, while the Court turned fiercely upon Latour and said:

"What do you mean by first telling us you killed Mr. Darrow by injecting poison into his circulation from a specially prepared hypodermic syringe, and then telling us that you did not strike him with this syringe. What do you mean, sir? Answer me!"

A sudden change came over M. Latour. All his

timidity seemed to vanish in a moment, as he drew himself up to his full height and faced the Judge. It seemed to me as if till now he had cherished a hope that he might not be forced to give the details of his awful crime, but that he had at last concluded he would be obliged to disclose all the particulars, and had decided to manfully face the issue.

Every eye was fixed upon him, and every ear strained to its utmost as he turned slowly toward the Judge and said with a calm dignity which surprised us all:

A. Your Honour is in error. I said that I made use of a specially constructed hypodermic syringe. I have not said that I struck Mr. Darrow with it. There is, therefore, nothing contradictory in my statements.

Again the prisoner had scored, and again the audience exchanged approving glances which plainly said: "He's clever enough for them all!"

Then the Court continued the examination.

Q. Were you upon the Darrow estate when Mr. Darrow met his death?

A. Yes, your Honour.

Q. Where?

A. Just outside the eastern parlour-window, your Honour.

Q. Did you strike the blow which caused Mr. Darrow's death?

A. No, your Honour.

Q. What! Have you not said you are responsible for his murder?

A. Yes, your Honour.

Q. Ah, I see! You had some other person for an accomplice?

A. No, your Honour.

Q. Look here, sir! Do you propose to tell us anything of your own accord, or must we drag it out of you piecemeal?

A. No power can make me speak if I do not elect to, and I only elect to answer questions. Commission for contempt will hardly discipline a man in my position, and may lead me to hold my peace entirely.

The Court turned away with an expression of disgust and engaged Jenkins and Maitland in a whispered conversation. The prisoner had again scored. There is enough of the bully in many judges to cause the public to secretly rejoice when they are worsted. It was plain to be seen that the audience was pleased with Latour's defiance.

Maitland now resumed the examination with his accustomed ease. One would have thought he was addressing a church sociable, – if he judged by his manner.

Q. You have testified to being responsible for the death of John Darrow. The instrument with which he was killed was directly or indirectly your handiwork, yet you did not strike the blow, and you have said you had no other person for an accomplice. Am I substantially correct in all this?

A. You are quite correct.

Q. Very good. Did John Darrow's death result from a poisoned wound made by the instrument you have described?

A. It did.

This reply seemed to nonplus us all with the exception of Maitland and Godin. These two seemed proof against all surprises. The rest of us looked helplessly each at his neighbour as if to say, "What next?" and we all felt, – at least I did and the others certainly looked it, – as if the solution of the enigma were farther away than ever.

Maitland proceeded in the same methodical strain.

Q. A blow was given, yet neither you nor any person acting as your accomplice gave it. Did Mr. Darrow himself give the blow?

A. No, sir.

Q. I thought not. Did any person give it?

A. No, sir.

The audience drew a deep inspiration, as if with one accord! They had ceased to reason. Again and again had we been brought, as we all felt sure, within a single syllable of the truth, only to find ourselves at the next word more mystified than ever. It would hardly have surprised us more if the prisoner had informed us that Mr. Darrow still lived. The excitement was so intense that thought was impossible, so we could only listen with bated breath for someone else to solve the thing for our beleaguered and discouraged minds. After a word with his colleague, Maitland resumed.

Q. A blow was given, yet no person gave it. Was it given by anything which is alive?

A. It was not.

You could have heard a pin drop, so silent was the room during the pause which preceded Maitland's next question.

Q. Did you arrange some inanimate object or objects outside the eastern window, or elsewhere, on the Darrow estate so that it or they might wound Mr. Darrow?

A. No, – no inanimate object other than the hypodermic syringe already referred to.

Q. To my question: "A blow was given, yet no person gave it. Was it given by anything which is alive?" you have answered: "It was not." Let me now ask: Was it given by anything which was at that time alive?

A. It was.

There was a stir all over the court-room. Here at last was a suggestive admission. The examination was approaching a crisis!

Q. And you have said it was not a person. Was it not an animal?

A. It was.

"An animal!" we all ejaculated with the unanimity of a Greek chorus. So audible were the exclamations of incredulity which arose from the spellbound audience that the crier's gavel had to be brought into requisition before Maitland could proceed.

Q. Did you train a little Capucin monkey to strike this blow?

A. I did.

A great sigh, the result of suddenly relieved tension, liberally interlarded with unconscious exclamations, swept over the court-room and would not be gavelled into silence until it had duly spent itself.

Even the Judge so far forgot his dignity as to give vent to a half-stifled exclamation.

Maitland proceeded:

Q. In order that this monkey might not attack the wrong man after you had armed him, you taught him to obey certain signals given by little twitches upon the cord by which you held him. A certain signal was to creep stealthily forward, another to strike, and still another to crawl quickly back with the weapon. When circumstances seemed most favourable to the success of your designs, – that is, when Miss Darrow's voice and the piano prevented any slight sound from attracting attention, – you gently dropped the monkey in at the window and signalled him what to do. When Mr. Darrow sprang to his feet you recalled the monkey and hastened away. Is not this a fairly correct description of what occurred?

A. It is true to the letter.

Q. And subsequently you killed the monkey lest he should betray you by exhibiting his little tricks, at an inopportune moment in a way to compromise you. Is it not so?

A. It is. I killed him, though he was my daughter's pet.

We were stricken aghast at Maitland's sudden grasp of the case. Even Godin was surprised. What could it all mean? Had Maitland known the facts all along? Had he simply been playing with the witness for reasons which we could not divine? M. Godin's face was a study. He ceased boring holes in Latour with his eyes and turned those wonderful orbs full upon Maitland, in whom they seemed to sink to the depths of his very soul. Clearly M. Godin was surprised at this exhibition of Maitland's power.

Browne, who throughout the trial had glared at Maitland with an unfriendliness which must have been apparent to everyone, now lowered blacker than ever, it seemed to me. I wondered what could have occurred to still further displease him, and finally concluded it must either be some transient thought which had come uncalled into his mind, or else a feeling of envy at his rival's prominence in the case, and the deservedly good reputation he was making. His general ill-feeling I, of course, charged to jealousy, for I could not but note his uncontrollable admiration for Gwen. I fully believed he would have given his own life – or anyone else's for that matter – to possess her, and I decided to speak a word of warning to George. After a short, whispered consultation with Jenkins and the prosecuting attorney, Maitland turned to the prisoner and said:

"That will do. M. Latour may leave the stand."

It seemed to the spectators that the affair was now entirely cleared up, and they accordingly settled themselves comfortably for the formal denouement. They were, therefore, much taken aback when Maitland continued, addressing the jury:

"The evidence against the prisoner would indeed seem overwhelming, even had we not his confession. Apart from this confession we have no incriminating evidence save such as has been furnished by the government's chief witness, M. Godin. As it is through this gentleman's efforts that Latour was brought within reach of justice, it is but natural that much should be clear to him which may be puzzling to those who have not made so close a study of the case. I think he will enlighten us upon a few points. M. Godin will please take the stand."

At this there was much whispering in the courtroom.. Maitland's course seemed decidedly anomalous. Everyone wondered why he should be at such pains to prove that which had been already admitted and which, moreover, since he was representing Latour, it would seem he would most naturally wish to disprove. M. Godin, however, took the stand and Maitland proceeded to examine him in a way which only added amazement to wonder.

Q. How long have you been at work on this case?

A. Ever since the murder.

Q. When did you first visit M. Latour's rooms?

A. Do you mean to enter them?

Q. Yes.

A. I did not enter his rooms until the day he was arrested. I went to other rooms of the same tenement-house on previous occasions.

Q. Have you reason to believe M. Latour ever saw you prior to the day of his arrest?

A. No. I am sure he did not. I was especially careful to keep out of his way.

Q. You are certain that on the several occasions when you say you entered his rooms you were not observed by him while there?

A. I did not say I entered his rooms on several occasions.

Q. What did you say?

A. I said I never was in his rooms but once, and that was upon the day of his arrest.

Q. I understand. Were you not assisted in your search for Mr. Darrow's murderer by certain library books which you discovered M. Latour had been reading?

A. I – I don't quite understand.

Q. M. Latour obtained some books from the Public Library for hall use, giving his name as – as –

A. Weltz. Yes, they did assist me. There were some also taken under the name of Rizzi.

Q. Exactly. Those are the names, I think. How was your attention called to these books?

A. I met Latour at the library by accident, and he at once struck me as a man anxious to avoid observation. This made it my business to watch him. I saw that he signed his name as "Weltz" on the slips. The next day I saw him there again, and this time he signed the slips "Rizzi." This was long before the murder, and I was not at work upon any case into which I could fit this "Weltz" or "Rizzi." I was convinced in my own mind, however, that he was guilty of some crime, and so put him down in my memory for future reference. During my work upon this present case this incident recurred to me, and I followed up the suggestion as one which might possibly throw some light upon the subject.

Q. Did you peruse the books M. Latour borrowed under the names of Weltz and Rizzi?

A. I did not.

Q. Did you not look at any of them?

A. No. It did not occur to me to examine their names.

Q. You probably noticed that there were several of them. Among the pile was one by Alexander Wynter Blyth entitled, "Poisons, Their Effects and Detection." Did you notice that?

A. No. I did not notice any of them.

Q. But after you became suspicious of M. Latour, did you not then look up the slips, find this work, and read it?

A. No. I have never seen the book in my life and did not even know such a work existed.

Q. Oh! Then the perusal of the books had no part in the tracking of M. Latour.

A. None whatever.

Q. Do you ever play cards?

A. Yes, sometimes, to pass the time.

Q. Do you play for money?

A. Sometimes for a small stake – just enough to make it interesting.

Q. Are you familiar with the house in which Mr. Darrow was murdered?

A. I have only such knowledge of it as I acquired at the examination immediately after the murder. You will remember I entered but the one room.

Q. And the grounds about the house? Surely you examined them?

A. On the contrary, I did not.

Q. Did you not even examine the eastern side of the house?

A. I did not. I have never been within the gate save on the night in question, and then only to traverse the front walk to and from the house in company with Messieurs Osborne and Allen. I was convinced that the solution of the problem was to be found within the room in which the murder was committed, and that my notes taken the night of the tragedy contained all the data I could hope to get.

Q. Was not this rather a singular assumption?

A. For many doubtless it would be; but I have my own methods, and I think I may say they have been measurably successful in most cases. [This last was said with a good-natured smile and a modest dignity that completely won the audience.]

At this point Maitland dismissed M. Godin and the court adjourned for the day. That night M. Godin made his first call upon Gwen. Their interview was private, and Gwen had nothing to say about it further than that her caller had not hesitated to inform her that he was aware a reward had been offered and that he considered he had earned it. Maitland questioned her as to what he had claimed as his due, but Gwen, with her face alternately flushed and ashen, begged to be permitted to keep silence.

This attitude was, of course, not without its significance to Maitland, and it was easy to see that M. Godin's visit had much displeased him. But he was not the only one who was displeased that night. I regret that my promise of utter candour compels me to bear witness to my own foolishness; for when Maitland found it necessary to take Jeannette into the back parlour and to remain there alone with her in earnest conversation one hour and twelve minutes – I happened to notice the exact time – it seemed to me he was getting unpleasantly confidential, and it nettled me. You may fancy that I was jealous, but it was, most likely, only pique, or, at the worst, envy. I was provoked at the nonchalant ease with which this fellow did offhand a thing I had been trying to work myself up to for several days, and had finally abandoned from sheer lack of courage. Why couldn't I carelessly say to her, "Miss Jeannette, a word with you if you please," and then take her into the parlour and talk a "whole history." Oh, it was envy, that's what it was! And then the change in Jeannette! If he had not been making love to her – well, I have often wondered since if it were all envy, after all.

The next morning M. Latour's trial was resumed, and Maitland again put M. Godin upon the stand. The object of this did not appear at the time, though I think the Judge fully understood it. Maitland's first act was to show the Judge and Jury a glass negative and a letter, which he asked them to examine carefully as he held the articles before them. He then passed the negative to M. Godin, saying:

"Please take this by the lower corner, between your thumb and forefinger, so that you may be sure not to touch the sight of the picture; hold it to the light, and tell me if you recognise the face." M. Godin did as directed and replied without hesitancy: "It is a picture of M. Latour." "Good," rejoined Maitland, taking back the negative and passing him the letter; "now tell me if you recognise that signature." M. Godin looked sharply at the letter, holding it open between the thumb and forefinger of each hand, and read the signature, "'Carl Cazenove.' I should say that was M. Latour's hand."

"Good again," replied Maitland, reaching for the paper and appearing somewhat disconcerted as he glanced at it. "You have smutched the signature; –

however, it doesn't matter," and he exhibited the paper to the Judge and Jury. "The negative must have been oily – yes, that's where it came from," and he quietly examined it with a magnifying glass, to the wonderment of us all. "That is all, M. Godin; thank you."

As the celebrated detective left the stand we were all doing our best to fathom what possible bearing all this could have upon Latour's confession. M. Godin for once seemed equally at a loss to comprehend the trend of affairs, if I may judge by the deep furrows which gathered between his eyes.

Maitland then proceeded to address the Court and to sum up his case, the gist of which I shall give you as nearly as possible in his own words, omitting only such portions as were purely formal, uninteresting, or unnecessarily verbose.

"Your Honour and Gentlemen of the Jury: John Darrow was murdered and the prisoner, M. Gustave Latour, has confessed that he did the deed. When a man denies the commission of a crime we do not feel bound to consider his testimony of any particular value; but when, on the other hand, a prisoner accused of so heinous a crime as murder responds to the indictment, 'I am guilty,' we instinctively feel impelled to believe his testimony. Why is this? Why do we doubt his word when he asserts his innocence and accept it when he acknowledges his guilt? I will tell you. It is all a question of motive. Could we see as cogent a motive for asseverating his guilt as we find for his insisting upon his innocence, we should lend as much credence to the one as to the other. I propose to show that M. Latour has what seems to him the strongest of motives for confessing to the murder of John Darrow. If I am able to do this to your satisfaction, I shall practically have thrown M. Latour's entire testimony out of court, and nothing of importance will then remain but the evidence of the government's witness, M. Godin."

A great wave of excitement swept over the room at these remarks. "What!" each said to himself, "is it possible that this lawyer will try to prove that Latour, despite his circumstantial confession, did not commit the murder after all?" We did not dare let such a thought take hold of us, yet could not see what else could explain Maitland's remarks. Is it any wonder, therefore, that we all waited breathlessly for him to continue? M. Godin's face was dark and lowering. It was evident he did not propose to have his skill as a detective, – and with it the Darrow reward, – set aside without a struggle – at least so it seemed to me. The room was as quiet as the grave when Maitland continued.

"I shall show you that M. Godin's testimony is utterly unreliable, and, moreover, that it is intentionally so."

This was a direct accusation, and at it M. Godin's face became of ashen pallor. I felt that he was striving to control his anger and saw the effort that it cost him as he fastened Maitland with a stiletto-like look that was anything but reassuring. George did not appear to notice it and continued easily:

"I shall prove to you beyond a doubt that, in the

actual murder of John Darrow, only one person was concerned, – by which I mean, that only one person was outside the east window when he met his death. I shall also show that M. Latour was not, and could not by any possibility have been, that person. [At this juncture Browne arose and walked toward the door. He was very pale and looked anything but well. I thought he was going to leave, but he reseated himself at the back of the room near the door.] I shall convince you that M. Latour's description of the way the murder was committed is false."

All eyes were turned toward Latour, but he made no sign either of affirmation or dissent. With his eyes closed and his hands falling listlessly in front of him, he sat in a half-collapsed condition, like one in a stupor. M. Godin shifted uneasily in his chair, as if he could not remain silent much longer. Maitland proceeded with calm deliberation:

"Mr. Clinton Browne – "

But he did not finish the sentence. At the name "Mr. Clinton Browne" he was interrupted by a sudden commotion at the rear of the room, followed by a heavy fall which shook the whole apartment. We all turned and looked toward the door. Several men had gathered about someone lying upon the floor, and one of them was throwing water in the face of the prostrate man. Presently he revived a little, and they bore him out into the cooler air of the corridor. It was Clinton Browne. The great tension of the trial, his own strong emotions, and the closeness of the room had doubtless been too much for him. I could not but marvel at it, however. Here were delicate women with apparently little or no staying power, and yet this athlete, with the form of a Mars and the fibre of a Hercules, must be the first to succumb. Verily, even physicians are subject to surprises!

When quiet had been fully restored Maitland continued:

"I was about to say when the interruption occurred that Mr. Clinton Browne and Mr. Charles Herne would both testify to the fact that a very sensible time elapsed between the delivery of the blow and the death of the victim. You will see, therefore, that I shall prove to your satisfaction that Mr. Darrow's death did not result from prussic acid, as stated by the prisoner. I shall show you that a chemical analysis of the wound made in my laboratory shortly after the murder gave none of the well-known prussic-acid reactions. I shall prove to you that John Darrow sprang to his feet after receiving the blow which caused his death. That he clutched at his throat, and that, after an effort consuming several seconds, he spoke disjointedly. I shall convince you that if he had been poisoned in the manner described he would have been dead before he could have so much as raised his hand to his throat. We have been very particular to make sure the exact nature of the poison which it is claimed was used, so there can be no possible doubt upon this point. I shall show you further that the little Capucin monkey which M. Latour says he killed is still alive, and I will produce him, if necessary, and will challenge M. Latour, or anyone else for that matter, to put him through the drill which it is claimed he has been taught. I shall inform you that, since I claim the monkey had no part in Mr. Darrow's death, I could not, during my examination of the prisoner, have been stating anything from knowledge when I spoke of the manner in which he had trained the animal, and gave details which M. Latour accepted as those of the murder. My sole effort was to state a plausible way, in order to see if the prisoner would not adopt it as the actual course pursued. I also coupled with this the killing of the monkey (though I knew the animal was still alive), that I might see if M. Latour would follow my lead in this also. You have seen that he did so; that he indorsed my guesses where they were purely guesses, and that he also accepted the one statement I knew to be false. I shall therefore ask you to consider about what the chances are that a series of guesses like those which I made would represent the exact facts as M. Latour has claimed, while at the same time you do not lose sight of the undeniable fact that upon the only detail regarding which I had positive information, M. Latour bore false testimony."

Here Maitland whispered to Jenkins, who in turn spoke to the sheriff or some other officer of the court. I would have given a good deal just then to have been able to translate M. Godin's thoughts. His face was a study. Maitland immediately resumed:

"It has been positively stated by M. Latour that he gambled with Mr. Darrow on Decatur Street between the 1st and 15th day of March. This is false. In the first place it can be shown that while Mr. Darrow occasionally played cards at his own home, he never gambled, uniformly refusing to play for even the smallest stake. Furthermore, Mr. Darrow's physician will testify that Mr. Darrow was confined to his bed from the 25th day of February to the 18th day of March, and that he visited him during that time at least once, and oftener twice, every day.

"Again; M. Latour asserts that he never saw M. Godin till the day of his arrest, and M. Godin asserts that he never entered M. Latour's rooms until that day. I have a photograph and here a phonographic record. The picture shows M. Latour's rooms with that gentleman and M. Godin sitting at a table and evidently engaged in earnest conversation. This cylinder is a record of a very interesting portion of that conversation – M. Godin will please not leave the room!"

This last was said as M. Godin started toward the door. The officer to whom Jenkins had recently spoken laid his hand upon the detective and detained him. "We may need M. Godin," Maitland continued, "to explain things to us.

"I invite your attention to the fact that M. Godin has testified that he was assisted in his search for Mr. Darrow's murderer by certain library slips which he saw M. Latour make out in two different names. He has also testified that he did not know even the names of any of the books procured on these slips, and that one of them, entitled 'Poisons, Their Effects and Detection,' he not only never read, but never even heard of. I shall show you that all of these books were procured with M. Godin's knowledge, and that most of them were read by him. I shall prove to you beyond a doubt that he has not only heard of this particular work on poisons, but that he has read it and placed his unmistakable signature on page 469 thereof beside the identical paragraph which suggested to Mr. Darrow's murderer the manner of his assassination!" M. Godin started as if he had been stabbed, but quickly regained his self-control as Maitland continued: "Here is the volume in question. You will please note the thumb-mark in the margin of page 469. There is but one thumb in the world that could have made that mark, and that is the thumb you have seen register itself upon this letter. It is also the thumb that made this paint smutch upon this slip of glass."

All eyes were turned upon M. Godin. He was very pale, yet his jaw was firmly set and something akin to a defiant smile played about his handsome mouth. To say that the audience was amazed is to convey no adequate idea of their real condition. We felt prepared for anything. I almost feared lest some sudden turn in the case might cast suspicion upon myself, or even Maitland. Without apparently noticing M. Godin's discomfiture, George continued:

"M. Godin has testified that he sometimes plays cards, but only for a small stake – just enough, he says, to make it interesting. I shall show you that he is a professional gambler as well as a detective.

"The morning after the murder was committed I made a most careful examination of the premises, particularly of the grounds near the eastern window. As the result of my observations, I informed Miss Darrow that I had reason to believe that her father had been murdered by a person who had some good motive for concealing his footprints, and who also had a halting gait. The weight of this person I was able to estimate at not far from one hundred and thirty-five pounds, and his height as about five feet and five inches. I also stated it as my opinion that the person who did the deed had the habit of biting his finger nails, and a particular reason for sparing the nail of the little finger and permitting it to grow to an abnormal length. This was not guesswork on my part, for in the soft soil beneath the eastern window I found a perfect impression of a closed hand. Here is the cast of that hand. Look well at it. Notice the wart upon the upper joint of the thumb, and the crook in the third finger where it has evidently been broken. M. Godin says he never entered the yard of the Darrow estate, except on the night of the murder in company with Messrs. Osborne and Allen, and that then he merely passed up and down the front walk on his way to and from the house, yet the paint-mark on this slip of glass was made by his thumb, and the glass itself was cut by me from the eastern window of the Darrow house – the window through which the murder was committed. This plaster cast was taken from an impression in the soil beneath the same window on the morning after the murder. The hand is the hand of M. Godin. You will note that one of this gentleman's feet is deformed and that he habitually halts in his walk."

We all glanced at M. Godin to verify these assertions, but that gentleman folded his arms in a way to conceal his hands and thrust his feet out of sight beneath the chair in front of him, while he smiled at us with the utmost apparent good nature. He would be game to the last, there was no doubt of that.

Maitland recalled our attention by saying:

"Officer, you will please arrest M. Godin!"

An excited whisper was heard from every corner, and many were the half-audible comments that were broken off by the imperative fall of the crier's gavel. So tense had been the strain that it was some time before complete order could be restored. When it was again quiet Maitland continued:

"Your Honour and Gentlemen of the Jury: We will rest our case here for to-day. To-morrow, or rather on Monday, we shall show the strange influence which M. Godin exercised over M. Latour, as well as M. Latour's reasons for his confession. We shall endeavour to make clear to you how M. Latour was actually led to believe he had murdered John Darrow, and how he was bribed to confess a crime committed by another. Of the hypnotic power of M. Godin over M. Latour I have indisputable proof, though we shall see that M. Godin by no means relied wholly upon this power. We shall show you also that sufficient time elapsed to enable M. Godin, by great skill and celerity, to make away with the evidences of his guilt in time to enable him to be present with Messrs. Osborne and Allen at the examination. In short, we shall unravel before you a crime which, for cleverness of conception and adroitness of execution, has never been equalled in the history of this community."

Maitland having thus concluded his remarks by dropping into a courteous plural in deference to Mr. Jenkins, the court adjourned until Monday, and I left Gwen in Maitland's charge while I hurried home, fearful lest I should not be the first to bring to Jeannette the glad news of her father's innocence, for I had not the slightest doubt of Maitland's ability to prove conclusively all he had undertaken.

I need not describe to you my interview with Jeannette. There are things concerning it which, even at this late day, when their roseate hue glows but dimly in the blue retrospect of the past, – it would seem sacrilege for me to mention to another. Believe me, I am perfectly aware of your inquisitive nature, and I know that this omission may nettle you. Charge it all up, then, to the perversity of a bachelor in the throes of his first, last, and only love experience. You must see that such things cannot be conveyed to another with anything like their real significance. Were I to say I was carried beyond myself by her protestations of gratitude until, in a delirium of joy, I seized her in my arms and covered her with kisses, do you for a moment fancy you could appreciate my feelings? Do you imagine that the little tingle of sympathy which you might experience were I to say that, instead of pushing me from her, I felt her clasp tighten about me, – would tell you anything of the great torrent of hot blood that deluged my heart as she lay there in my arms, quivering ecstatically at every kiss? No! a thousand times no! Therefore have I thought best to say nothing about it. Our love can keep its own secrets. – But alas! this was long ago, and as I sit here alone writing this to you, I cannot but wonder, with a heavy sense of ever-present longing, where on this great earth Jeannette – 'my Jeannette,' I have learned to call her – is now. You see a bachelor's love-affair is a serious thing, and years cannot always efface it. But to return to the past:

Jeannette, I think, was not more pleased than Gwen at the turn affairs had taken. Indeed, so exuberant was Gwen in her quiet way that I marvelled much at the change in her, so much, indeed, that finally I determined to question Alice about it.

"I can understand," I said to her, "why Gwen, on account of her sympathy and love for Jeannette, should be glad that M. Latour is likely to be acquitted. I can also appreciate the distaste she may have felt at the prospect of having to deal with M. Godin under the terms of her father's will; but even both of these considerations seem to me insufficient to account for her present almost ecstatic condition. There is an immediateness to her joy which could hardly result from mere release from a future disagreeable possibility. How do you account for it, sis?" Alice's answer was somewhat enigmatical and didn't give me the information I sought. "Ned," she replied," I'll pay for the tickets to the first circus that comes here, just to see if you can find the trunks on the elephants." Do my best, I couldn't make her enlighten me any further, for, to every question, she replied with a most provoking laugh.

Maitland called and spent most of the next day, which was Sunday, with us, and we all talked matters over. He did not seem either to share or understand Gwen's exuberance of spirits, albeit one could easily observe that he had a measure of that satisfaction which always comes from success. More than once I saw him glance questioningly at Gwen with a look which said plainly enough: "What is the meaning of this remarkable change? Why should it so matter to her whether M. Latour's or M. Godin's death avenges her father's murder?" When he left us at night I could see he had not answered that question to his own satisfaction.

CHAPTER III

The Devil throws double sixes when he turns genius heliward.

The next morning after the events last narrated I was utterly dumfounded by an article which met my gaze the instant I took up my paper. It was several moments before I sufficiently recovered my faculties to read it aloud to Gwen, Alice, and Jeannette, all of whom had noticed my excitement, and were waiting with such patience as they could command. I read the following article through from beginning to end without pause or comment:

M. Godin Anticipates the Law. – The Real Murderer of John Darrow Writes His Confession and Then Suicides in His Cell. – Contrived to Mix His Own Poison Under the Very Nose of His Jailer! – The Dorchester Mystery Solved at Last. – Full Description of the Life of One of the Cleverest Criminals of the Century.

At 4.30 this morning M. Godin was found dead in his cell, No. 26, at Charles Street Jail. The manner of his death might still be a mystery had he not left a written confession of his crime and the summary manner of his taking off. This was written yesterday afternoon and evening, M. Godin being permitted to have a light on the ground that he had important legal documents to prepare for use on the morrow. We give below the confession in full.

"I am beaten at a game in which I did my own shuffling. I never believe in trying to bluff a full hand. Had I had but ordinary detectives with whom to deal, I make bold to say I should have come off rich and triumphant. I had no means of knowing that I was to play with a chemist who would use against me the latest scientific implements of criminal warfare. It is, therefore, to the extraordinary means used for my detection that I impute my defeat, rather than to any bungling of my own. This is a grim consolation, but it is still a consolation, for I have always prided myself upon being an artist in my line. As I propose to put myself beyond the reach of further cross-examination, I take this opportunity to make a last statement of such things as I care to have known. After this is finished I shall sup on acetate of lead and bid good-night to the expectant public.

"Lest some may marvel how I came by this poison, and even lay suspicions upon my jailers, let me explain that there is a small piece of lead water-pipe crossing the west angle of my room. This being Sunday, I was permitted to have beans and brown bread for breakfast. I asked for a little vinegar for my beans, and a small cruet was brought to me. I had no difficulty in secreting a considerable quantity of the vinegar in order that I might, when occasion served, apply it to the lead pipe. This I have done, and have now by me enough acetate of lead to kill a dozen men. This form of death will not be particularly pleasant, I am aware, but I prefer it to its only alternative. So much for that.

"I was horn in Marseilles, and my right name is Jean Fouchet. My father intended me for the priesthood, and gave me a good college education in Paris. His hopes, however, were destined to disappointment. In college I formed the habit of gambling, and a year after my graduation found me at Monte Carlo. While there I quarrelled with a gambling accomplice and ended by killing him. This made my stay in France dangerous for me, and I took the first opportunity which presented itself to embark for America.

"Familiarity with criminals had made me familiar with crime, and I added the occupation of detective to my profession of gambling. These two avocations had now become my sole means of support, and I plied my trades in New York, Boston, and Philadelphia for several years, during which time I became a naturalised citizen of the United States.

"When the Cuban rebellion broke out I could not restrain my longing for adventure, and joined a filibustering expedition sailing from New York. I did this from no love I bore the Cuban cause, but merely for the excitement it promised. While handling a heavy shot during my first engagement I accidentally dropped it upon my left foot, crushing that member so badly that it has never regained its shape. This deformity has rendered it impossible for me to conceal my identity. Three months after this accident I was taken prisoner by the Spanish and shipped to Spain as a political malefactor. A farce of a trial was granted to me, not to see whether or not I was guilty, but simply to determine between the dungeon and the garrote. It would have been far better for me had I been sentenced to the latter instead of the former.

"As a political offender I was doomed to imprisonment at Ceuta, an old Moorish seaport town in

Morocco, opposite Gibraltar and upon the side of the ancient mountain Abyla. This mountain forms one of the 'Pillars of Hercules,' the Rock of Gibraltar being the other. It is almost impregnable, and is used by Spain as Siberia is used by Russia, only it is far, far more horrible. The town was built by the Moors in 945, and nowhere else on earth are there to be found an equal number of devices for the torture of human beings. If anyone thinks the horrors of the Inquisition are no longer perpetrated let him get sent to Ceuta: I have good cause to believe that the Inquisition itself is far from dead in Spain. Alas for the person who is sent to Ceuta! The town is small, and, to guard against possible attack, the Moors constructed a chain of fortresses around it. It is in the black cellars of these disintegrating fortresses that the dungeons are located. They are in tiers to the depth of fifty or sixty feet, and are hewn out of the solid rock. They are reached through narrow openings in the stone floors of the fortresses, and when one of these horrible holes is opened the foul odor of filth and decomposition is utterly overpowering. Some of these dungeons contain as many as thirty or forty men. I was placed in a cell reserved for solitary confinement. I have never been a man who regarded life seriously, or feared to risk it upon sufficient occasion, but my heart froze within me when the horror of my situation was revealed to me. A stone box perhaps eight feet square – as I lay upon the floor I could touch its opposite sides with my hands and feet – had been prepared for my entrance by cutting a slit in one of its walls just large enough for the passage of my body. Through this narrow opening I was dropped into the total darkness within. A blacksmith followed and welded my fetters, for locks and keys are never used. A chain having a heavy weight pendant from it was riveted to my ankle, and an iron band was similarly fastened to my waist. This band was fastened by a chain to an iron ring deeply sunk in the solid rock. When these horrible preparations were completed the blacksmith left me and a mason bricked up the slit through which I had entered, leaving only a hand-breadth of space for air and the thrusting through of such scraps of food as were to be allowed me. Language is powerless to describe the feelings of a man in such a position. He realises that his only hope is in disease – disease bred of the darkness, the dampness, the starvation, and the horrible filth. He says to himself: 'How long, O God! how long?' – For hours I remained prone and inert – how long I do not know; night and day are all one in the dungeons of Ceuta. Then I began to think. Could I escape? I felt that all power of thought, all cleverness would soon desert me, and I said to myself: 'If anything is to be done, it must be done at once.' I knew not then what long-drawn horrors a mortal could endure. Whenever I attempted to walk the iron mass fastened to my leg would 'bring me up short,' often, in my early forgetfulness of it, throwing me prone upon my face. After a little I learned to move with a halting gait, striding out with the free limb and pausing to pull my burden after me with the other. This habit, learned in the squalor and darkness of the dungeon hells of Ceuta, I have never been able to unlearn.

"It was many days before I could see how anything short of a miracle could enable me to escape. I tried to calmly reason it all out, and every time came to the same horrible conclusion, viz.: I must rot there unless help came to me from without. This seemed impossible, and all the horrors of a lingering death stared me in the face. Every two or three days one of the jailers would come to the slit in the masonry and leave there a dish of water and a few crusts of bread. I tried on one occasion to speak with him, but he only laughed in my face and turned away. Finally I hit upon a plan which seemed to offer the only possible means of escape. In my college days I was well acquainted with M. Charcot, and even assisted in some of his earlier hypnotic experiments. The subject interested me, and I followed it closely till I became something of an adept myself. There were in those days but few people I could not mesmerise, provided sufficient opportunity were allowed me for hypnotic suggestion. I determined to see if any of this old power still remained with me, and, if so, to strive to render my jailer subservient to my will. But how should I keep him within ear-shot long enough to work upon him? Clearly all appeals to pity were useless. I must excite his greed, nothing else would reach him. This was not an easy thing to do without a sou in my possession, yet I did it. When I heard his step I crawled to the opening in the wall and mumbled in a crazy sort of a way about a hidden treasure. At the word 'treasure' I saw him pause and listen, but I pretended not to be aware of his presence and rambled on, in a loose, disjointed fashion, about piracies committed by me and the great amount of booty I had secreted. My plan worked perfectly. The jailer came to the aperture in the wall and called me to him. Muttering incoherently, I obeyed. He asked me what offence brought me there, and I, with a good deal of intentional misunderstanding, told him I was a pirate and a smuggler. He asked me where the treasure I had been talking about was hidden. My reply, – I remember the exact words in which I couched it, – made him mine completely. I said: 'We buried it near Fez – Treasure? I don't know anything about any treasure.'

"To all the many questions he then asked me I returned only incoherent replies, but I was careful to be again raving about buried riches upon the next visit. In this way I kept him by me long enough to influence him, and in less than a month he was completely subject to my will. I tested my power over him in divers ways. Any delicacy I wished I compelled him to bring me. In this way I was enabled to regain a portion of my lost strength. When I concluded the time had come for me to make good my escape, I caused him to come to my cell at midnight and remove the bricks from the slit while I put on the disguise he had brought me. Once out of my stone tomb we carefully walled it up again and then departed to find my imaginary hidden treasure. We made our way without trouble to Algiers, for my companion had money, and sailed thence via Gibraltar for England. During the trip my companion jumped overboard and was drowned in the Bay of Biscay. Thus I was completely freed from Ceuta and its terrible pest-hole.

"From England I sailed to New York, reaching America penniless and in ill health. Things not going to my liking in New York, I came to Boston and took up my old callings of gambler and detective. It was at this time that I saw John Darrow's curious notice in the newspaper, offering, in the event of his murder, a most liberal reward to anyone who would bring the assassin to justice.

"Mon Dieu! How I needed money. I would have bartered my soul for a tithe of that amount. It was the old, old story, only new in Eden. Ah! but how I loved her! She must have money, money, always money! That was ever her cry. When I could not supply it she sought it of others, and this drove me mad. If, I said to myself, I could only get this reward! This was something really worth working for, and if I could but get it, she should be mine only. I at once set to work upon the problem.

"It was not an easy thing to solve. I might be able to hire a man to do the deed for me, but he would hardly be willing to hang for it without disclosing my part in the transaction. It was at this time that I first met M. Latour on Decatur Street. He at once impressed me as being just the man I wanted, and I began to gradually subdue his will. In this circumstances greatly aided me. When I found him he was in very poor health and without any means of sustenance. His daughter was able to earn a little, but not nearly enough to keep the wolf from the door. Add to this that he had a cancer, which several physicians had assured him would prove fatal within a year, that he was afflicted with an almost insane fear that his daughter would come to want after his death, and you have before you the conditions which determined my course. My first thought was to influence him to do the deed himself, but, recalling the researches of M. Charcot in these matters, I came to the conclusion that such a course would be almost certain to lead to detection, since a hypnotic subject can only be depended upon so long as the conditions under which he acts are precisely those which have been suggested to him. Any unforeseen variations in these conditions and he fails to act, exposes everything, and the whole carefully planned structure falls to the ground. When, therefore, the time came which I had set for the deed, I found it possible to drug M. Latour, abduct him from his home, and to keep him confined and unconscious until I had killed Mr. Darrow in a manner I will describe in due course. As soon as I had committed the murder and established what I fondly believed would be a perfect alibi in my attendance at the examination, I secretly conveyed the still unconscious M. Latour to his rooms and awaited his return to consciousness. I then asked him how he came in such a state and what he was doing in Dorchester. He was, of course, ignorant of everything. Little by little I worked upon him till he came to believe himself guilty of John Darrow's murder.

"I had availed myself of his interest in the subject of cancer to get him to the library. It is one of my maxims never to take an avoidable risk, for which reason I made Latour apply for the books I wanted, as well as for the medical works he desired to peruse. As he was ambidextrous, I suggested the use of the two names Weltz and Rizzi, the former to be written with his right and the latter with his left hand. I was actuated in all this by two motives. First, I was manufacturing evidence which might stand me in good stead later, as well as minimising somewhat my own risk in getting the information I needed; and, secondly, I was getting Latour into a good atmosphere for my hypnotic influence. Not a word of all these matters did he relate to his daughter, whom he loves with a devotion I have never seen equalled. Indeed, it was this very affection that made my plan feasible. When I had convinced him he was a murderer I showed him Mr. Darrow's curious advertisement offering a reward, should he be assassinated, to anyone bringing about the conviction of his assailant.

"'In a year,' I said to him, 'you will die of cancer, if your crime be not previously discovered and punished. Your daughter will then be penniless. How much better for you to permit me in a few months to accuse you of the murder. You then confess; I claim and secure the reward and secretly divide with you; you are sentenced; but as considerable time will transpire between this and the date set for your execution, you in the meantime will die of cancer, leaving Jeannette well provided for.'

"I think my influence over him would have been sufficient to have compelled him to all this, could he have reasoned out no benefit accruing to himself or daughter by such a course, but with circumstances thus in my favour my task was an easy one. The public knows all it need know of what occurred after this. This man, Maitland, was in the next room to Latour's, overheard our conversation, and even phonographed our words and photographed our positions. It has always been a matter of pride with me to gracefully acknowledge that three aces are not so good as a full house, therefore I confess myself beaten, though not subdued.

"I consider this the very best tribute I can pay to the genius of the man who has undone me. I take my punishment, however, into my own hands.

"In my haste to have done with all this and to start on my long and chartless journey, I had well-nigh forgotten to tell just how I killed Mr. Darrow. No hypodermic syringe had anything to do with it. The while plan came to me while reading that fatal page upon which I left my telltale thumb-signature in my search for some feasible plan of making away with my victim. I need not go into particulars, for I know perfectly well that this Maitland knows to a nicety how the thing was done. The Daboia Russellii, or Russell's viper, is one of the best known and most deadly of Indian vipers. I procured one of these reptiles at the cost of great delay and some slight risk. That is the whole story. On the night of the murder I took the viper in a box and went down to the water-front, near the Darrow estate. Here I cut a small pole from a clump of alders, made a split in one end of it, and thrust it over the tail of the viper. It pinched him severely and held him fast despite his angry struggles to free himself and to attack anything within his reach. All that remained to be done was to thrust this through the window into the darkened room and to bring the viper within reach of Mr. Darrow. This I did, being careful to crouch so as not to obstruct the light of the window. When I heard my victim's outcry I withdrew the pole, and with it, of course, the viper, and made good my escape. That the reptile bit Mr. Darrow under the chin while his back was toward the window was mere chance, though I regarded it as a very lucky occurrence, since it seemed to render the suicide theory at first inevitable.

"I had had some fear lest the hissing of the viper might have been heard, for which reason I hazarded the only question I asked at the examination, and was completely reassured by its answer. I should perhaps state that my purpose in keeping in the background at this examination was my desire to avoid attracting attention to my deformed foot and my halting gait. This latter I had taken pains to conceal at my entrance, but I knew that the first step I took in forgetfulness would expose my halting habit. I had no fear of either Osborne or Allen, but there was something about this Maitland that bade me at once be on my guard, and, as I have said before, I never take an avoidable risk. For this reason I sat at once in the darkest corner I could find and remained there throughout the examination. I thought it extremely unlikely, though possible, that an attempt might be made to track the assassin with dogs, yet, since that is precisely the first thing I myself would have done, I decided that the risk was worth avoiding. I accordingly set the boat adrift to indicate an escape by water, and then waded along the beach for half a mile or so, carrying the pole, boards, etc., with me. As I kept where the water was at least six inches deep I knew no dog could follow my trail. At the point where I left the water I sat down upon a rock and put on my stockings and shoes, thoroughly saturating them at the same time with turpentine, and pouring the remainder of the bottle upon the rock where I had sat. As I had known prisoners escaped from Libby Prison to pass in this way undetected within twenty feet of bloodhounds upon their trail, I felt that my tracks had been well covered, and made all possible haste to get ready to attend the examination with the special detail.

"And now I have finished. Before this meets any other eye than mine I shall be dead – beyond the punishment of this world and awaiting the punishment of the next. Lest some may fancy I do not believe this, – thinking that if I did I could not so have acted, – let me say there is no moral restraining power in fear. Fear is essentially selfish, and selfishness is at the bottom of all crimes, my own among the rest. I leave behind me none who will mourn me, and have but one satisfaction, viz.: the knowledge that I shall be regarded as an artist in crime. I take this occasion to bid the public an adieu not altogether, I confess, unmixed with regrets. I am now on that eminence called 'Life'; in a few minutes I shall have jumped off into the darkness, and then – -all is mystery."

When I had finished reading this article we all remained silent for a long time. Gwen was the first to speak, and then only to say slowly, as if thinking aloud: "And so it is all over."

CHAPTER IV

It often happens that two souls who love are, like the parts of a Mexican gemel-ring, the more difficult to intertwine the better they fit each other.

You may be assured that, after reading M. Godin's confession, we looked forward to seeing Maitland with a good deal of interest. We knew this new turn of affairs would cause him to call at once, so we all strove to possess our souls in patience while we awaited his coming. In less than half an hour he was with us. "The news of your success has preceded you," said Gwen as soon as he was seated. "I wish to be the first to offer you my congratulations. You have done for me what none other could have done and I owe you a debt of gratitude I can never repay. The thought that I was unable to carry out my father's wishes, – that I could do nothing to free his name from the reproaches which had been cast upon it, was crushing my heart like a leaden weight. You have removed this burden, and, believe me, words fail to express the gratitude I feel. I shall beg of you to permit me to pay you the sum my father mentioned and to – to – " She hesitated and Maitland did not permit her to finish her sentence.

"You must pardon me, Miss Darrow," he replied, "but I can accept no further payment for the little I have done. It has been a pleasure to do it and the knowledge that you are now released from the disagreeable possibilities of your father's will is more than sufficient remuneration. If you still feel that you owe me anything, perhaps you will be willing to grant me a favour."

"There is nothing," she said earnestly, "within my power to grant for which you shall ask in vain."

"Let me beg of you then," he replied, "never again to seek to repay me for any services you may fancy I have rendered. There is nothing you could bestow upon me which I would accept." She gave him a quick, searching glance and I noticed a look of pain upon her face, but Maitland gave it no heed, for, indeed, he seemed to have much ado either to know what he wanted to say, or knowing it, to say it.

"And now," he continued, "I must no longer presume to order your actions. You have considered my wishes so conscientiously, have kept your covenant so absolutely, that what promised to be a disagreeable responsibility has become a pleasure which I find myself loth to discontinue. All power leads to tyranny. Man cannot be trusted with it. Its exercise becomes a consuming passion, and he abuses it. The story is the same, whether nations or individuals be considered. I myself, you see, am a case in point. I thank you for the patience you have shown and the pains you have taken to make everything easy and pleasant for me; and now I must be going, as I have yet much to do in this matter. It may be a long time," he said, extending his hand to her, "before we meet again. We have travelled the same path – " but he paused as if unable to proceed, and a deadly pallor overspread his face as he let fall both her hand and his own. He made a heroic effort to proceed.

"I – I shall miss – very – very much miss – pray

pardon me – I – I believe I'm ill – a little faint I'd – I'd better get out into the air – I shall – shall miss – pardon – I – I'm not quite myself – goodbye, good-bye!" and he staggered unsteadily, half blindly to the door and out into the street without another word. He certainly did look ill.

Gwen's face was a study. In it surprise, fear, pain, and dismay, each struggled for predominance. She tried to retain her self-control while I was present, but it was all in vain. A moment later she threw herself upon the sofa, and, burying her face in the cushions, wept long and bitterly. I stole quietly away and sent Alice to her, and after a time she regained her self-control, if not her usual interest in affairs.

As day after day passed, however, and Maitland neglected to call, transacting such business as he had through me, the shadow on Gwen's face deepened, and the elasticity of manner, whereof she had given such promise at Maitland's last visit, totally deserted her, giving place to a dreamy, faraway stolidity of disposition which I knew full well boded no good. I stood this sort of thing as long as I could, and then I determined to call on Maitland and give him a "piece of my mind."

I did call, but when I saw him all my belligerent resolutions vanished. He was sitting at his table trying to work out some complicated problem, and he was utterly unfitted for a single minute's consecutive thought. I had not seen him for more than two weeks, and during that time he had grown to look ten years older. His face was drawn, haggard, and deathly pale.

"For Heaven's sake, George," I exclaimed, "what is the matter with you?"

"I've an idea I'm spleeny," he replied with a ghastly attempt at a smile. This was too much for me. He should have the lecture after all. The man who thinks he is dying may be spleeny, but the man who says he is spleeny is, of the two, the one more likely to be dying.

"See here, old man," I began, "don't you get to thinking that when you hide your own head in the sand no one can see the colour of your feathers. You might as well try to cover up Bunker Hill Monument with a wisp of straw. Don't you suppose I know you love Gwen Darrow? That's what's the matter with you."

"Well," he replied, "and if it is, what then?"

"What then?" I ejaculated. "What then? Why go to her like a man; tell her you love her and ask her to be your wife. That's what I'd do if I loved – " But he interrupted me before I had finished the lie, and I was not sorry, for, if I had thought before I became involved in that last sentence, how I feared to speak to Jeannette – well, I should have left it unsaid. I have made my living giving advice till it has become a fixed habit.

"See here, Doc," he broke in upon me, "I do love Gwen Darrow as few men ever love a woman, and the knowledge that she can never be my wife is killing me. Don't interrupt me! I know what I am saying. She can never be my wife! Do you think I would sue for her hand? Do you think I would be guilty of making traffic of her gratitude? Has she not her father's command to wed me if I but ask her, even as she would have wed that scoundrel, Godin, had things gone as he planned them? Did she not tell us both that she should keep her covenant with her father though it meant for her a fate worse than death? And you would have me profit by her sacrifice? For shame! Love may wither my heart till it rustles in my breast like a dried leaf, but I will never, never let her know how I love her. And see here, Doc, promise me that you will not tell her I love her – nay, I insist on it."

Thus importuned I said, though it went much against the grain, for that was the very thing I had intended, "She shall not learn it first through me." This seemed to satisfy him, for he said no more upon the subject. When I went back to Gwen I was in no better frame of mind than when I left her. Here were two people so determined to be miserable in spite of everything and everybody that I sought Jeannette by way of counter-irritant for my wounded sympathy.

Ah, Jeannette! Jeannette! to this day the sound of your sweet name is like a flash of colour to the eye. You were a bachelor's first and last love, and he will never forget you.

CHAPTER V

*All human things cease – some end. Happy are
they who can spring the hard and brittle bar of
experience into a bow of promise. For such,
there shall ever more be an orderly gravitation.*

My next call on Maitland was professional. I
found him abed and in a critical condition. I blamed
myself severely that I had allowed other duties to
keep me so long away, and had him at once removed to the house, where I might, by constant attendance in the future, atone for my negligence in
the past. Despite all our efforts, however, Maitland
steadily grew worse. Gwen watched by him night
and day until I was finally obliged to insist, on account of her own health, that she should leave the
sick room long enough to take the rest she so
needed. Indeed, I feared lest I should soon have two
invalids upon my hands, but Gwen yielded her place
to Jeannette and Alice during the nights and soon
began to show the good effects of sleep.

I should have told you that, during all this time,
Jeannette was staying with us as a guest. I had convinced her father that it was best she should remain
with us until the unpleasant notoriety caused by his
arrest had, in a measure, subsided. Then, too, I told
him with a frankness warranted, I thought, by circumstances that he could not hope to live many
weeks longer, and that every effort should be made
to make the blow his death would deal Jeannette as
light as possible. At this he almost lost his self-
control. "What will become of my child when I am
gone?" he moaned. "I shall leave her penniless and

without any means of support."

"My dear Mr. Latour," I replied, "you need give yourself no uneasiness on that score. I will give you my word, as a man of honour, that so long as Miss Darrow and I live we will see that your daughter wants for none of the necessities of life, – unless she shall find someone who shall have a better right than either of us to care for her." This promise acted like magic upon him. He showered his blessings upon me, exclaiming, "You have lifted a great load from my heart, and I can now die in peace!" And so, indeed, he did. In less than a week he was dead. I had prepared Jeannette for the shock and so had her father, but, for all this, her grief was intense, for she loved her father with a strength of love few children give their parents. In time, however, her grief grew less insistent and she began to gain something of her old buoyancy.

In the meantime, Maitland's life seemed to hang by a single thread. It was the very worst case of nervous prostration I have ever been called to combat, and for weeks we had to be contented if we enabled him to hold his own. During all this time Gwen watched both Maitland and myself with a closeness that suffered nothing to escape her. I think she knew the changes in his condition better even than I did.

And now I am to relate a most singular action on Gwen's part. I doubt not most of her own sex would have considered it very unfeminine, but anyone who saw it all as I did could not, I think, fail to appreciate the nobility of womanhood which made it possible. Gwen was not dominated by those characteristics usually epitomised in the epithet 'lady.' She was a woman, and she possessed, in a remarkable degree, that fineness of fibre, that solidity of character, and that largeness of soul which rise above the petty conventionalities of life into the broad realm of the real verities of existence.

It occurred on the afternoon of the first day that Maitland showed the slightest improvement. I remember distinctly how he had fallen into a troubled sleep from which he would occasionally cry out in a half-articulate manner, and how Gwen and I sat beside him waiting for him to awaken. Suddenly he said something in his sleep that riveted our attention. "I tell you, Doc," he muttered, "though love of her burn my heart to a cinder, I will never trade upon her gratitude, nor seek to profit by the promise she made her father. Never, so help me God!"

Gwen gave me one hurried, sweeping glance and then, throwing herself upon the sofa, buried her face in the cushions. I forbore to disturb her till I saw that Maitland was waking, when I laid my hand upon her head and asked her to dry her eyes lest he should notice her tears.

"May I speak to him?" she said, with a look of resolution upon her face. I could not divine her thoughts, as she smiled at me through her tears, but I had no hesitancy in relying upon her judgment, so I gave her permission and started to leave the room.

"Please don't go," she said to me. "I would prefer you should hear what I have to say." I reseated myself and Gwen drew near the bedside. Maitland was now awake and following her every motion.

"I have something I want to say to you," she said, bending over him. "Do you feel strong enough to listen?" He nodded his head and she continued. "You have already done a great deal for me, yet I come to you now to ask a further favour, – I will not say a sacrifice – greater than all the rest. Will you try to grant it?"

The rich, deep tones of her voice, vibrant with tender earnestness, seemed to me irresistible.

"I will do anything in my power," the invalid replied, never once moving his eyes from hers.

"Then Heaven grant it be within your power!" she murmured, scarcely above a whisper. "Try not to despise me for what I am about to say. Be lenient in your judgment. My happiness, perhaps my very life, depends upon this issue. I love you more than life; try to love me, if only a little!"

I watched the effect of this declaration with a good deal of anxiety. For fully half a minute Maitland seemed to doubt the evidence of his senses. I saw him pinch himself to see if he were awake, and being thus reassured, he said slowly: "Try – to – love – you! In vain have I tried not to love you from the moment I first saw you. Oh, my God! how I adore you!" He reached his arms out toward her, and, in a moment, they were locked in each other's embrace.

I saw the first kiss given and then stole stealthily from the room. There was now no need of a doctor. The weird, irresistible alchemy of love was at work and the reign of medicine was over. I did not wish to dim the newly found light by my shadow, and, – well, – I wanted to see Jeannette, so I left.

I need not tell you, even though you are a bachelor, how fast Maitland improved. Gwen would permit no one else to nurse him, and this had much to do with the rapidity of his recovery. In a month he was able to go out, and in another month Gwen became Mrs. Maitland. A happier pair, or one better suited to each other, it has never been my privilege to know. As I visited them in their new home I became more and more dissatisfied with bachelor existence, and there were times when I had half a mind to go straight to Jeannette and ask her advice in the matter. Ah, those days! They will never come to me again. Never again will a pink and white angel knock so loudly at my heart, or be so warmly welcomed. I wonder where she is and if she is thinking of me.

And now I may as well stop, for my narrative is over, and I hear someone coming along the hail, doubtless after me. It is only Harold, so I may add a word or two more. I am writing now with difficulty, for some frolicsome individual has placed a hand over my eyes and says, "Guess." I can just see to write between the fingers. Again I am commanded, "Guess!" so I say carelessly, "Alice." Then, would you believe it, someone kisses me and says: "Will you ever have done with that writing? The children wish me to inform you that they have some small claim upon your time." You see how it is. I've got to stop, so I say, as becomes an obedient gentleman: "Very well, I will quit upon one condition. I have been wondering where on earth you were. Tell me what

you have been doing with yourself. I have been re-
peating in retrospect all the horrors of bachelordom."

"Why, Ned dear," my wife replies, "I've only
been down-town shopping for Harold and little
Jeannette. Bless me, I should think I'd been gone a
year!"

"Bless you, my dear Jeannette," I reply; "I should
think you had," and I draw her down gently into my
lap and kiss her again and again for the sake of the
conviction it will carry. She says I am smothering
her, which means she is convinced.

You see I have learned some things since I was a
bachelor.